NOT MY VALENTINE

Murder on a special night

TONY BASSETT

Published by The Book Folks

London, 2025

ISBN 978-1-80462-339-8

www.thebookfolks.com

NOT MY VALENTINE is the seventh standalone mystery in the Detectives Roy and Roscoe crime fiction series by Tony Bassett.

The full list of books is as follows:

MURDER ON OXFORD LANE
THE CROSSBOW STALKER
MURDER OF A DOCTOR
OUT FOR REVENGE
HEIR TO MURDER
IT NEVER RAINS
NOT MY VALENTINE

Details about these books can be found at the back of this one.

Lydia, who was approaching thirty but looked younger, reached for her black clutch bag, next to their steaming cups of coffee, and fumbled for her silver phone.

'I don't recognise this number,' she grumbled as she pressed the answer key.

'Hello?' she said.

'Is that Lydia?' asked an educated female voice.

'Yes.'

'This is Clare, your next-door neighbour. Do you remember? You gave me your phone number in case of emergencies.'

'That's right,' she said with a smile.

'Well, I don't want to alarm you, but someone's been acting suspiciously outside your house.'

'How do you mean?' asked Lydia as her smile faded.

'Someone was sitting across the street in a car for several hours yesterday,' said Clare. 'They were in a black Mercedes with tinted windows. I glanced out of my window just after ten o'clock and it was still there when I checked an hour later. It eventually left at about four o'clock.'

Lydia shrugged her shoulders. 'Why do you think this has anything to do with me?'

Roman became concerned and interrupted her. 'What is it, Lydia? What's the matter?'

She raised a finger, signalling for him to be quiet.

'Well, the driver – a man – was looking across at your house every time I checked on the car. And at about half past two, I heard the driver's door creak open while I was cleaning our windows upstairs. Whoever it was had gone to your front door and was peering through the glass panel next to it.'

'What did the person look like?' asked Lydia.

'I'm sorry. I didn't get a very good look. Whoever it was, they were dressed in dark clothes. I thought I'd ring you. I thought you ought to know.'

Lydia nodded. 'Very good of you, Clare. You're an angel.'

Clare continued, 'I mean, if something strange happened outside my place while I was away, obviously it would be great if you could let me know. This is what neighbours are for.'

'I agree,' said Lydia. 'I suppose it's possible it was something to do with my mother. She's been away having hospital treatment. Did you know?'

'Yes. She was meant to be moving in with you, wasn't she? You mentioned a couple of weeks ago that she was in hospital.'

Roman was listening to every word spoken in her soft, mellow tones and trying to interrupt. Eventually, Lydia had to ask Clare to wait for a moment. She lowered her phone and briefly explained about the whole incident.

'Could I have a word with your friend?' he suggested.

She nodded and passed him the handset.

'Clare, this is Roman Makepeace,' he said. 'I'm a friend of Lydia's. This sounds quite alarming. Did you by any chance take a note of the registration number?'

'No, I didn't. I'm a bit short-sighted and it was on the other side of the street,' said Clare. 'But if it comes back, I'll be sure to go outside and make a note of it.'

'Good,' he said. 'The way it's been described to me, this could be something or nothing. This person might have a totally genuine reason for parking outside Lydia's house. Maybe they're from the local council or it's something to do with her mother's healthcare. They aren't there this morning?'

'No.'

'All right,' he said. 'I'll just hand the phone back to Lydia.'

As he passed her the handset back, she gently scolded him. 'It's all right, darling, I can take care of myself.'

She patted him on the arm before resuming the conversation.

Chapter 1

Before she received the troubling phone call, it had been one of the happiest days Lydia Squires could remember.

As she sat at the cafe table in her floral-patterned spring dress, she seemed like a woman in love.

All her plans were working out. The man beside her appeared to be smitten with her, despite their whirlwind courtship of just six weeks.

She swept her long, blonde hair away from her sparkling blue eyes before turning towards him and kissing him on the cheek. He slipped his right hand round her shoulder and kissed her passionately on the lips.

Pedestrians were strolling past on their way to the traffic-free public square in front of Birmingham Snow Hill railway station.

But Lydia and her partner, Roman, a handsome, well-groomed man in his early thirties, ignored them. Their lips remained locked together as though they were a pair of love-struck teenagers until Lydia's mobile phone disturbed the peace of the mild Sunday morning.

After a few seconds had passed, the man drew back.

'Aren't you going to answer that call?' he asked in a warm, confident voice.

'How are you keeping anyway?' Clare asked. 'I haven't seen much of you.'

'That's right,' said Lydia. 'I'm very well. We were out all day yesterday, going round the shops. We're actually about to get on a train.'

'Oh, I'm sorry. I'd better not keep you,' said the neighbour.

'No, it's all right,' said Lydia. 'We're going on the steam train from Snow Hill.'

'Oh, I saw something online about that. It's a Valentine's special, isn't it?'

Lydia nodded. 'Yes.'

'And your friend Roman is taking you, is he? Lucky old you,' said Clare. 'I probably won't recognise you when I see you next.'

'Why's that?'

'After travelling on the love train, you'll have such a broad smile on your face and a twinkle in your eye.'

'Get along with you,' said Lydia, laughing out loud. 'Look, Clare, thank you so much for taking the time and trouble to let me know about the strange visitor. Let's hope there's an innocent explanation.'

'I'm sure there is,' said Clare. 'Enjoy your trip, you pair of lovebirds.' Then she hung up.

'So what do you make of that?' Lydia asked while sipping from her cup of coffee, which was now lukewarm.

'I'm sure it's nothing to worry about,' Roman said, sweeping some of his ginger hair away from his face. 'Come on. It's nearly five to ten. If we're going to ride on this steam train, we'd better get a move on.'

As they walked across the square, the pair glanced up at the cluster of six-storey office buildings crowded into this corner of the city's commercial district – lofty cathedrals of gleaming glass.

They made their way through the ticket barrier and climbed down the steps to the southbound platform.

'Here we are – the Shakespeare Express,' Roman announced.

There before them stood a vintage steam train that was set to depart for Stratford-upon-Avon within the next fifteen minutes. The passenger excursion train – just for today rebranded as the 'Valentine's Express' – was due to reach speeds of at least sixty miles an hour while hauling seven coaches through rolling Warwickshire countryside.

A few minutes later, they clambered aboard the second coach and made themselves comfortable at their table seats.

Then Lydia's phone rang again and Clare's number flashed up on the screen.

'Yes. What is it, Clare?' Lydia asked.

'I just thought I'd let you know the car's back,' she said.

Chapter 2

Detective Sergeant Sunita Roy was gripped with anticipation as Tom Vickers' Audi A3 headed further and further into the heart of the city. He'd promised her that this Sunday would prove a day to remember and her mind was flooded with a myriad of thoughts.

Were they going to the National Sea Life Centre or the zoo? Valentine's Day was nearly upon them. Were they destined for somewhere romantic? Was her boyfriend, a detective inspector with the same force, finally going to…? No, that was surely unlikely.

She hoped his promise of a memorable day would not end in disappointment like the time he took her fishing on a remote riverbank for an entire day without catching a single fish.

The detective sergeant, who was slim with silky, black, flowing hair and lustrous, dark eyes, turned towards him in the passenger seat.

'We're obviously going on some kind of trip – is it a canal boat?' she asked.

'Sunita, I've told you countless times already,' he replied with what she felt was a rather infuriating tone. 'I want to surprise you. We're nearly there.'

'Will we be near the shops?'

'You'll find out soon enough.'

After parking on the fifth floor of a multi-storey car park, the tall, stocky inspector, who was slightly overweight with short, brown hair, led her into the station beneath and down the stairs. The steam train was hissing and spluttering by the platform, like a great steel beast with plumes of steam gushing from its nostrils.

'Oh, Tom,' said Sunita. 'How wonderful. A steam train!'

'I just thought it would be great to try something different for Valentine's.' he explained with a smile. 'So I thought we could take a trip and have a meal in the Pullman's dining car at the same time.'

'You're such an old romantic,' she said, kissing him on the cheek.

'Not so much of the old,' he said while opening a carriage door and helping her on board. Then Vickers hauled himself up behind her into the carriage.

The pair found their table seats in the second coach, across the aisle from a couple of similar age to them – a ginger-haired man in a light-blue suit and a blonde woman in a green floral dress.

Vickers flashed a smile towards them. 'All right?' he asked.

'Yeah,' replied the man. 'You know you've only just made it, don't you? Train's due off any second.'

'Never mind. We'll still have a bostin' time,' said Vickers as the locomotive released a surge of steam and they drew away from the platform.

'I love the old steam trains,' said the man. 'Have you done this trip before?'

'No,' said Vickers. 'To be honest, we both work long hours. Don't get much chance for pleasure trips. This is our first weekend off together in weeks.'

'Months,' said Sunita with a broad grin.

'Are you two married?' asked the woman.

Sunita shook her head. 'No,' she said, 'but I live in hope.'

The couple laughed.

'We've only just met,' said the woman. 'I'm Lydia. Lydia Squires. This is Roman.'

'I'm Sunita and this is Tom,' said Sunita. She was reluctant to mention they worked for the police – a frequent conversation-stopper.

'We're having a meal later on in the Pullman car,' said Vickers.

'So are we,' said Roman. 'It's brilliant. Well worth it. I've had silver-service dinners on here twice before. You won't regret it.'

There was a pause in the conversation. Sunita glanced out of the window. They had just roared through another suburban station. That must be the fourth or fifth they had passed, she told herself. Now woods and fields came into view.

Sunita turned to her boyfriend. 'It isn't Valentine's Day officially till Tuesday,' she said quietly.

'I know,' he said. 'But it would be pointless running this train on a Tuesday when everyone's at work, wouldn't it?'

'I suppose so,' said Sunita. 'We'll both be working then anyway. I tell you what, Tom – this is one of your better ideas.'

She reached across the table and clasped his hand. 'Thank you, Tom.'

Roman interrupted them. 'Do you know what you're having to eat yet?' he asked Vickers.

'No. Haven't seen the menu.'

'I'd recommend the pan-fried cod,' Roman continued. 'Lydia can't decide between the vegetarian curry and duck leg with ratatouille.'

Lydia's mobile phone began to ring. She stared down at the handset before glancing towards her boyfriend.

'It's the neighbour again,' she whispered while answering the call with a cordial, 'Yes, Clare?'

A faint buzzing could be heard as the neighbour presented a brief report which pleased Lydia.

'Thank you, Clare,' she said. 'And you've got the registration number? Good. Can you hold on a second?'

Lydia put the phone on the table and searched her bag for a pen.

'Have you got a piece of paper?' she asked Roman.

'Will the cafe receipt do?' he asked.

She nodded and picked up her phone again.

'Can you give me that number slowly, Clare?' she asked.

After jotting down the car number on the back of the receipt, Lydia thanked Clare and hung up.

'She got a better look at the mystery visitor,' she told Roman. 'It's a guy. He tried the front door this morning and now he's gone. But at least she's got his car number.'

The two detectives could not help overhearing the conversation between their two fellow passengers. The pair gazed into each other's eyes. Both their minds were swarming with questions. But they said nothing.

Roman felt a duty to explain.

'Lydia here is a little concerned,' he told the detectives. 'There's a mystery guy who's been keeping a vigil outside her house while she's been away. I've tried to tell her not to worry.'

'That's a little alarming,' Vickers agreed. 'But, more often than not, there's a simple explanation.'

'That's what I've tried to tell her,' said Roman, reaching across and fondling his partner's hand. 'I'm wondering if it's a debt collector, chasing your old parking tickets.'

'I always pay them on time,' said Lydia.

'Could be all sorts of explanations,' said Sunita. 'You haven't done something newsworthy lately, have you, Lydia, or won the lottery? Maybe it's someone from the press.'

'Hold on. I know what it is,' said Vickers. 'You've forgotten to return your library book.'

'Don't be flippant, Tom,' said Sunita as a smile crept over her partner's face.

'Whatever it is, it's a little worrying,' Roman admitted.

'Yes, I can understand you both feeling like that. So what exactly has the man been doing?' asked Sunita. 'Has he been knocking on your door at odd times?'

'I didn't know anything until my neighbour called me a few moments ago,' said Lydia, before explaining about the black Mercedes and telling her she now had the car number.

'That's good,' said Sunita. 'I'd suggest you go to your local police station. Tell them what's happened and get them to check the registration.'

'Thanks. That's a good idea.'

'Whereabouts do you live?' asked Vickers.

'In Worcester,' said Lydia.

The two detectives glanced at each other. Her address was narrowly inside the district covered by their force, Heart of England Police.

'The neighbour could just go along to see the guy, dumbo Columbo, and ask what he wants,' suggested Vickers. 'You know, "I couldn't help noticing you. Is there anything I can do to help?"'

Lydia rolled her eyes. 'Oh, I've been a fool. I know who this could be,' she said. 'There's a guy at my company who seems to have some kind of crush on me. I'm sure he followed me home one afternoon after work. I thought all

that had come to an end after one of the bosses warned
him off. But maybe that's started up again.'

A waiter dressed in black approached them. 'If you've
booked for our dining experience, you'll be pleased to
know we're now serving lunch in the dining car at the rear
of the train,' he announced before walking away.

Chapter 3

The landlord and landlady of the Five Bells in the heart of
Worcester had made an effort to ensure that that
Valentine's night would prove a memorable one.

Bunting made from sparkling red hearts and cupid
figures had been draped above the entrance and around
the wood-panelled walls of the oak-beamed, city centre
pub. All the tables in the dining section at the rear were
decked out in red tablecloths. A red rose in the centre of
each one was surrounded by tiny, multi-coloured hearts.
Each table also featured a solitary red candle, adding a final
touch to the romantic, dimly lit atmosphere.

As soon as Roman Makepeace and Lydia Squires
arrived, a waitress in a black uniform escorted them across
the oak floor to the corner table they had booked a week
earlier.

After ordering a bottle of sauvignon blanc, Roman
leaned forward and clasped his sweetheart's hand.

'So what's been happening in your world since our train
ride on Sunday?' he asked.

'Not a great deal,' she said, straightening the creases in
her black chiffon dress with her other hand. 'I told you I
went to the police station, didn't I?'

'You told me you gave them the car number and they
said they'd get back to you.'

She nodded. 'Yes. They still haven't got back to me.'

Roman shrugged his shoulders.

'You were telling me social services have been trying to find your mother a care home,' he said.

'Yes. I'm due to visit her and maybe I'll get someone from the hospital to call the council.'

Roman shook his head.

'You'd have thought they could have written or phoned. Anyway, there's no sense worrying. You'll find out in due course.'

They chose identical dishes from the menu – duck liver pâté, beef Wellington and chocolate torte.

Afterwards, while sipping brandy coffees, they discussed their plans for the rest of the week. They were going to the cinema on Friday night and, on Saturday afternoon, visiting Roman's parents in Sutton Coldfield.

At about ten o'clock, Roman looked at his watch.

'I'm afraid I'm going to have to call it a night. As I told you last week, I've got to get to the office early tomorrow,' he said. 'We've got two coaches leaving at about half past seven.'

'Roman, it's been a lovely evening,' she replied.

His eyes had been fixed to his phone for the previous few minutes. He glanced up.

'I've just been reading a report on *Birmingham Live*. The M5 motorway is blocked south of Worcester and all surrounding roads are gridlocked,' he said.

'Will you manage to get home all right?' she asked.

'I should be fine,' he replied. 'The roads are clear north of the city.'

As Roman paid for their meal, one of the waiters presented Lydia with a red rose. Then, after collecting their coats, they set off on foot for her home, a quarter of a mile away. Walking hand in hand with her cherished new boyfriend, she felt as secure as she had, years before, as a child in her father's arms.

The semi-detached house in tree-lined Balmoral Gardens was in complete darkness when they arrived there, fifteen minutes later.

'I must have forgotten to leave a light on,' Lydia moaned. 'I usually leave the one in the hall on.'

Roman didn't reply. He wrapped his arms around her and kissed her tenderly under the glow of the nearby lamp post and the waning crescent moon. She kissed him back passionately and they remained standing there, by her wooden front gate, for a few minutes. Then he eased himself away.

'I'd better say goodnight,' he said while walking with her to the front door.

She took a key from her handbag and opened it before turning round.

She smiled. 'Goodnight then,' she said, drawing herself towards him again and kissing him on the lips.

Finally, Roman broke free and, while repeatedly turning his head and waving, he made his way back to the pavement and along the road to his silver Porsche Boxster. Lydia watched from the doorway, smiling and waving, until she saw him get in the car and set off on the forty-mile journey back to his home in Coleshill.

Still clasping the rose along with her clutch bag, Lydia stepped into the hallway and at once sensed that something was wrong. After turning the hall light on, she thought she could detect a faint trace of body odour.

Was it her imagination or was there a light flickering in the kitchen at the back of the house?

'Is there anybody there?' she called, taking a few steps forward.

There was no reply. The house was as still as a monastery at prayer.

She was now close to the foot of the stairs. The living-room door was on her left and the kitchen door straight ahead. How she wished she had invited Roman in. This talk about the mystery visitor had unnerved her a little.

Roman was strong and tall. He was athletic. She would have felt safe with him beside her.

She tried to think in a more positive way.

'There's no one here,' she told herself. 'I must have left one of the kitchen lights on when I went out instead of the hall light. Yes. That's how it must have been.'

She advanced gingerly towards the kitchen door. She pushed and it creaked open.

Lydia was alarmed when she stepped inside the faintly lit room. Resting on the centre of the kitchen table was a silver pocket torch which did not belong to her. A ray of light from it was illuminating the sink and window beyond.

Suddenly, to her horror, something moved in the shadows. A hooded figure that was standing by the back door.

Then, as she stood riveted to the spot, a muffled, low-pitched voice loomed from the darkness.

'So here you are at last,' it said.

Lydia's heart was pounding. Her mouth was dry and she was breathing erratically. She dropped her clutch bag and flower onto the table. The flower rolled across the tabletop and fell to the floor.

'Who are you?' she asked the person standing by the other side of the table, her voice shaking. 'What do you want?'

'I wanted to see your face,' said the voice.

Surely this must be someone playing a joke, thought Lydia. Any moment now one of her colleagues would spring out, laughing and shouting, 'Surprise!'

But the darkness endured and no one burst forward in a jocular manner.

As Lydia's eyes adjusted, she realised the hooded figure was dressed in black and wearing a face mask.

Without warning, the intruder darted forward and snatched up the torch. Lydia stood motionless for a moment by the kitchen door, shocked by the intrusion into her home and disoriented by the torch beam.

But then she bravely steeled herself for action. As the figure hurtled round the table and careered towards her in the dim light, Lydia grabbed her opponent's arm and jerked hard. The forward momentum sent the assailant crashing onto the floor.

Before she could decide on her next move, the agile attacker sprang back up and struck her several times in the neck and chest.

'What have you done, you bastard?' Lydia screamed.

'I done it because of what you done,' came the angry retort as Lydia became aware she was being stabbed with some kind of knife.

Her assailant watched while Lydia tumbled to the floor. Then, seconds later, the figure fled into the hall and escaped through the front door.

Chapter 4

Just before a quarter to eleven that night, a police car with its blue overhead light flashing raced along Balmoral Gardens and screeched to a halt outside number sixty-seven.

The next-door neighbour, a plump, middle-aged woman in a baggy top and jeans, was standing anxiously by the door.

The car's driver, PC Nina Kaur, jumped out and ran through the gate, closely followed by PC Graham McDonald.

'Are you Clare Robbins?' asked Kaur, an enthusiastic young constable with ambitions to join CID.

'Yes,' said the neighbour. 'I heard Miss Squires screaming about twenty minutes ago. The 999 operator told me not to go in for safety reasons.'

'You acted correctly,' said McDonald as she handed him the key. 'The lady's called Lydia Squires?'

'That's right.'

He unlocked the door and the pair marched inside the freshly painted hall.

'Police!' shouted Kaur. 'Nobody move.'

The kitchen door in front of them was ajar but swinging to and fro in a light breeze that was wafting through the house and knocking the door against the lock.

Kaur called out, 'Lydia! Are you about?'

Her cry was met by silence. She stepped towards the kitchen and pushed the door. Little could have prepared her for the shocking scene that lay before them.

The hunched figure of a woman in a grey coat was lying on the floor covered in blood. She lay on her back with her head towards the kitchen door. A rose had been placed across her chest.

'Oh my God! What's happened?' Kaur exclaimed as the neighbour approached the kitchen door.

'Is it a grey coat?' shouted the neighbour, glancing across at the body. 'Oh for Christ's sake. I hope it's not Lydia.'

McDonald, turned round to face her.

'Come on, Mrs Robbins,' he said. 'I think you should leave.'

He escorted her back to the gate.

At the same time, Kaur ran forward into the room, knelt down and raised Lydia into her arms. Lydia's black chiffon dress had been slashed around the chest. There was a pool of blood on the floor beneath her. Her eyes were open and lifeless. The constable lowered her upper torso to the floor and checked for a pulse.

'There's nothing that can be done for her,' she said quietly as her colleague returned. 'She's dead.'

McDonald now realised why the kitchen door had been swaying. A pane had been smashed in the back door, creating a through-draught. Fragments of glass were strewn around the doormat.

'We'd better call the control room,' he muttered.

While Kaur fussed over the body, he reached inside his jacket for his radio and made an urgent call to Heart of England Police headquarters. After he finished, he cast his eyes round the kitchen.

'Looks like a burglary,' he said. 'Maybe she interrupted them.'

His colleague didn't seem to be listening. Then she glanced up.

'Whoever killed her must have done it in a frenzy,' she said. 'This lady's been stabbed several times. It looks like the work of a maniac.'

'Yes. Someone with a passion has done this. Some evil bastard,' said McDonald. 'But if they act in this way – on the spur of the moment and in an irrational way – the chances are they've made mistakes. It won't be long before our forensic people nail them.'

His phone began to ring.

'We've been asked to attend 67 Balmoral Gardens. Lady believed badly injured,' said the caller from the ambulance service.

'She's actually died,' said McDonald.

'We've still got to come,' said the caller. 'Where's the body?'

After giving full details to the ambulance service, he turned his attention to Kaur.

'You know we ought to vacate the room and not touch anything in here,' said the constable, who was standing by the kitchen door. 'We must try and preserve the crime scene.'

The pair left the house and walked to the gate, where Clare Robbins was waiting for them.

'Is she definitely dead?' she asked.

'Yes, I'm afraid so,' said Kaur.

Clare began crying into her hands.

'This is probably all my fault,' she wailed. 'I heard Lydia shouting at someone. If I'd used the key that she'd lent me and let myself in, maybe I could have helped her.'

'And you might have got yourself killed in the process,' said Kaur. 'No, you did the right thing. Whoever did this was desperate. I'm sure they wouldn't have thought twice about attacking you as well. Then we'd have been dealing with an even worse incident.'

'Come on,' said McDonald. 'I think you should leave everything up to the police now, Mrs Robbins. I'll escort you back home.'

While he was attending to the neighbour, Kaur stepped back inside the house and decided to inspect the rest of the ground floor. She entered the bright, modern living room at the front. It was sparsely furnished with a beige three-piece suite, a glass bookcase in the corner, a small table, a low-level sideboard containing ornaments and a wide-screen television beside the bay window. There was an open brick fireplace and three Valentine's cards lined up on the mantelpiece above it.

She strolled over and peered inside each card in turn. None had been signed with a name.

McDonald burst into the hall, calling her name. 'Nina! I've got an idea where the killer might have got the murder weapon,' he told her. 'One of the kitchen drawers is half open and all the cutlery's been scattered about inside.'

Chapter 5

Bleary-eyed Sunita Roy hauled herself out of bed in her darkened bedroom and peered at her bedside clock. She was perturbed to find it was nearly nine o'clock and annoyed that her partner had gone off without waking her.

Sunita, who should have risen from her bed an hour earlier, ran into her en suite bathroom and quickly showered.

'This is what comes from having a late night,' she told herself while becoming conscious of a developing headache.

Tom Vickers had taken her for a Valentine's meal in the nearby town of Queensbridge and she had had more wine than she normally drank. He had also presented her with chocolates and flowers. In return, she had handed him a grey pullover and some aftershave.

I shouldn't complain, she thought to herself as she got dressed. After all, it was her second Valentine's meal within three days.

She had only just descended the stairs in her five-bedroom house in Shawley Green when her phone rang and she saw from the photograph appearing on her handset that her boss, DCI Gavin Roscoe, was calling.

'Good morning, sir,' she said.

'Don't bother coming into the office,' said Roscoe, Head of CID. 'There's been a murder in Worcester. Woman's been viciously stabbed to death.'

'Sounds shocking,' she said.

'Yes. Victim's in her late twenties. She lived with her widowed mother, who's in hospital right now. Your friend, PC Kaur, found the dead woman in a pool of blood on the kitchen floor after a 999 call from a neighbour. It looks like whoever it was broke in through the back door. Could be a burglary gone wrong.'

'What's the address, sir?'

'It's 67 Balmoral Gardens in a suburb called Barbourne. Dead woman is Lydia Squires.'

She nearly dropped the phone.

'Are you sure, sir?'

'Yes, of course. Why?'

'It's just that Tom and I met a woman last Sunday with that name. She was in her late twenties.'

'Might be her,' said Roscoe.

* * *

PC Nina Kaur was on duty outside 67 Balmoral Gardens when Sunita Roy arrived.

The sergeant weaved her way through a crowd of reporters and photographers gathered on the pavement outside.

'Any news on the victim?' one of the reporters called out to her.

'Do you know when the name will be released?' asked another.

'I'm sorry,' Sunita replied. 'A senior officer might be making a statement later.'

She and Kaur hurried up the path and went inside.

'You look shattered,' Sunita told her.

'Not surprising,' said the constable. 'I haven't stopped since seven o'clock last night.'

'You *are* keen.'

'No, we're just short of staff.'

'Is Dr Reynolds here yet?' asked Sunita.

'Yes. He's been examining the body for a while,' said Kaur.

'I couldn't see his car.'

'He's had to park down the road. The SOCOs have been here for several hours.'

Sunita gazed at her surroundings. Lydia Squires' home was a grey, semi-detached house on three storeys standing in a row of similar Victorian properties. She could see a side gate down an alley which gave access to the back of the four-bedroom house.

'The next-door neighbour, Clare Robbins, called 999 last night after she heard screaming,' said the constable. 'The victim's brother-in-law, Aiden Pagett, has been here, checking the contents.'

'I know,' said Sunita. 'I've seen statements from both Mr Pagett and Mrs Robbins.'

Sunita watched as the chief inspector, a tall, stout man, strode along the pavement towards her.

'Come on, Sergeant,' he said after greeting the two women. 'Let's see what we've got.'

As soon as they reached the front door, the crime scene manager stopped them in their tracks.

'Sorry, sir. We're not letting anyone enter the kitchen from the hallway at present,' he explained.

'All right,' said Roscoe. 'We'll just stick our noses into the living room, shall we?'

The two detectives left the bright hallway and stepped into the living room, a through-room with light-green walls and a matching patterned carpet.

'The neighbour says Lydia had spoken about going out for dinner on Valentine's Day,' said Roscoe.

'Yes, sir,' said Kaur. 'Clare Robbins bumped into Lydia on Monday. She told her Lydia's boyfriend was taking her for a Valentine's meal at the Five Bells but they weren't intending to stay out late as it was a midweek night.'

'That's very helpful,' said Roscoe. 'But now we must go and see Dr Reynolds before he leaves.'

Sunita followed the chief inspector out of the front door, down the side alley and into the rear garden, which consisted of a lawn surrounded by shrubs and trees. Through the open back door they could see into the kitchen, where portly, middle-aged pathologist Dr Silas Reynolds, dressed in white overalls, was crouched over a body.

'Silas, how's it going?' asked Roscoe.

'You always turn up when all the hard work's done,' Reynolds replied as he turned his head towards the two detectives.

'Is it all right to come in?' asked Roscoe.

'Yes. Our scenes of crime chums have finished in here,' said the doctor. He made sure a plastic sheet over the corpse was covering the victim's head. Then he stood up and ventured towards them.

'Well, I'm afraid this poor lady has been subjected to a frenzied attack, old fruit,' said Reynolds.

'Definitely murder then?'

'No doubt at all,' said the pathologist.

Chapter 6

In her seven years with Heart of England CID, law graduate Sunita Roy had seen the bodies of countless murder victims shortly after their demise. But viewing the corpse was always unsettling. As she and the chief inspector stood talking to the pathologist in the draughty kitchen, she braced herself for this burden which was a necessary part of the job.

'I've counted at least nine stab wounds to the abdomen, neck and chest,' Dr Reynolds was saying. 'The most serious one was on the left-hand side of the woman's neck. The carotid artery has been partially severed. That's one of two arteries supplying blood to the brain, face and neck. Although I've got more tests to do, this was a significant injury and it's highly likely it was this that led to her death. That along with the haemorrhagic shock produced by the multiple wounds.'

The chief inspector suggested they should both view the body.

'You particularly, Sergeant,' he said. 'You need to establish it's the same woman you met on the steam railway.'

He strode to the other side of the kitchen, stooped down and raised the edge of the plastic sheet. He spent a few seconds staring down at the woman's face and her gruesome injuries before letting the sheet slip back.

'Not pleasant,' he remarked as he rejoined his colleagues.

Sunita, somewhat reluctantly, followed his lead, stepping across the room and raising the sheet.

There was no doubt in her mind. It was the same woman she had met on the train on Sunday – the same long hair and blue eyes. A young woman in the first throes of love. A young woman on the threshold of an exciting new life. Now all her young hopes and dreams gone, lost to oblivion.

She dropped the sheet back.

'Yes,' she said. 'It's the same woman Tom and I met on the train. She was with a guy called Roman. She'd been warned about a stranger seen hanging about outside here. Looks like he may have found her.'

'Write me a report on that for the files,' said Roscoe.

'Sounds as though you've got an intriguing start to the case already,' Reynolds remarked.

Roscoe nodded.

'Dr Reynolds,' said Sunita, 'do you have any idea what kind of weapon would have caused these wounds? A kitchen knife has gone missing.'

'Too early to say, Sergeant,' he replied. 'But a kitchen knife could have done the job. Each wound is approximately 1.7 cm long by 0.6 mm. Each one has a clearly pointed edge with the opposite edge squared off.'

'We haven't had a chance to obtain precise information on the missing knife yet,' she said.

'Certainly, there's no sign the incisions that pierced this lady's flimsy dress were made by a weapon with a serrated edge, if that helps.'

'Are there any signs of defensive wounds on the victim – you know, signs that she put up a fight?' Sunita asked.

'Too early to say,' said Reynolds. 'There may be skin cells from the attacker under the victim's fingernails, but she may have been taken totally by surprise. Or she may have been too shocked to react.'

'Perhaps the attacker acted extremely quickly, denying her the opportunity to fight back,' Sunita suggested.

Reynolds shrugged his shoulders.

Roscoe, who had been patiently listening to the conversation, interrupted to say, 'Silas, what time would you say the victim died?'

Reynolds looked down, stroked his chin and thought for a moment.

'Rigor mortis is well set in. It has extended to arms and legs, so I'd estimate that she died between eight and twelve hours ago,' he said.

'So between 9.30 p.m. and 1.30 a.m.?' said Roscoe. 'We received the 999 call at around ten thirty.'

'That sounds right,' said Reynolds.

'Dr Reynolds, a pane of glass has been broken in the door,' said Sunita. 'Do we know how it was smashed?'

'Yes. Dr Ling from forensics identified a house brick in the back garden which we found on the path by the door. It looks as though it was used to smash the glass. After smashing the pane, it would have been simple for someone to put their hand through, turn the key and open the door.'

'So there could be DNA or prints on the brick?'

'They've bagged it up now, of course, but there could be,' Reynolds agreed. 'The only other result they had was finding tiny globules of spittle on the kitchen table. That suggests the killer was speaking with some force to the victim across the table. You never know. That might also give us some DNA.'

He began putting his thermometer, syringes, a handsaw, sterile swabs, a small torch and a camera away in his brown leather 'murder bag'.

Sunita was casting her eyes around the kitchen, engrossed in thought.

'Strange burglary,' she remarked. 'The suspect breaks in, searches around and finds a knife. Then what? Presumably they might have looked for valuables of some kind around – jewellery or gadgets. But there aren't any signs that they've searched the place. It doesn't sound like a standard burglary. It sounds like someone was waiting for Lydia Squires.'

'Good points you make there, Sergeant,' said Roscoe.

'I'm also thinking that, if the killer arrived here with murder on their mind, how come they didn't bring a weapon with them? They could easily have shopped for a knife and brought it along. Using a knife belonging to the victim's family seems rather odd.'

'I see what you're saying, Sergeant,' said Roscoe. 'If we accept the theory that the intruder used a kitchen knife to kill Miss Squires, it appears they then ran off with it. So it follows that there's a good chance they disposed of it nearby. This means that one of our main priorities now is to find that knife.'

'Yes, sir,' Sunita said, 'finding that knife is crucial.'

'I'm going to head back to CID now,' said Roscoe. 'I'm going to make PC Kaur responsible for keeping us informed of the progress of all the external searches. Meanwhile, Sergeant, I've got a list of jobs for you. I'd like you to have a good look round the house. After that, call round at the Five Bells and see if you can pick up anything useful there. Then I think you should have a chat with the brother-in-law. We need to know as much as we can about this young woman's life in the weeks leading up to the murder. In addition, I'll get DC Khalid to speak to Miss Squires' employer.'

* * *

As she cast her eyes round the living room, Sunita Roy felt she would rank it as comfortable but requiring updating.

As she gazed at the fireplace, her eyes drifted upwards and rested on the three Valentine's cards on the mantelpiece.

One, signed 'Guess who?' and showing two love-struck cows, was captioned, 'You're udderley adorable.' A second, with two enamoured hedgehogs covered in sticking plasters, bore the scribbled greeting 'Who?' The third card with roses on the front was inscribed with a capital letter

R. Almost certainly one that her boyfriend, Roman, sent, she decided.

After photographing the greetings inside the cards, Sunita climbed the stairs and found Dr Alice Ling, the senior forensic scientist, crouched on the landing examining the door to the front bedroom.

'We're nearly finished,' she remarked, peering at the sergeant over her wire-framed glasses.

Sunita stepped past her and entered the bright, airy main bedroom, which had a bay window overlooking the street. She decided this must be the mother's bedroom since there was a Zimmer frame beside the single bed and a hot-water bottle on top of a bedside cabinet.

'Which is Lydia's room?' she asked.

'The one at the back,' replied Dr Ling, pointing to the far side of the landing. 'Don't worry. It's all right for you to go in there. Oh, before you ask, we've removed Miss Squires' phone and tablet.'

Sunita pushed the back bedroom door and stepped into a space with a predominantly pink colour scheme. Although the walls were grey, the bed covers, pillows and curtains were all pink. There were fashion magazines on the bedside table. There was an electronic keyboard standing by the far wall and a hi-fi system on a table in the corner. She opened a wardrobe door to find an array of outfits in bold, bright colours including satin dresses with sequins and faux fur.

Sunita glanced round to find Dr Ling had followed her in.

'I thought you'd be interested in these,' she told the sergeant quietly, handing her a collection of handwritten letters. 'They're all from someone called Vernon Bainbridge.'

Sunita found there were altogether three brief letters presented in spidery writing on small sheets of expensive-looking white notepaper.

'There's no address given,' said Dr Ling. 'Envelopes that they came in were all postmarked January.'

Sunita read part of the first one.

> *Hi Gorgeous One,*
> *Why do you keep avoiding me? When I saw you in the canteen I only wanted to have a brief chat, Lydia. It would be great if we could go for a meal together and continue our conversation.*

Sunita turned to the second note and read the opening lines.

> *Hi Gorgeous One,*
> *I've just learned you have blocked my emails. I can't understand why. I thought you had feelings for me.*

She glimpsed a third note.

> *Hi Gorgeous One,*
> *Writing these notes is the only way I know to express my deep love for you.*

Two of them were signed 'Vernon' and one was signed 'Vernon Bainbridge'. She scrolled through the images of the cards on her phone. The words 'Guess Who?' on the one with love-struck cows matched Bainbridge's handwriting.

'Did you know I ran into Lydia three days ago,' Sunita told her.

'Did you?'

'Yes. She mentioned a guy at the shoe company where she worked who'd been stalking her. I'm guessing that's him.'

'Sounds like it,' said Dr Ling. 'We've bagged up some letters relating to Miss Squires' job. She worked for Hinkley and Evans in Saltley. She was secretary to a company director. Oh, and I've got some photographs of her. Thought you could do with some.'

She handed the sergeant a head-and-shoulders photograph of Lydia Squires and an envelope.

'Have you seen any mention of a guy called Roman?' asked the sergeant.

'No, nothing. The only other thing we found was this note on the mantelpiece. Thought it might be important.'

Dr Ling handed her a scrap of paper and walked away. Sunita read the words 'Mercedes A-Class' followed by a car number.

Before she left the house, Sunita spent a few minutes talking to Dr Reynolds, who was preparing for the victim to be placed in a body bag and removed to a hospital mortuary.

Then, as she was about to leave the kitchen, her eyes suddenly rested on a red object on the kitchen floor, pressed up against the body.

She bent down and touched something delicate lying by the body. She slid her hand down beside the victim's black dress and drew out a rose, dripping in blood.

Chapter 7

Sunita Roy had never ventured inside the Five Bells pub before, but knew precisely where it was – positioned in the heart of the city, close to one of the two railway stations. She spent nearly five minutes knocking on the main door of the premises without anyone answering.

Finally, she heard the sound of footsteps before a gruff male voice growled, 'We're not open yet.'

'Police,' Sunita yelled back through the door. 'I need to speak to you.'

She heard bolts being drawn back before the heavily built grey-haired landlord, Charlie Coverdale, poked his head round the entrance.

'What are we meant to have done this time?' he asked.

'I'm DS Roy from Heart of England Police,' she explained. 'We're investigating a murder.'

'We've had no trouble here.'

'Don't worry,' she said. 'It happened some distance away in Balmoral Gardens. It's just that it happened last night and we believe the victim had a meal here earlier on.'

'You'd better come in.'

The publican, who had been cleaning the wooden floor, moved his bucket of soapy water to one side and placed his mop in it. Although initially suspicious of his visitor, Coverdale proved to be a genial man who became more relaxed as their conversation progressed.

'So what would you like to know, Sergeant Roy?' he asked.

'Do you recognise this lady?' she asked, slipping the photograph from its envelope.

'Oh my God,' he said. 'Is that the lady that's been murdered?'

'I'm afraid so.'

'Yes, I remember her very well. Her partner phoned and booked the table last week. They were a lovely couple. I'll show you the table they had.'

He led her into the rear section of the pub and showed her the corner table.

'They had a bottle of sauvignon blanc and both had the beef Wellington, if my memory serves me correctly. They didn't stay long. They left around ten o'clock.'

'Do you hand out red roses to ladies on Valentine's Day?'

'Yes. Why do you ask?'

'I just needed to clear up that point. A flower was found near the body.'

'Oh my God. A rose denoting love lying beside a murder victim. That's so tragic.'

'I know. What about the man she was with? Do you remember his name?'

'Roman Makepeace. He paid a small deposit by credit card when he booked the table and then paid for the meal with the same card. My wife took a call yesterday morning from someone wanting to confirm the booking.'

Why does that name Makepeace strike a chord? Sunita thought to herself.

'Anyway,' she said, 'I just wanted to find out if anything unusual happened while they were here. You know, there wasn't an argument, as far as you're aware?'

'No, definitely not.'

'You didn't see them being followed by anyone when they left?'

'We were way too busy, Sergeant. The place was heaving. Look, as far as I could tell, they were a devoted couple enjoying a romantic meal on Valentine's Day. Nothing untoward happened. Believe me.'

* * *

After leaving the Five Bells, Sunita took her mobile out of her coat pocket and carried out some online research while walking back to her car. She was interrupted when her phone began ringing. Tom Vickers' image appeared on the handset's screen.

'Have you heard what happened?' she said as she answered the call.

'That's why I'm ringing,' said Vickers, who was using a 'hands-free' while driving. 'I'm on my way to headquarters and I've just found out about Lydia Squires, the woman on the train.'

'Yes, stabbed at least nine times. Tom, it's horrible.'

'Do you think it was that stranger that was hanging round her place?' he asked.

'Who knows? Too early to say, but I've just had another shock. You know the guy she was with on the train? His full name's Roman Makepeace.'

'Oh my God,' said Vickers. 'Is he related to that drugs baron?'

'Yes. I've just been having a look online. He's the son of Axel Makepeace, who runs the West Side Gang.'

* * *

While Sunita set off to buy an early lunch, Tom Vickers was thirty miles away, driving into the police car park at their St James Street headquarters. As he was climbing the stairs just before half past twelve, the familiar Birmingham accent of the chief inspector boomed out from behind him.

'Morning, Tom. You all right?' asked Roscoe.

Vickers turned his head while reaching the quarter landing, midway up the stairs.

'Morning, guv,' Vickers replied with a broad smile. 'Yes, bearing up.'

'On top of this gruesome murder in Worcester, I hear the chief super wants us to take a fresh look at a cold case,' said Roscoe.

'Yes. That's why I've come in,' said Vickers.

'I'm just going to hang up my coat and then I'll see you up there,' said Roscoe.

A few minutes later, the pair met on the second-floor landing and approached the office of Chief Superintendent Nicola Norris.

'Come straight in,' she shouted through the open door. 'I want to get straight down to business.'

The two detectives found the grey-haired, sixty-five-year-old policewoman at the side of her large oak desk, tapping away on a computer keyboard.

Norris, who had been injured in a horse-riding accident years before, manoeuvred her wheelchair to a more central position at her desk and peered at them over her reading glasses.

'I'll come straight to the point,' she said, after the two detectives had found chairs. 'Tom, you know about this matter already, but I believe you're totally in the dark, Gavin. So I'll go over the basics. The assistant chief constable has asked us to take another look into the missing councillor, Debbie Portman.'

Roscoe immediately remembered the macabre case. Eight years earlier, an independent member of Queensbridge Town Council and a former mayor, Councillor Debbie Portman, disappeared without trace after a violent incident at her home on the northern outskirts of the town. Bloodstains were found on a carpet together with fragments of a smashed antique vase.

Evidence at the time strongly pointed to the involvement of a well-known local criminal, Todd Styler, a paving contractor who dabbled in drugs. Styler and his workmate, Zak Bridges, had a job laying a patio at the Portmans' house. There was a row over the fee. But the evidence against Styler was mostly circumstantial. He had an alibi for the night of the disappearance, and, with the absence of a body, police were forced to drop the case.

'Debbie Portman's body was thought to have been buried close by. Among the locations searched were the grounds of King's Milton Primary School,' Norris stated.

'That's the school that had been shut down, wasn't it?' said Roscoe.

Norris nodded. 'That's right. At the time, the school was right next door to the councillor's house. It had fallen into disrepair and was cited as a possible hiding place for a body – either in the buildings or in the grounds. And of course Jakeman's Wood is close by, where our search teams also spent a lot of hours without success.'

'That was such a long while ago, but it's started to come back to me now,' said Roscoe.

'Yes, a lot of time has passed, Gavin,' said Norris. 'But her family have never given up hope and neither has our force. The detective who led inquiries back then,

DCI Ainslie Hill, felt the best hope of a conviction lay in tracking Styler's movements on the night of the murder with the help of phone records. But that proved a dead end.'

Roscoe nodded. 'Like a lot of the leads we had on that case. I remember it well. I was a DI at the time. Styler claimed he'd lost his phone and no signal could be found.'

'Yes. Well, there have been considerable advances in the technology relating to mobile phone analysis since those days,' Norris continued. 'And for that reason we've taken a decision to reopen the case. This is why Tom's here. He's been working hard for the past few days to obtain data that will hopefully give us more precise information about the locations where Styler's phone might have travelled that night.'

Roscoe glanced towards the inspector.

'Any definite progress so far, Tom?' he asked.

'Not so far, guv,' Vickers admitted. 'But the chief superintendent is correct in what she's been saying. There have been major advances in cell tower data analysis and we're hopeful of getting a map of Styler's phone movements that night. It will only give us the general location of his phone, of course. But any help in narrowing down the search area could lead to a breakthrough.'

Chapter 8

The street in Saltley where footwear firm Hinkley and Evans had been manufacturing shoes since the 1930s had seen better days.

Firms either side of the red-brick shoe factory had closed long ago. Their grimy windows, some broken, and shuttered doors told of abandoned trades or firms that had now closed down. But the directors of the family shoe firm still proudly boasted in their annual report, available online, of how they were 'keeping step in the footwear world'.

DC Omar Khalid, an earnest detective in his twenties with black, curly hair, who had been researching the company in advance, found a parking space in the street for his blue Ford Focus. He walked to the main entrance on Thursday morning and stepped inside.

A young dark-haired woman, sitting at a computer behind a curved graphite-grey reception desk, asked if he had an appointment.

'No, but I need to see your boss urgently,' he explained, producing his warrant card. 'I'm DC Khalid from Heart of England CID.'

'Oh, police?' she said, rising to her feet. 'Can I ask what it's about?'

'It's about the death of a member of your staff.'

After making an internal phone call which Khalid could not hear, she directed him to the lift and told him to travel to the second floor.

On arrival a few minutes later, he was greeted by a tall man in a navy-blue suit who was wearing black-framed glasses.

'You're the fellow from CID, I take it?' said the man.

'Yes, sir. DC Khalid.'

'Good. I'm Mervyn Hinkley, managing director. I gather you have some distressing news for us?'

'I'm afraid so,' said the detective.

'You'd better come into my office.'

He led Khalid along the corridor, past several doors, until they reached a large room at the end. Hinkley found his visitor a comfortable seat before settling himself into an executive-style chair behind a vast oak desk.

'I understand your secretary is a lady named Lydia Squires. Is that correct, sir?' said Khalid.

'Yes. What exactly has happened? She didn't come in yesterday, nor phoned in sick. Is she all right?'

'I'm sorry to tell you she's been found dead at her home.'

'Oh my God. How terrible,' said Hinkley. 'Her poor mother must be devastated. When did this happen?'

'Her body was found on Tuesday night, sir, at about eleven o'clock.'

'She's only been working here for three months but in that time she's really impressed us. Absolutely brilliant woman. I don't know how we're going to manage without her. This is all very sudden, DC Khalid. She seemed well when she left work on Tuesday afternoon. We wondered when she failed to turn up yesterday if her mother had become ill again as she's been in hospital.'

'I'm afraid Miss Squires has been murdered. That's why I thought it was important to come here, see her place of work and to speak to you.'

'This is horrendous,' said Hinkley. 'Absolutely dreadful. If I can help the police in any way at all, I obviously will. Can I ask how she died?'

'I can't disclose all the details but I'm afraid it was a violent death, sir.'

'How awful.'

'Have there been any incidents at work recently involving Miss Squires?' asked the detective.

'No. Thankfully, everything's been running smoothly.'

'No arguments with anyone? Nothing to suggest she was unhappy about anything?'

'Well, no. We run a happy ship, DC Khalid. She's a lady with a very amiable, positive nature. She gets on well with everybody. Nothing is too much trouble.'

'So you can't think of anyone who might have a motive for killing her?'

'No, not at all. She was a first-rate secretary and popular with everyone.'

Khalid leaned back in his chair and, for a moment, stared out of the window behind the director's desk into the busy street below.

'We heard there's been at least one individual who's been bothering Miss Squires. Stalking her probably wouldn't be overstating the case. A guy by the name of Bainbridge – Vernon Bainbridge.'

Hinkley grimaced. 'Oh, that was more of a misunderstanding when she first came here. He's a rather immature guy who had some kind of crush on Miss Squires and tried to show her affection. As soon as he understood she wasn't interested in him, it all stopped.'

Khalid shook his head. 'I'm not sure if that's strictly true, sir. We understand he wrote several letters to Miss Squires last month.'

Hinkley frowned. 'Bainbridge works in our customer service department. I went and had a quiet word with him before Christmas when I found out how distressed Miss Squires was becoming as a result of this unwanted attention. I warned him that he'd got a choice: he could either desist with his obsessive behaviour and leave Miss Squires alone or I'd dismiss him and refer the matter to police. I understood from Miss Squires that he had desisted and that therefore the whole matter had resolved itself.'

'Well, as I say, he sent her at least three letters and expressed his love for her.'

'I can't believe that the man would do that. Especially after the stern way I spoke to him.'

'We'll need to interview him, of course. Is he in work today?'

'I'll find out for you,' Hinkley assured him.

After Hinkley confirmed with his secretary that Bainbridge was in his office and obtained the man's home address in Northfield for Khalid, the director turned to the detective with a smile.

'Is there anything else you need to know?'

'You don't happen to know what kind of car Mr Bainbridge drives, do you?' asked Khalid.

'No. I'm afraid not,' said Hinkley.

'Would you like me to invite Mr Bainbridge up here, so you can chat to him in relative comfort?'

Khalid shook his head. 'No. That won't be necessary. You mentioned he was in customer services. I'd rather drop in while he's in his department.'

'Very well. I'll show you down there personally,' Hinkley said. 'It's a large building. I don't want you getting lost.'

He strode to the door, opened it and beckoned the detective to follow him.

They took the lift to the ground floor. Hinkley led Khalid along a corridor until they reached a brightly lit office where more than a dozen members of staff were sitting in front of computers with headsets on.

After inviting Khalid to wait by the door, he stepped across the room and tapped on the shoulder of a man in his thirties.

Vernon Bainbridge, a man of medium height with long, fair hair in a ponytail, had been engrossed in a phone conversation. But seeing his boss standing behind him and noticing the visitor by the door, he extricated himself from his call.

He followed Hinkley out of the room.

'This is a detective from Heart of England Police, Vernon,' said Hinkley. 'He'd like to talk to you. Now, Detective, if you don't mind, I'll leave you in the hands of our employee. If you need any more help, this is my card. Call me any time you like during office hours.'

He handed the visitor a small white card.

'Thank you. You've been very helpful,' said Khalid.

As Hinkley walked away, Khalid quickly assessed Bainbridge and could see why Lydia had become concerned by his past pursuit of her. The employee was a solemn-faced man with a reddish, pimply face and, as he approached him, he detected a faint whiff of body odour.

'What's this all about?' Bainbridge demanded.

'Look, is there somewhere we can go to have a chat?' asked Khalid.

'We can go into the reception area, if you like,' Bainbridge suggested.

He led Khalid back along the corridor until they reached the reception desk near the entrance. They stepped across the room to a set of beige sofas in the corner and sat down opposite each other.

'Now first of all, Mr Bainbridge, could you tell me what car you drive?' asked Khalid, taking care to keep a clear distance from his malodorous companion.

'Yes, but where's all this going?' asked Bainbridge.

'Sorry. I should have said. I'm investigating the death of a work colleague of yours, Lydia Squires.'

'Is she dead?'

'Yes. I'm afraid she is.'

Bainbridge shook his head repeatedly as he turned pale. 'No, no, no,' he said under his breath. He put his hands to his face, stood up and stepped around the room in a daze.

'I haven't seen anything in the news about it,' he said.

'I think her name was only being officially released to the media today.'

'How did she die?'

'She was murdered.'

'My God. That's terrible. I really loved that woman. Where did she die?'

'In Worcester.'

'So she was killed at her home?'

'I'm not able to discuss all the details of the incident.'

Bainbridge returned to his seat and placed his head in his hands.

'Can you give me a minute?' he asked.

He stood up and walked about the room again, staring down at the light-green carpet. Then he resumed his seat.

'I'm sorry if this has come as a shock,' said Khalid while Bainbridge began to compose himself. 'Listen, could you tell me what car you drive?'

'A grey Toyota Yaris,' he replied.

'Have you recently been using a different car?'

'No,' he replied indignantly. 'Why do you want to know all this?'

'We've discovered you had a fascination for this lady. You sent her letters and it's believed you followed her to her house on occasion.'

'Oh, that's not true,' he said.

'Your boss seemed to think you had some kind of crush on her,' said Khalid. 'He had to give you a warning.'

'It was all a misunderstanding. I really liked Lydia. We chatted once or twice and I thought she was encouraging me to take things further. As soon as I realised she didn't feel the same way about me, I broke off contact.'

'Really?' said Khalid. 'We believe you've turned up several times at her house over the past few days.'

'That's total nonsense. Why would you say that? I've been at home or out with my mates.'

'How did you know she lives in Worcester?'

'She must have told me.'

'You completely deny having use of another car?'

'Of course.'

Bainbridge leaned forward and placed his head in his hands again.

'This is ridiculous,' he said. 'Someone in a car is spotted outside Lydia's house and immediately police think it's me. Well, I can tell you straight. As soon as Mr Hinkley pointed out to me that my approaches to the lady were unwelcome, I immediately ended all communication.'

Khalid frowned on hearing this.

'My sergeant's told me you sent Lydia a Valentine's card.'

'No,' Bainbridge insisted.

'You knew exactly where she's been living, didn't you? And you've been visiting her house.'

'No.

'On Valentine's Day, you couldn't keep away. You went round there in the evening and confronted her in her house.'

'No. Of course not.'

'Where were you between 10 p.m. and 10.45 p.m. on Tuesday?'

'I was at my father's place,' he said.

After a brief pause, he glanced up at the detective.

'For God's sake,' he said, 'you think I murdered her, don't you?'

Chapter 9

Aiden Pagett, Lydia Squires' brother-in-law, lived in a sumptuous, two-bedroom ground-floor apartment in a sought-after district of West Bromwich with views across open fields.

Sunita Roy was immediately impressed as she parked her newly acquired grey C-Class Mercedes outside the building in Trinity Drive and strolled up the concrete path to the smart, partly glazed front door.

According to his police statement, thirty-two-year-old Pagett had married Lydia's older sister a year earlier. He worked as an office manager while she worked nights in a biscuit factory. They had no children.

As she waited for the door to be opened, Sunita gazed round, wondering why there was no car on the drive.

Perhaps he doesn't drive, she thought to herself. Or maybe he owns one of the vehicles parked across the street.

The door was opened by a solemn man with receding dark hair and a small beard. Looking relaxed in a T-shirt and jeans, he was of medium height, bony and with a long jaw.

'Mr Pagett?' she asked.

'Yes.'

'DS Roy,' she explained. 'Heart of England CID. Sorry. I know it's a bad time, but I'd like to talk to you about your sister-in-law.'

'Come in,' he said with a resigned look.

She followed him into an immaculately presented living room with light streaming in through white venetian window blinds. There were several watercolour paintings of Warwickshire landscapes around the walls.

'We're finding it hard coming to terms with our loss,' he said in a soft voice. He picked up some motoring magazines from a light-brown sofa and invited her to sit down.

'I understand you're married to Lydia's sister, Allison,' said Sunita, taking a small black notebook and pen from her pocket.

'That's right.'

'Is she not around at present?'

'She's asleep. She's had some sleeping pills. Allison has taken the loss of her sister very badly. Thankfully, her bosses at work have been very understanding and let her take the week off.'

'Could you give me her phone number?'

He obliged by taking her notebook and writing a number on the open page with a pen.

'That's her mobile,' he said.

Sunita began taking notes while Pagett made himself comfortable in an armchair next to a table piled with dirty food plates and coffee mugs.

'We want to build up a picture of what kind of person Lydia was,' she said.

'What the police call victimology,' said Pagett, who began fidgeting with his pen.

'Yes, that's right. How did you know that?'

'I think I read about it in a true crime magazine.'

'Often studying the life of the victim helps to solve the crime,' said Sunita. 'How long had you known Lydia?'

'Only about a year,' he said, shrugging his shoulders, 'but I got to know her fairly well over that time. Did you know she was a club and pub singer as well as working as a secretary?'

'No, I didn't. Did she have regular singing work?'

'She's been singing recently with a pub band. Would you like a tea or coffee, by the way?'

'No. I'm all right,' she said.

Pagett continued, 'She's been singing with a band called the Urban Renegades. I could play you a video and show you how good she is but, to be honest, I'm not in the right frame of mind right now.'

'I completely understand. Do you happen to know if she owns the house in Balmoral Gardens where she lived?'

'She was renting it.'

'You wouldn't know who the landlord is?'

He paused before giving a reply. 'No, sorry.'

'How long has she actually lived there?'

'Since October or November, I think. She moved there with her mother, Judith, about the same time she started working for Hinkley and Evans.'

Sunita raised an eyebrow. 'So not very long then?'

'No,' he said with a shake of his head.

'Do you happen to know which hospital her mother is in?'

He wore a blank expression.

'I think it's either Worcestershire Royal Hospital or Queensbridge General. Sergeant Roy, do the police have any idea who might be behind this terrible business?'

'It's only just happened, so any thoughts on who might be responsible could only be speculation,' she said.

'Do you think she interrupted a burglar?' he asked pensively.

'That's one line of inquiry we're pursuing. But it's not the only theory.'

'What other theories do you have?'

'I'm sorry. My hands are tied. I can't speak about that at the moment. Mr Pagett, can I ask whether Miss Squires was from Worcestershire originally?'

'She and Allison grew up in Staffordshire. Look, I'm sorry. I'm not really the best person to ask about Lydia. You should come back when Allison is around.'

Sunita wrote a few details in her notebook before glancing back at her host, wondering if he was being totally honest with her. During her brief meeting with Lydia on the train, she hadn't detected any Midlands accent.

'Not to worry. We'll just press on,' she said. 'So, growing up, did Allison and Lydia have any siblings?'

'They were the only two.'

'Any idea what their parents did?'

'Their father was a human resources manager and their mother a dental receptionist.'

'What sort of education did they have?'

'They went to a grammar school but neither went to university. As I say, you'd be a lot better off talking to Allison when she's about. She'd be able to tell you much more than me.'

Sunita nodded. He appeared unsettled and ill at ease. She sensed he did not welcome her presence. However, she was keen to continue her questioning.

'How did both sisters come to live in this part of the West Midlands?' she asked.

'They both moved from Staffordshire for work reasons.'

'Where was she working before she landed the job with the shoe firm?'

'I'm not sure. All I know is it was secretarial work.'

'And where was she living before Balmoral Gardens?'

'I don't know.'

Sunita took these details down before steering the conversation towards Lydia's social life.

'Are you aware that she was dating a guy called Roman Makepeace?'

Pagett looked as startled as an army general who's spotted a wave of enemy planes approaching.

'I'm sorry,' he said. 'I wasn't aware you knew about that. Yes, we *did* know about her friendship with Roman, but she only got to know him recently and their relationship was only in its early stages.'

'I know about their relationship personally because my partner and I met them on the Valentine's Express a few days ago,' said Sunita. 'We could see how close they'd become.'

'Yes, well, that's all over now, isn't it?'

'Do you happen to know about her earlier relationship history? I mean, did she have a boyfriend before she met Mr Makepeace?'

'Well, there was a guy called Dominic Jenks, who was the bass player in the band. She was seeing him, off and on, before she met Roman.'

'I can't imagine he was too pleased when she started seeing her new guy.'

Pagett shrugged his shoulders.

'Less than delighted, I suppose,' he admitted, 'but I met Dominic at one of their gigs. He was a quiet, unassuming guy. I can't imagine he'd have harboured any long-term resentment – certainly not enough to warrant killing her.'

Sunita nodded.

'We need to know if your sister-in-law had any enemies. Do you know if anyone has made threats against her? Have any strange incidents happened recently?'

'She was quite a private person and, if anything like that had happened, I'm not sure we'd have known about it. She might have confided in Allison, but Lydia was the kind of independent woman who got on with life and tried not to be burdened by people who might be harbouring jealousies or grievances.'

'Do you know how she and Mr Makepeace first got to know each other?' she asked.

'I think they got together through online dating. He took her out a couple of times. You'll have to ask Allison. She's more clued up than me. I know she was singing with the band at the Crown and Sceptre pub in Queensbridge in early January and he came to watch her. They started going out together regularly soon after that.'

'He's going to be absolutely devastated when he finds out she's dead,' said Sunita. 'I should imagine he must have heard by now.'

He glanced down at the oak floor before turning back to her.

'Do you know, if I were you, I wouldn't go bothering Roman for the moment,' said Pagett. 'Things are a bit raw for him. Leave him for a while to grieve.'

Sunita shrugged her shoulders.

'I wish I could, but this is a murder investigation. We can't leave any stone unturned. Listen, you've been very helpful, but I'll have to go. Could you do me a favour? Could you ask Allison to call me?'

She stepped towards him and handed over her visiting card.

'Yes, of course,' said Pagett.

Sunita was preparing to leave and thinking of the long journey back to her office when something caught her eye.

As she stepped towards Pagett's front door, she stopped in her tracks. In a corner, leaning against the wall by a row of coats and partly hidden at the end of a bookcase, stood a shotgun.

Chapter 10

As she travelled back to the CID office, Sunita Roy could not stop thinking about the account Aiden Pagett had given her. There were still considerable gaps in her knowledge of the murder victim's family and she suspected that Pagett was holding back for some reason.

By the time she reached the open-plan CID office, most of her colleagues were returning from lunch. She noticed the chief inspector had erected a new whiteboard on the far wall. She strolled across to find he had pinned three photographs up – Lydia Squires, Roman Makepeace and Vernon Bainbridge.

She hung up her fawn coat and was switching on her computer when Detective Constable Brett Dawson, breathing heavily and holding a half-eaten sandwich, burst through the doors and hurried towards her.

Dawson smiled broadly as he greeted his colleague.

'You look pleased with yourself, Brett,' Sunita said, as she glanced up.

'I've just found a shop opposite the Five Bells pub where they've got a CCTV camera,' he said. 'So I'm going to go through the footage now. I thought I'd see if Lydia and Roman were being watched or followed.'

'Good thinking,' she said.

'Did you have any luck with Aiden Pagett, Sarge?'

'I spent half an hour over there, but I don't really know what to make of him,' she replied. 'There were gaps in his information about Lydia. Do you know she only moved to the Worcester area a few months ago? And, surprisingly, she sang with a band in her spare time.'

'You're kidding.'

'No. Do you know he behaved strangely when I mentioned the name Roman Makepeace? He acted as though the relationship between Lydia and Roman was a state secret and seemed shocked I knew about it.'

Dawson shrugged his shoulders. 'A lot of people in the Midlands must be aware of the Makepeace family. By reputation, if nothing else.'

'I suppose so,' she agreed. 'As I was about to leave, I noticed he had a shotgun near the front door.'

'Has he got a certificate for it?'

'He claims he has. He says he'll bring it to a police station when he's found it. It's a Beretta A400. He says his family have a farm and it's used to control pests.'

Dawson, an amiable, usually enthusiastic detective with spiky blond hair, sat down at the desk beside her. He looked as gloomy as an undertaker caught in the rain.

'I'm afraid we've drawn a blank on the knife, Sarge,' he said. 'No sign of it in the nearby streets. It could have been thrown in the Severn or into a lake.'

She nodded. 'Anything on the cameras in Balmoral Gardens?'

'We picked up a figure in dark clothing, scuttling along the street, but it was too blurred to be of any use. There's been more luck with cars, though. Many of the parked cars obviously belonged to residents or people with genuine reason to be in the vicinity at around ten thirty in the evening on Valentine's Day. But there are two vehicles that sparked interest.'

'That's encouraging,' she said. 'Have you had any time to look into the ownership of Lydia's house?'

'I'm having problems getting hold of her bank statement, but, during our house-to-house, it came up that the landlady is a woman called Bina Patel, who owns a string of properties in the area.'

'We need to speak to her,' Sunita said. 'What's the position regarding Lydia's phone?'

'John in digital forensics is still working on it,' said Dawson. 'But it looks as though most of her calls were either to or from her boyfriend.'

The chief inspector's office door sprang open and her boss's head appeared.

'Sergeant, have you got a moment?' he asked.

Sunita stepped nimbly into Roscoe's room, closing the door behind her, and drew up a chair.

'We've set up an incident room for the Squires murder with a bank of phones in Tom Vickers' old office. I've put DC Hopkirk in charge.'

'That's excellent, sir,' she said.

'I'm also getting the media team to put out an appeal for any shopkeepers with CCTV in the vicinity of Balmoral Gardens to come forward, and for any motorists with dashcams.'

'Great idea, sir,' she said.

Then she explained how she had discovered Lydia Squires' boyfriend was Axel Makepeace's son. She also told him about Aiden Pagett.

He listened attentively. But he was eager to impress her with details of a possible suspect.

'I'm very interested in this fellow Bainbridge,' he said when she had finished. 'Omar Khalid's had a chat with him. Bainbridge claims he stopped taking an interest in Lydia Squires after his boss gave him a talking to, but Omar doesn't believe him and I'm inclined to share his opinion. After all, it's been shown he sent Lydia a Valentine's card.'

He strode out of the office and waved his hand.

'DC Khalid, have you got a moment?' he yelled.

The sullen-faced detective stood up and made his way to the chief inspector's room.

'Come in and tell us about Mr Bainbridge,' said Roscoe, slipping back into the executive chair behind his desk.

'Well, as I said on the phone, sir, he insists he didn't go to see Lydia Squires on Valentine's Day and that he was at his father's house at the time of the murder,' said Khalid, taking a chair beside the sergeant. 'But I got the clear impression he was extremely upset on being asked about Lydia and I believe he might have been obsessed with the woman. On the most romantic night of the year, would he have left her alone? There's a good chance he wouldn't.'

'I agree,' said Roscoe.

He turned towards Sunita. 'Sergeant, there's something I haven't told you. The black Mercedes seen by the neighbour – it's owned by Bainbridge's father, Eric Tait. He works as a caretaker at the city hall. Bainbridge has been telling Omar that he drives a grey Toyota Yaris and vehemently denies using any other car. We're certain that's a lie.'

Roscoe stared out of the window at the cars parked in rows outside the police headquarters. He cast his eyes across to the park beyond, where children were playing on swings and slides. He glanced back at his sergeant.

'So it appears Bainbridge has been borrowing his father's car in order to visit 67 Balmoral Gardens,' said Roscoe. 'Perhaps his reasoning was that he'd stand a better chance of staying under the radar if he didn't make his visits to Miss Squires' street in his usual car. He probably didn't want to risk losing his job. I'm thinking that he must have bitterly regretted not being in Miss Squires' company that night. So, if he saw that she was with another man, that might have provoked him into attacking her.'

Sunita nodded.

'Sir, how is it that Bainbridge has a different name from his father?' she asked.

'Shall I explain, sir?' said Khalid. He faced Sunita.

'I made a call to our family history researcher in Birmingham,' he said. 'His parents separated when he was small and, when he started school, he used his stepfather's surname. As a teenager, he reconnected with his real father, who lives in the same city, and they've since become close.'

While continuing their discussion, all at once there was a knock, and Dawson's head appeared in the doorway.

'I'm sorry if I'm interrupting,' he said.

'That's all right, Dawson,' said the chief inspector. 'What is it?'

'I thought you'd be interested to know I've picked up Lydia and Roman on a camera outside the Five Bells and there's a guy in a black Mercedes who looks like he's watching them.'

'That's excellent, Dawson,' said Roscoe.

'The camera's outside a shop which is a short distance from the pub. You can see the couple walking hand in hand. Then there's this Mercedes with tinted windows moving slowly behind them. The guy behind the wheel bears more than a passing resemblance to Vernon Bainbridge.'

* * *

Later that day, DI Vickers knocked on Roscoe's door.

'I've made some good progress on the Portman case,' he said as the chief inspector beckoned him in.

'Our digital forensic specialist, John Hepworth, has come up trumps,' said Vickers. 'John applied to the court for permission to obtain call data records and he's been able to use mobile downloads, connection records from the phone's network and call data records. He's also benefited from the historical ANPR information, CCTV camera stills and vehicle tracking data. He's been able simultaneously to map location details, time schedules and link data. He's created a detailed map of the movements of Todd Styler's phone on the night Debbie Portman disappeared.'

Roscoe nodded.

Vickers continued. 'Styler's phone was located by his service provider in Bedivere Road, Queensbridge, which is where Councillor Portman lived. It also pinged on the southern section of Jakeman's Wood.'

Roscoe leaned back on his chair. 'Those were areas we searched before,' he said.

'Well, that's not strictly correct, guv. Before, we only had a steer regarding the school grounds and the woods generally. This more precise phone data helps us pinpoint Styler's movements with greater accuracy.'

'All right,' said Roscoe. 'I suppose we need to launch a fresh land search.'

'John says he was lucky in that Styler used his phone a lot. He sent a number of texts that night, which meant he had more data to work on.'

'All those drug deals,' Roscoe murmured.

'No. I'm sure he'd have used a different phone – probably a burner phone – for pushing his drugs,' said Vickers.

'We were fairly confident Debbie Portman had been killed and her body buried somewhere close to the Portmans' house,' said Roscoe. 'But back then the area we needed to search was too vast. There wasn't enough information available to investigators because no telecoms mast was close by.'

'That's right,' said Vickers, 'but cellular analysis has come on by leaps and bounds. Simply through the passage of time, our ability to use mobile phone data to track suspects down has advanced tremendously, guv.'

'So where do you suggest we go from here?' asked Roscoe. 'Bring in a cadaver dog?'

'That's exactly what I was thinking, guv,' said Vickers. 'I've made inquiries with the dog section and they've got a springer spaniel called Flint that sounds ideal.'

Their conversation was interrupted by a call on Roscoe's landline that he recognised as coming from DC Khalid.

'What is it, Khalid?' asked Roscoe. 'I'm in a meeting.'

'Dawson and I are having problems finding Vernon Bainbridge, sir,' said the constable. 'He's not at work. After a bit of persuasion, his landlady in Watermill Lane let us search her home and he's not there either.'

Chapter 11

The coach firm run by Roman Makepeace's family was based in a shabby backstreet in the industrial town of Smethwick, four miles west of Birmingham city centre.

Tribune Coaches, founded by Roman's grandfather, Gustave Makepeace, in 1959, had once been one of the most successful travel companies in the West Midlands. After a steady decline in the popularity of continental coach holidays, Tribune and its many rivals had been facing a financial struggle.

Sunita passed run-down auto repair shops, back-to-back terraced houses and gloomy shuttered shops in Tilehurst Street until she reached the marginally more impressive coach depot, a large 1930s building.

She drove in past the open wrought-iron gates and parked her car beside two blue coaches.

'I really hope Roman's at work,' she told herself as she stepped into the yard and was greeted by the smell of diesel oil and other industrial fumes. 'He might have been given time off to cope with his grief.'

As soon as she entered the small front office and approached the counter, she spotted Roman sitting in a smart grey suit at a desk in the corner. Before she could call out to him, a tubby man acknowledged her with a smile.

'Can I help?' he asked.

'I wanted a quick word with Roman,' she said.

The minute the words passed her lips, Roman glanced up and their eyes met.

Puzzled, he stood up and stepped towards the counter. 'I know you, don't I?' he said.

She nodded. 'Yes. Sunita Roy. We met on the steam train on Sunday.'

'I remember,' he said.

'I'm really sorry to call on you at such a sad time.'

'Yeah, well…' he said, leaning forward onto his desk with his head in his hands. 'Nothing can bring her back. I've just come into work today to give me something to do. To try and keep my mind off it.'

'I didn't mention to you on the train but both Tom and I work for the police,' she said, producing her warrant card from her coat pocket. 'And, by coincidence, it's my job to talk to you about Lydia.'

'Oh really?' he said. 'Yes, that *is* a coincidence.'

He turned to his work colleague, who was typing on a computer keyboard.

'Sajid, I'm just going to take the detective outside,' said Roman. 'She wants to talk to me about – well, you know.'

'Yes, of course,' said Sajid, raising a hatch in the counter so that Roman could pass through. 'Take as long as you like.'

Since it was a chilly afternoon, Sunita invited him to sit in the car with her, a suggestion he readily agreed to. While clambering into the passenger seat, he appeared rather tense. She thought he had the strained look of a prisoner steeling himself for interrogation.

'As you probably realise, I thought the world of Lydia,' said Roman, 'and I was absolutely devastated when I found out what happened to her. Whoever it was who did for her, they must have been in the house when we were saying goodnight at her front gate. I keep going over that night in my head. I keep thinking that, if only I'd gone inside with her, things could have been so different.'

'You might have both been attacked,' said Sunita.

'Well, it might have been me that was killed – not her,' he said. 'Or together we might have turned the tables on the attacker. Anyway, it's pointless to talk like that now. We can't turn back the hands of time. She's gone…'

He glanced down at the car's footwell.

'I've just come back to work after taking all yesterday off. Honestly, Sunita, I don't think I'm ever going to get over losing Lydia. She meant absolutely everything to me. I know I'd only known her a month or so but I was sure she was the right girl for me. Perhaps I'm just a fool with little experience of the world but I had ideas of the two of us being together for the rest of our lives.'

'I'm so sorry,' said Sunita. 'This has obviously been extremely hard for you.'

'It has.'

'Could you tell me about what happened the last time you saw her?'

'Yes. I took her to the Five Bells pub at about seven o'clock,' he said. 'I left my car by her house and we walked there because it was a pleasant night. We had a nice meal and a bottle of wine. Then I mentioned I had an early start in the morning and I walked her back. After kissing her goodnight, I drove off.'

'We believe someone followed you through the streets in a car,' she said.

'What? I don't know anything about that. What sort of car?'

'A black Mercedes with tinted windows.'

'That sounds like the car Lydia was complaining about.'

'So you didn't notice you were being followed?' she said.

'No. Lydia was the most incredible woman, Sunita. She had the most amazing eyes and I was totally locked into conversation with her. I don't know if I'll ever get over losing her. My life seems so empty without her.'

Roman broke down and wept uncontrollably. Then he wiped his eyes with the palms of his hands and tried to regain his composure.

'Are you all right?' she asked. 'Would you like me to come back at another time?'

'No. It's OK,' he said. 'She's constantly on my mind anyway. I may as well talk to someone. I've got to talk about it at some point.'

'What time did you kiss Lydia goodnight and drive off?'

'I'm not sure. Maybe ten thirty?'

'What did you do after you left Balmoral Gardens? Did you go directly home?'

'Yes,' he said. 'I drove straight back to my flat.'

'Where's that?'

'Kipling Street, Coleshill.'

'How long did that take you?'

'About three quarters of an hour. I went straight to bed because I had an early start the next morning.'

'Did you have a girlfriend before you met Lydia?' said Sunita.

'Well, yes. There's a woman called Sophie Bishop that I was involved with for a couple of years, but things had been going downhill for a while and it wasn't too much of a surprise to her when I decided to end it.'

Sunita grimaced. 'After two years, it must have been hard for her, being told it was over.'

'Actually, she didn't take it too badly and she's moved on with her life now anyway. She's settled down with a guy and lives in Northfield.'

Sunita jotted down the details in her notebook.

'Roman, can you think of anyone with a grudge against Lydia? Is there anyone who might have wished her harm?'

He shook his head.

'I've been thinking about this terrible business ever since it happened. I can't think of anyone who might have wished her harm. I really can't.'

'Your family are well known throughout the Midlands, aren't they? I'm not talking about the coach firm.'

He scowled. 'No. I know what you're referring to. Somehow or other, we've got a bit of a bad reputation because of things that have been said by ignorant people.

Things that have been said in the press and on TV. They think my father's a gangster.'

'There have been a few court cases in which your father has been alluded to and he has convictions for drug offences,' Sunita said.

She immediately regretted her remarks. He was clearly becoming annoyed and, as a result, might refuse to help her further.

'That was a long time ago,' he snapped. 'If you're trying to get me to say something against my family, I won't. They've tried to make out that my father is some kind of mafia boss. Well, it's nonsense. He's just an honest businessman trying his best to make a living. And if you want to check that with him, that's his car arriving now. So you'll be able to fire any other questions at him, won't you?'

Chapter 12

A dark-green Jaguar coasted through the iron gates and came to a halt in the centre of the coach firm's forecourt. With the engine still purring, the driver, a tall man in a grey uniform with a peaked cap, walked round to the rear door and helped his passenger out.

As Sunita and Roman got out of the detective's car, she at once recognised the portly, middle-aged newcomer as Roman's father, Axel. He had the same swarthy appearance and straggly, greying hair she had seen in newspaper reports and in police photographs.

Leaning heavily on a walking stick, he manoeuvred his way towards them.

'What's happening, lad?' he demanded.

'This lady's a detective sergeant from Heart of England Police, Dad,' Roman replied.

'Oh yeah? And what's she doing here?'

'She's been asking me about Lydia,' he explained.

'I'm DS Roy,' said Sunita, holding out her hand.

'Very, very sad what happened to her,' Axel Makepeace said without shaking it. 'Well, why are you chatting out here? It would be much more comfortable in my office. Why don't you both come inside with me now?'

Sunita was about to point out that she had nearly completed her interview. Then she decided it would be foolish to mention that. Here was a brief chance to spend a few minutes with a feared underworld figure known to head a major Midlands crime syndicate. Surely this was not an opportunity to be squandered.

While the chauffeur drove away in the Jaguar to find a parking space, Roman's father led them into the building and they followed as he slowly negotiated his way up a flight of stairs to the first floor, where he led them through a door marked 'Managing Director'.

She found herself in a vast, brightly lit office with a large maple desk by the far windows.

After finding them comfortable seats, Axel Makepeace settled himself behind his desk and glared at his son and their visitor. His eyes were as cold as a Moscow winter.

'What have you been telling this detective, Roman?' he asked.

His son shrugged. 'Only how devastated I was to hear Lydia had died at the hands of some intruder,' he said, 'and that we'd had a pleasant Valentine's Day dinner at the Five Bells before it happened.'

Axel Makepeace leaned back on his chair. 'In the ordinary course of events, I'll be honest – I ain't got much time for coppers,' he said. 'They've accused me in the past of all kinds of things I've never done and, generally speaking, once my lawyer has been involved, I've been let home without a stain on me character. What was your name again?'

'I'm Detective Sergeant Sunita Roy,' she said.

'Well, Sergeant Roy, I'm fully aware that you people occasionally have your uses. Who is it that comes and knocks on the door to tell you your old granny's been knocked down by a careless driver, Roman?'

'The police, Dad.'

'Not an easy job for anyone, breaking this sort of news to family and then dealing with the consequences,' said the businessman, brushing locks of his hair away from his eyes with his right hand.

'Of course, we never got that. Roman's not next of kin. But I know you people have a tough job dealing with grief and I sympathise with you and your colleagues.'

He turned towards Sunita. 'My boy's been destroyed over this tragedy, Sergeant Roy. I only met the young lady once myself but I could see how close they'd both become. She was a charming young woman and I could completely understand my boy being enamoured with her. And this is one of those occasions when my family and me want to give the force as much help as we can.'

Sunita gazed into his eyes. 'Could I ask where you were yourself on Tuesday night, sir?' She wondered if this was too direct a question. Should she perhaps have phrased it in a different way?

But the businessman did not seem troubled by this approach.

'Since it was Valentine's, I took my dear wife Klara to the Santos Cocktail Bar round the corner from where we live,' he replied. 'Then we returned home. I'm sure the owner of the bar, Sergio, would be happy to vouch for us being there.'

Then, his mobile phone rang. 'Excuse me one moment,' he said. He removed the silver handset from his pocket and answered it.

'I'm in a meeting,' he said, looking as flustered as one of his drivers caught in a mile-long jam. 'Call me later.'

He turned his attention back to the detective.

'Sorry. Where were we?' he said. 'Oh yes. You were asking for my whereabouts.'

He waited for a coach to roar out from beside the building and pass through the gates before continuing.

'Our driver took us from our home in Hanover Drive, Sutton Coldfield to the bar in the town centre at 9 p.m.,' he explained. 'He picked us up just before 11 p.m. Does that answer your question?'

Sunita said that his reply covered the issue perfectly.

'I don't suppose you'd be too interested in my opinion, but since you're here, I'll give it to you anyway,' said the businessman.

'Roman here believes that, considering it was Valentine's, this was likely to have been a crime of passion committed by someone with strong feelings for Lydia. He's told me about visits by a mystery caller and believes that that person might be responsible for the death.'

Roman nodded. 'That's right, Dad.'

'Obviously, that's one of our lines of inquiry,' said Sunita. 'But this investigation is in its very early stages and other theories are likely to emerge as time passes.'

Makepeace nodded. 'Yes. Of course. I can understand that. I know how you people operate. I've got one or two close friends in the police who've helped me to understand over the years how the system works.'

He paused, then continued, 'I'm afraid I don't agree with my son's theory that this murder was the work of a jilted lover. To me, it's obvious what happened. I believe your killer was one of our local villains. Knowing that it was Valentine's Day and folk were likely to be out for the evening with partners, he toured the streets, sussing out targets. Roman tells me there was a side gate giving easy access to the back of the house. In my opinion, this toerag broke in, hunting for rich pickings. Then, when Lydia came back early, he struck out at her in a panic to get away.'

* * *

Just before eight o'clock that Thursday evening, Tom Vickers drove into the village of Shawley Green. He passed St Michael's Church, turned into Old School Lane and drove on until he reached the third house in the street. A sign made from slate saying *Ashiyana* – which meant 'beautiful home' – had been screwed to the wall beside the entrance gates. His car trundled across the gravel forecourt and drew to a halt outside Sunita Roy's red front door.

Sunita lived in a rambling, five-bedroom house in the heart of the village. She had bought the former eighteenth-century school house after an inheritance from an eccentric uncle.

Sunita ran out of the house to greet him.

'Come inside,' she said, kissing his cheek. 'I've got lots to tell you.'

She led him into her spacious living room containing a grand piano, two cream leather settees and a Chippendale dining table and chairs.

'So you finally decided to buy that piano then?' Vickers remarked as he sunk down into one of the settees.

'Yes,' she said. 'Don't you think it suits the room? Now all I've got to do is learn to play it! Tom, I wanted to tell you about Aiden Pagett.'

'That's Lydia's brother-in-law.'

'Yes. You know I saw a shotgun near his front door?'

'You told me.'

'Well, he still hasn't come forward with the certificate for it.'

'He'll have to request a replacement from his local police.'

'Yes, but it's made me suspicious. He claims it's for controlling pests on a relative's farm but we don't even know if there *is* a farm in the family.'

'You need to do some digging,' said Vickers. 'Funnily enough, that's exactly what *we're* going to be doing tomorrow.'

'Digging?' she asked as she sat down beside him.

'Yes. There's a team of us going out to the woods near Debbie Portman's old place with the cadaver dog, Flint.'

'And you're hoping Flint is going to have a flash of inspiration?'

He grinned. 'We hope so,' he said.

'I met Axel Makepeace today,' she said.

'You're such a name dropper.'

'I know. He was surprisingly helpful. Last time we tried to interview him, four years ago, we couldn't get past his lawyer. But he claims he and his family want to help us find Lydia's killer. He also said something really worrying – that he's got "one or two close friends in the police" and that, through them, he's "learnt how the system works."'

'It makes the blood curdle to hear an arch villain speak like that,' said Vickers. 'He's suggesting he's got some colleagues of ours in his pocket and there's also a veiled threat there.'

'I felt a bit intimidated when he said that,' she admitted.

'I'm afraid you just have to ignore it,' he said.

'Can I get you a drink, Tom?' she asked.

'A Scotch and water would go down well,' he said.

As she stepped across the room to the bookcase where she kept bottles of wine and spirits, she said, 'The DCI is convinced Vernon Bainbridge killed Lydia, but I've got my doubts. I'm not sure he would have the physical strength, from what Khalid has said.'

'That's a good point,' said Vickers.

'We're probably looking in the wrong direction,' Sunita continued. 'I've been wondering if Roman could be as crooked as his father. He says all the right things and this helps make people like him. But it's dawned on me that there might have been a problem in his relationship with Lydia. I'm not sure whether to believe him about the time he says he left her. I'm wondering if they had a row and he killed her. Then maybe he smashed the pane in the door to make it look like a botched burglary.'

Chapter 13

Omar Khalid arrived in Worcester as the sun began to emerge from behind the clouds just before nine o'clock on Friday morning. He drove into the quiet residential street on the Warndon housing estate and parked.

A white Volkswagen Golf was parked halfway down Lime Tree Drive. Khalid walked towards it and tapped on the passenger window before opening the door and slipping inside.

'Morning, Brett,' he announced. 'I didn't wake you, did I?'

'No, not at all,' Dawson said. 'I was just resting my eyes. There's been no movement at the house but one of the neighbours told me last night they think they saw Vernon Bainbridge briefly in the back garden, along with his father. I called the DCI to let him know.'

Khalid glanced down the road towards a red-brick, semi-detached property.

'You don't have a brilliant view from here,' complained Khalid, who had often harboured doubts about his colleague's competence. 'There were at least two cars parked on the forecourt when I drove past the place last night and, if our chum Bainbridge came out of the front door and jumped into one of them, you wouldn't be able to see that from here.'

'Oh, I can see well enough,' replied Dawson, who had parked thirty metres away from the target house. 'In any case, if I came any closer, they might spot me and realise they're being watched.'

'Have you seen anything of either of them yourself since you came here last night?' asked Khalid.

'Only the old man, Eric Tait. He turned up at ten o'clock in his Mercedes but no sign of Vernon. His grey Yaris hasn't moved.'

Khalid shrugged. 'That all suggests he might be in the house.'

'I suppose so,' Dawson admitted. 'I'm wondering if we should go and knock on the door?'

'No, we'll have to wait till the DCI gets here. He was arranging last night for someone to pick up a search warrant. I don't expect he'll be long.'

An hour later, the chief inspector's blue BMW drew into the street followed by two patrol cars.

Roscoe stepped across the street and spoke to the two detectives through Dawson's open window.

'No movement at all?' he asked.

'No, sir,' Dawson replied. 'Tait arrived here last night, but I haven't seen anything of Bainbridge.'

'Right, we'd better go and make our presence known,' said Roscoe, beckoning officers from the patrol cars to follow him as well as the two detectives.

He marched down the street as confidently as a bailiff about to deliver court papers. He stepped across the block-paved forecourt and rang the doorbell.

A stout, middle-aged man in a T-shirt and jeans drew open the door and scowled at the contingent of police.

'Mr Tait?' said Roscoe, brandishing his warrant card. 'DCI Roscoe, Heart of England CID.'

'What do you want?' the suspicious householder demanded.

'We're looking for your son. We've reason to believe he's on your premises. His car's here.'

'I haven't seen him for a while.'

'I'm afraid we've got a warrant to search these premises,' said Roscoe.

'On what grounds?'

'We're investigating a murder, Mr Tait, and have reason to believe your son may be involved or have important information for us.'

'Let me see the warrant.'

Roscoe produced the document from the pocket of his coat, which he handed to Tait.

As he gazed at the warrant, Tait grumbled, 'I suppose I don't have any choice.'

The waiting officers, who included PC Nina Kaur, followed Roscoe into the three-bedroom house. Kaur and two colleagues were sent upstairs to check the first-floor rooms, while Khalid was sent to inspect the loft. Roscoe left Dawson and one remaining constable to scour the ground floor while he himself headed out into the rear garden.

After satisfying himself that the elusive customer service assistant was not hiding in the brick-built garden shed, behind a wood pile or inside an outside toilet, Roscoe stepped back into the house.

Kaur and Dawson informed him they had found no trace of the wanted man. But when Roscoe called out Khalid's name, there was no response.

'I know he pulled down the loft ladder, sir,' said Kaur.

'Would you mind going up and having a word with him?' said Roscoe. 'There's no sense in me keeping all these officers here on a wild goose chase. If our man isn't holed up in the loft, I think we'll have to knock this on the head.'

A few minutes passed. Grey-haired Tait was pacing up and down in the living room, muttering to himself. Most of the group of officers, who were gathered in Tait's dingy kitchen and hallway, could hear Kaur calling Khalid's name.

Finally, there came a reply. 'Just coming,' said a muffled voice from the depths of the insulated loft.

Then, with his face, hands and clothing peppered in dust, the detective descended the stairs, coughing.

'Sorry, sir,' he told Roscoe. 'No sign of the man, but there was an old trunk that I needed to check and a couple of old wardrobes.'

One by one, the officers began to troop out of the front door. But as he was about to leave, Roscoe remembered they had not looked inside the garage. He made Tait open the doors. Sitting before their eyes was the black Mercedes which had featured in their investigation.

Having brushed all the dust off his clothes, Khalid stepped forward, opened the nearside rear passenger door and gazed around. Then he tried the boot release lever.

'The boot's locked, sir,' he said.

Roscoe called for Tait.

'Where's the remote to open the Mercedes?' he demanded.

'I've no idea,' he replied. 'My son uses the car. It's wherever he left it.'

'Mr Tait, you were seen arriving home in this car last night at round ten o'clock,' said Roscoe. 'Kindly fetch the remote.'

'I put the key fob on a hook in the hall. It's not there, so my son must have it. I don't know where he is.'

The chief inspector's eyes twinkled as he was possessed by a sudden idea.

'Khalid, you've got knowledge of mechanics, haven't you?' he said.

The curly-haired detective broke into a smile. 'I've got my City and Guilds Level 1,' he said.

'I think we can probably access the boot by removing one of the rear seats,' said Roscoe.

'Yes but I'm not sure I can put it back in afterwards,' said Khalid.

Tait looked at the chief inspector in alarm.

'You can't do it that way,' Tait insisted. 'Anyway, why on earth would you want to get into the boot?'

'Mr Tait,' said Roscoe. 'I'm convinced that your son is hiding from us. We've tried everywhere else so there's a good chance he's in the boot of your car.'

'I don't suppose it would make any difference if I swore on my children's lives that he wouldn't be so stupid as to hide in the boot of a car,' he said.

'No, it wouldn't,' said Roscoe. 'So you've got a choice. Either you quickly find the remote and open the boot for us or I let our Level 1 mechanic loose on your car.'

Tait spent a minute pondering over the options. Then he shook his head and pulled the key fob out of his trouser pocket. He pressed it and the lid sprang open.

A figure dressed in black was lying before them. He was staring up at his audience with an anxious expression on his face.

Chapter 14

Tom Vickers was becoming dejected.

The springer spaniel Flint, under the control of his handler Mark Davenport, had spent a solid two hours sniffing his way round the southern part of Jakeman's Wood. And not once had the liver-and-white dog pressed his nose to the ground and barked to alert them to a potential discovery.

A second dog handler had arrived with a second cadaver dog, a short-haired, fawn-coloured Belgian Malinois called Luther, who had also failed to detect any scent.

The team of officers and volunteers, who had been at the site since 8.30 a.m., were all, like Vickers, showing signs of becoming disillusioned. Now he was considering whether to admit defeat and send everyone home.

When he had first arrived that morning on the eastern outskirts of Queensbridge, the inspector had been feeling optimistic about the task they faced in searching for the missing councillor's body. With so much work done in narrowing down the search area, he had been encouraged to believe that they would finally find her corpse. After twenty years in the force, he felt that, in a way, he was putting his reputation on the line. Moreover, he had given the missing woman's family renewed hope that her body might be found and they might finally achieve closure. There was a great deal at stake.

He recalled his arrival in Bedivere Road just before eight o'clock. He had glanced from his car at the Portmans' detached house, where Councillor Portman was believed to have met her final moments. He had then passed the abandoned school, which had now been purchased by a developer and was due to be converted into flats.

He'd turned left into the lane that led to the wood and, after travelling for around fifty metres, entered the car park. He had found Davenport leaning against the side of his white van, holding Flint on a lead.

'Let's hope Flint's old spark hasn't deserted him,' Vickers had told him.

There was a bonhomie among the men and women who had assembled at the edge of the wood. Despite their sombre objective, the team had set to work enthusiastically, creating a grid of washing lines across a large glade with holes in the ground, a metre apart, in order to assist the dogs. This clearing – a large stretch of open scrubland speckled with bracken and gorse – had been identified in advance by Vickers as the prime location.

Davenport had been confident that, if the woman had been buried there, at least one of the two dogs would find her.

'If you dropped a bottle of Scotch in Loch Lomond, they'd find it,' the handler had boasted. 'Their sensory system is three hundred and fifty times better than a human's. A dog like Flint or Luther can smell a body that's been buried for decades and can cover one and a third kilometres a day. They can detect a body that's buried up to five metres below ground.'

'I hope for all our sakes that the body's not five metres down,' grumbled Vickers.

On the whole, the inspector had been heartened by the handler's staunch defence of the dogs' abilities.

He had watched in fascination as first Flint and then Luther were released. With their tails wagging like ships' propellers, the pair had set to work with their noses pressed close to the woodland floor, their heads constantly turning from side to side.

The pair had covered the northernmost part of the target area without giving any sign of having detected the faintest whiff of buried human remains.

By midday, Vickers was on the point of calling it a day. Perhaps they should consider returning at a later time with ground-penetrating radar.

But then, unexpectedly, Flint's tail stopped wagging and his head appeared transfixed. He barked furiously before glancing round at Davenport. This was like Elgar to Davenport's ears.

'He's found something!' Davenport shouted in excitement.

The team of police staff and volunteers, who had stopped for a tea break, ended their conversations. All eyes were on the dog.

The spot where the animal stood, barking furiously, was at the edge of the clearing, covered in bracken and close to a gorse bush.

'Get the spades!' shouted Vickers as he hurried across to the spot and studied the soil, pressing his fingers into the damp clay.

The team began to gather round.

'There's been a bit of light rain this week,' he announced as Davenport rewarded Flint by tossing him his red ball. 'But the ground's still quite hard. Anyway, let's make a start.'

Two constables collected spades and set to work, removing the first clods of earth from the ground.

Half an hour later, one of two volunteers who had replaced them struck something hard. The digging stopped to allow Vickers to bend down and retrieve a woman's high-heeled shoe from the soil.

Davenport, who by now had shut Flint in the back of his van, peered over the inspector's shoulder.

'Is it what we've been looking for?' he asked awkwardly.

Vickers nodded and frowned.

'Yes,' he said, 'Debbie Portman was wearing a shoe like this the night she went missing.'

Chapter 15

The chief inspector strode through CID until he reached Khalid's desk near the back of the office.

'Are you ready to come and have a chat with Mr Bainbridge?' Roscoe asked the detective, who was peering at his screen.

'Yes, sir,' said Khalid, who began switching off his computer.

'His brief's had a long chat with him and he's decided to make a clean breast of things.'

'That's good to hear, sir. Hopefully, this shouldn't take long.'

'In my experience of police interviews, I'd never allow myself to believe that,' moaned his boss. 'There's always a chance he'll change his mind halfway through.'

They made their way to one of the interview rooms on the ground floor, where they found Vernon Bainbridge sitting motionless, hunched across the table. His solicitor, Saleema Siddiqui, was beside him, attempting to make conversation.

After turning on the digital recorder, Roscoe, who was carrying an envelope containing photographs, took his seat opposite their suspect and Khalid sat down facing the lawyer.

'Just to remind you you're not under arrest,' said Roscoe. 'But we may charge you with an offence at a later date, depending on the answers you give. Is that understood?'

Bainbridge said nothing, obliging the chief inspector to repeat his question.

At last, Bainbridge glanced up and hissed, 'Yes.'

'I'd like to ask first of all why you were hiding in the boot of the Mercedes,' said Roscoe.

Bainbridge raised himself up from the table and stared into his questioner's eyes. 'It was such a warm day, I wanted somewhere cool to chill out,' he replied.

'If you carry on like this, we might have to arrest you formally and charge you with stalking,' he warned.

'You're very touchy this morning,' said Bainbridge. 'Didn't you sleep well?'

'Why did you hide in that car when you obviously knew we wanted to speak to you about the murder of Lydia Squires?' said Roscoe.

'I don't know. It seemed a good idea at the time,' he insisted.

'It obviously makes police officers like myself suspicious if someone we want to talk to is at pains to avoid us. It suggests someone who's got something to hide.'

'I've got nothing to hide. I'm here now speaking to you, aren't I?'

Saleema Siddiqui, a slim, solemn-faced woman with her black hair tied behind her head, interrupted.

'Chief Inspector, my client wishes to be completely open with you. He knows he behaved foolishly in concealing himself in the car – that's right, isn't it, Mr Bainbridge? My client has realised he ought to assist you as best he can and wants to give you a clear statement which will show he's always behaved properly.'

'That remains to be seen,' said Roscoe. 'The next thing I want to speak to you about, Mr Bainbridge, is your personal living arrangements. You've been renting a room in Watermill Lane. But, although we've called round on several occasions, we've never found you there. Instead, we found you at your dad's place. Are you trying to avoid us?'

'I've decided to move back in with me dad for financial reasons. Just haven't got round to sorting things out with the landlady yet.'

'Now a neighbour has informed us you called round at Miss Squires' address several times last weekend,' said Roscoe sternly. 'We've shown her photographs of yourself and she's confirmed it was you she saw. She's also identified your father's car. You denied this before. Are you still denying this was you?'

Bainbridge shrugged. He shook his head and stared down at the floor. 'All right. I called round in the hope of seeing her but she wasn't around.'

'What was your intention?' asked Roscoe.

'I just wanted to chat to her. I wanted to ask her out.'

'Despite knowing your feelings for her weren't reciprocated and that you were risking the wrath of your employer?'

'Yes. I suppose I've been a fool.'

Roscoe tutted. 'This brings us round to what happened last Tuesday night, Valentine's Day,' he said. 'Where were you that evening, Mr Bainbridge?'

'I was round my dad's.'

Roscoe exhaled and pulled a face. 'We know that's not true. You were caught on camera driving your father's black Mercedes to Worcester and waiting outside the Five Bells.'

'No,' he insisted, screwing up his face.

Roscoe sighed. 'Take a look at these photographs.' He opened the large envelope which he had placed on the table in front of him, and pulled out some black-and-white images.

'These clearly show your face at the wheel of the car,' said Roscoe as the suspect glanced at the pictures.

'It's you behind the wheel, isn't it?' he said. 'When Miss Squires and her friend, Mr Makepeace, left at around ten o'clock, you were waiting for them outside and followed them along the street. Don't try and deny it.'

Bainbridge tutted.

'All right. It was me,' he said with a scowl. 'I was jealous. It should have been me eating and drinking with her on Valentine's Day – not that cretin, the coach-booking clerk. I wanted to see if they were both going to go into her house. I wanted to see if he was going to stay the night.'

'But he didn't, did he?' said Khalid. 'He left her at the garden gate and drove away.'

'Yes,' said Roscoe. 'As soon as he'd gone and Miss Squires had entered the house, you broke in through the back and murdered her.'

'Don't be ridiculous. I drove away. I've read the press reports. It's being suggested someone lay in wait for her. If I followed them from the pub, I wouldn't have had time to get inside, hunt round for a weapon and wait for her. You should be looking for the real killer – the person who ambushed her. It can't have been me. It doesn't make sense.'

Roscoe looked at Khalid. The two detectives appreciated that their suspect had a point. If Bainbridge had followed the couple all the way from the pub, he wouldn't have had time to break in and stab her. Would he?

Roscoe shook his head. 'This is the issue that concerns me,' he said. 'You've admitted you were jealous. You've admitted believing it should have been you with her that night. So you must have had a tremendous urge to call in on her when you realised her boyfriend was having an early night and had left the scene.'

'No. I was satisfied he wasn't staying over. That was the thing that consumed my mind. Once I knew he wasn't going to be sleeping with her, I was relieved and happy to call it a night myself.'

'That's hard to believe,' said Khalid. 'You've lied constantly to us. You denied to me having use of a second car. You insisted you'd followed your boss's advice and broken off all contact with Miss Squires. Here you were chasing after her late at night and, shortly after she returns home, she's found savagely stabbed to death. Why should we believe your denials?'

Bainbridge sat back in his chair.

'I'd never have harmed a hair on that woman's head,' he said loudly. 'It says in the press she was stabbed. There's no way I'd have stabbed her. I loved her and thought she was playing hard to get.'

'You killed her in a fit of pique because she'd chosen Makepeace over you,' Khalid insisted.

'No, of course not.'

'So what happened?' asked Roscoe. 'Did you meekly just head off back to your father's place with your tail between your legs?'

'No. I didn't.'

'What did you do then?'

Bainbridge glanced at Siddiqui before returning his gaze to the chief inspector.

'I followed Makepeace's car.'

Chapter 16

On Saturday morning, as the sun's rays began glinting from behind the clouds, Sunita Roy rose early. She caught a glimpse of her garden while opening the curtains in which the first daffodils were about to open their yellow blooms.

She spent the first hour of the day working on her laptop, carrying out research into Warwickshire pub bands. She discovered the Urban Renegades were listed on a website run by a Birmingham talent agency. It gave a mobile number for one of the band members, lead guitarist Nathan Gardener. She tried to call him, but the phone went to voicemail, so she left a message.

After breakfast, she set off on the journey to Northfield in the hope of interviewing Sophie Bishop, Roman Makepeace's previous girlfriend.

She had only travelled a few miles before her phone rang. She recognised the number that appeared on the screen.

'Is that DS Roy?' asked a man with a strong Black Country accent.

'That's right,' she replied after stopping her car by the side of the road. 'You must be Nathan. You can probably imagine why I wanted to speak with you.'

'Of course,' he said. 'You're calling about Lydia. We're all in a state of shock. Such a lovely woman. If there's anything members of the band can do…'

'Thank you. Because of your knowledge of her time with the band, do you know if she was bothered about anything? I mean, can you think of anyone who might have had a grudge against her or reason to harm her?'

'No, she were such a lovely lass. None I can think of.'

'How did she become your singer?'

'She came to one of our gigs in Brum during the summer. She was with another woman and offered to sing a couple of rock classics. We were really knocked out. She had a beautiful voice. It wasn't long before she agreed to become part of the band and came to rehearsals regularly. She fitted in really well. We had a lot of laughs and we found she had a heart of gold, so you can imagine how devastated we all are.'

After obtaining contact details for all the band members and ending the call, Sunita decided to continue with her initial plan of visiting Sophie Bishop. Then she would travel to Willenhall, thirty miles away near Coventry, and try to speak with bass guitarist Dominic Jenks.

Sophie Bishop lived with her new boyfriend in a quiet cul-de-sac of detached houses called Floyd Close, which was a short distance from Northfield railway station.

Their 1960s house had been freshly painted in white, had venetian blinds in every window and there was a block-paved forecourt in front with room for several vehicles. A Ford Fiesta was taking up the middle space.

Sunita Roy strode up to the grey composite front door and pressed the bell. A tall woman in her mid-thirties in a turtleneck sweater and jeans greeted her. She had attractive blue eyes and a gentle smile. The smile faded as soon as she saw the police warrant card being held up.

'Yes?' she said as she stood in the open doorway.

'Sophie Bishop?' Sunita asked.

'Yes.'

'DS Roy, Heart of England CID. We're investigating a death and I'd like to ask you a few questions.'

'Whose death?' asked Bishop, whose unkempt blonde hair and lack of make-up suggested she had only just got up.

'A woman called Lydia Squires.'

'What's it got to do with me?' Bishop demanded.

'Well,' said Sunita, 'she's been associating with a man called Roman Makepeace, and I understand the pair of you recently split up.'

Bishop sighed. 'I suppose you'd better come in,' she said, glancing up and down the street. 'I was about to head off to the gym. I suppose I can go later.'

She led the sergeant through an elegant hall and into a light, stylish lounge. The place was as immaculate as a developer's showhouse and Sunita was impressed.

She took a seat on a cream settee. A Yamaha keyboard was standing close to the wall, next to a white marble fireplace.

'Yes, I was in a relationship with Roman,' Bishop explained as she stood in the centre of the room beside a white, fleecy rug. 'But I finished with him several months ago. We were in a bit of a rut and I stopped trusting him with other women. All the excitement had gone out of our relationship too. Then I met Chris, who was much more husband material.'

Sunita, who was taking details down in her small notebook, asked, 'Do you remember exactly when you broke up with Roman?'

'I think it would have been around October.'

'And at what point did you become involved with Chris?'

'At around the same time.'

'So you live here together now? You're cohabiting?'

'Yes. I'm not sure you need to put it like that but, yes, we're living together. Have been since Christmas Eve.'

'OK,' said Sunita.

'I know what you're thinking,' said Bishop, sitting down on a chair beside patio doors bordered by chintz curtains. 'You're thinking it sounds a bit rushed – that I got together with Chris on the rebound. But it wasn't like that. He's an amazing guy. He's thoughtful and fairly well off. He's got far more going for him.'

'What does he do for a living?'

'He's involved in television production. He's a cameraman.'

'And what do you do?'

'My main job is working as a manager in a sports shop.'

'Whereabouts is it you work?'

'Only up the road in Dudley. It's a shop called Good Life Sports and Leisure.'

'How long have you been there?'

'A couple of years. I was working for Roman's father at Tribune Coaches before that.'

'I see. So what was your reaction when you found out Roman was seeing Lydia Squires?' asked Sunita.

'I thought, good luck to him.'

'How did you actually find out?'

'One of our mutual friends told me. I can't remember who it was now. But I was quite fine with it. Actually I was glad he'd been able to move on with his life as I had.'

'His new life hasn't moved on very far,' Sunita pointed out.

'I know. Incredibly sad, isn't it?' said Bishop, looking directly into her visitor's eyes. 'I feel a lot of sympathy for him. He'd found new happiness and then this happens.'

Sunita put her notebook down.

'I need to ask you where you were on Valentine's night,' she told Bishop.

'That's an easy one,' she replied with an air of confidence. 'I was playing keyboards at the theatre in Tewkesbury.'

She picked her phone up from a nearby coffee table and showed the sergeant a photograph of her with a group of musicians. Sunita noticed it timestamped 11.15 p.m.

A smile flickered across Sunita's face.

'Really? You're a musician?'

'Yes. I play in a small orchestra. Have you heard of the musical *Dawn of Rock*?'

The sergeant nodded, not wishing to appear ignorant.

'Vaguely,' she said. In reality, modern music was as much a mystery to her as accounts of the Mary Celeste or the Yeti.

'We were performing along with singers and dancers until ten thirty,' Bishop continued.

'So there'll be dozens of people who can account for your presence?' said Sunita.

'Exactly.'

The detective frowned. 'This is a part-time job, is it?'

'Music's more of a hobby.'

'What did your Chris think about you going off to perform on your first Valentine's since you got together? Wouldn't he have preferred a romantic night – just the two of you?'

'He's in the media world, so he understands these things. But he got me some red roses, which are in the dining room, and that lovely card up there.'

Sunita stood up.

'May I?' she said.

'Of course.'

The detective stepped across to the mantelpiece and peered at the red double hearts on the front of the card, which were entwined with the message 'Together Forever'. Inside were the handwritten words 'Evermore in harmony. All my love, Chris'.

'Lovely words,' said Sunita. 'Clever words.'

'Yes. He's a sweetheart,' she said.

Sunita made a quick calculation in her head. Tewkesbury is at least fifteen miles from Worcester. If Sophie Bishop had left the theatre promptly at ten, she would have had no time to commit the crime – even if she had wanted to. In addition, the motorway and nearby roads had been heavily congested following a chemical spillage, which would have made it impossible for her to have travelled there.

'I think I've got everything I need,' said Sunita as she made her way out of the front door. She paused to hand

Bishop her calling card. 'Please let me know if anything else occurs to you that could help our investigation.'

She was about to drive away when Brett Dawson phoned her.

'We've just had a call from a member of the public,' he said. 'A kitchen knife's been found in a hedge.'

Chapter 17

The discovery of a bloodstained white bag containing what appeared to be a knife had been made by a twelve-year-old schoolboy, David Turnbull.

Sunita learned that he and his mother, Linda, had been walking along a quiet street of detached houses in Worcester – a few streets away from Balmoral Gardens – when he noticed the white object. It had been secreted in a hedge behind some black railings.

Out of curiosity, his mother later told police, David had reached through the bars and tugged at the plastic. The pair, who were on their way to the high street shops, were astonished when the rolled-up bag slipped out and tumbled onto the pavement. As soon as Linda Turnbull picked it up and saw it contained a knife, she screamed.

'I knew straight away it might be the missing murder weapon,' she told the police operator when she dialled 999 on her phone. 'I like to keep up with the news and realised it might be the weapon police had been searching for.'

Police advised her to wait at the scene of the discovery, in Springwell Lane, and not to handle the bag any further.

Once it had been collected, the bag and the knife were conveyed to the forensics department at St James Street.

Sunita Roy, after being informed of the breakthrough, was hopeful that it might lead to a swift resolution of the case. She spent a few minutes speaking to Dr Ling before calling Dawson back.

'We should get results on the knife back by Monday morning at the latest, Brett,' she told him.

'Brilliant.'

'Listen, are you free at the moment?' she asked.

'Well, I've managed to find an address for Lydia Squires' landlady. It's in Worcester so I wondered if you wanted me to go over there today?'

'No. That can wait. I'm going to see Dominic Jenks – you know, Lydia's previous boyfriend. I could do with you coming along. I'm not far from your place at the moment.'

'That's fine. I'll be ready in five,' he said.

'Make that ten,' she said. 'I'm not totally sure of the way.'

As soon as she arrived in Dawson's tree-lined street in Kings Heath, she saw him standing outside his terraced house, waving at her in a bright-red zip-up jacket.

'Another cold day, Sarge,' he complained as he jumped into the passenger seat and they drove away. 'You didn't take long.'

'I was only down the road in Northfield.'

She explained about her meeting with Sophie Bishop and how she had been performing in Tewkesbury at the time of the murder.

'So another blind alley,' he said. 'Let's hope we have more luck with this Dominic guy.'

'While I think of it, Brett, don't wear that bright jacket again when you're on a job with me. We need to be subtle and discreet when we're questioning suspects.'

'Sorry, Sarge. It was all I could find in a hurry. By the way, I like your new car.'

More than three quarters of an hour passed before they reached the Coventry suburbs and found their way to Dominic Jenks' first-floor flat, located in a quiet street on the edge of the city.

'We've taken a bit of a chance. I hope he's in,' said Sunita while parking her car.

'Well, it's Saturday morning. People tend to either have a lie-in or go shopping,' said Dawson.

'I usually wash my hair,' she said.

'There's always one, Sarge,' he said cheekily.

She glanced up at the flat, which was in a block of six. Dominic Jenks had a small balcony overlooking a car park and the countryside beyond.

They entered through the main door, climbed the stairs and rang the bell.

Soon afterwards, a tall, slim man with receding hair drew back the half-glazed door.

'Yes?' he said.

'DS Roy and DC Dawson, Heart of England CID,' said Sunita. 'Are you Dominic Jenks?'

'Yes.'

'Nathan Gardener gave us your address. We wanted a word with you about Lydia Squires.'

Strangely, he looked as calm as a boat drifting in a windless sea. Sunita wondered if Gardener had warned him to expect their visit.

'You'd better come in,' he said. 'I heard what happened, obviously. It's been all over the news. But I don't know if I'm going to be of much help.'

'I gather you went out with Lydia a few times,' said Sunita as the pair followed Jenks along a narrow hallway and into a small living room.

'I suppose we were fairly close around November,' he said.

'Did she come round here much?'

'Only once. She didn't like to travel too far from her home. I don't blame her. Either we'd go to her place or we'd meet at a pub in Warwick, the King's Arms.'

Without being invited, the two detectives sat down on a beige settee beneath a painting of a guitar. Jenks leaned against a tiled fireplace.

'We've heard Lydia was quite a glamorous lady,' said Dawson. 'You got to know her. What was she really like?'

'She was confident, pretty and had a bubbly personality. Everyone was her friend. To be truthful, I couldn't believe it when she showed so much interest in me. Maybe she felt safe with me, I don't know. I suppose, as the singer she was the main face of the band and a lot of men tried it on with her. In the end, I got the feeling she just wanted to be around someone tall to protect her when we did the gigs.'

'How did it all end?' asked Sunita.

'When she met Roman Makepeace.'

Dawson interrupted to say, 'We've been told they met online.'

'I don't know about that. All I know is that, at one of our gigs, the creep came over to the front and watched her singing. Then he bought her a drink and they chatted.'

'So you didn't think much of him?' said Dawson.

'He was a slimy toerag, in my opinion, and certainly not good enough for her. You know who his father is, don't you? That gangster Axel Makepeace, who's spent more time behind prison bars than Captain Cook spent navigating the world.'

'Oh,' said Sunita. 'So your nose was put out when Lydia switched her attentions to him?'

'Well, I wasn't happy about it, obviously, but I just had to accept things, didn't I? That woman was a law unto herself, like.'

The pair were both staring at Jenks. He looked uncomfortable.

'Don't get me wrong,' he said. 'I'd no quarrel with Lydia. I was devastated when I heard she was dead. But I'd no time for that Makepeace fellow.'

'If you'd had you way, you'd have continued to be Lydia's regular boyfriend?' said Sunita.

'Yes. If I'd had my way, we'd still be together and she'd probably still be alive. The thing is Lydia was a strong, independent woman, like. I'm not sure she thought I met her high standards.'

'Besides going on dates, you performed in the band together. So you must have seen quite a bit of her. I mean, you must have had rehearsals as well as gigs.'

'We had a laugh and a joke, but we were never what I'd call properly together.'

'Do you know of anyone with reason to harm Lydia?' asked Sunita.

'No. She was a terrific girl and, you know, if things had been different, I'd have loved to have had a proper relationship with her.'

Sunita glanced across the room at their host. 'Dominic, I need to know where you were on Valentine's night,' she said. 'I take it the band wasn't performing anywhere?'

'No. We had lots of offers for that night but the guy who plays the drums was ill, so we didn't do any midweek dates that week.'

'So what did you do?'

'I can't remember offhand. I think that was the night I had to rush over to my grandmother's place a few miles away because her dog was ill and I had to take him to the vet,' he said.

'This is very important,' said Sunita. 'Do you keep a diary or calendar? If you called your grandmother, would she remember?'

'No. I wouldn't have written anything down and she never remembers anything,' said Jenks. 'I don't know. Perhaps I was here on my own all night.'

Chapter 18

Axel Makepeace's Jaguar swept into the peaceful, tree-lined avenue as the sun was about to set over the town of Sutton Coldfield on Sunday evening.

The family's large, detached home, like so many in the street, was shrouded from prying eyes by high walls and hedges. The businessman's chauffeur pressed a remote device to open the black metal gates before proceeding up the drive towards the ten-bedroom house.

'That will be all, Davies,' said Makepeace, raising his hefty frame from the back seat and heaving himself out of the car.

He turned his key in the reinforced front door and headed through the vast hallway and into the dual-aspect drawing room with its imposing, ornate pillars and four glittering chandeliers. Two full-size sash windows, glazed in bulletproof glass, gave views of the front lawn. Patio doors across the room, also bullet-resistant, overlooked a terrace and landscaped rear gardens. Roman was sprawled out on one of the two white settees close to the marble fireplace.

'Good to see you, son,' he said, placing his briefcase on the floor by the door. 'You had another early start, didn't you?'

'Yes,' Roman replied. 'We had those two coaches leaving early for the Cornish Charm Tour.'

'Another jostling jamboree of happy customers,' said Makepeace, as he sat down on the second settee.

'It wasn't all smiling faces. There were a couple who turned up late and didn't get the seats they'd wanted,' said Roman.

'Sod 'em. We've got their money, haven't we?'

'Yes, Dad.'

'So you just thought you'd call round and see how your mum and dad were getting on?'

'Yes. Plus I thought I might have left my phone charger here, but it's not. I'll have to buy another one.'

'How are you feeling now? You seem a bit more cheerful than last time I saw you.'

Roman moved into an upright position on the settee. He felt as gloomy as if he'd spent a rainy night in the Lickey Hills.

'I'm a little better now, Dad,' he lied. 'I had been thinking about going to the doctor for antidepressants, but I don't think I'll be doing that now.'

'Good lad,' said Makepeace. 'The Makepeaces are men of grit. We don't let a little bad luck blight our lives.'

'Dad,' Roman snapped. 'You seem to be dismissing my girlfriend's death as something minor.'

'I'm not saying that, son. What I'm trying to say is that we don't let the tragic side of life get us down. We soldier on. That's the kind of people we are.'

Makepeace stood up and stretched himself. He took a few steps round the room.

'Despite feeling a little better, I still can't stop thinking about her,' Roman continued.

'You've got to pull yourself together, young man,' said Makepeace. 'She was a nice girl. I liked her, but you've got to face reality. She's gone. She's not coming back, and you've got to move on. There are plenty of other nice girls out there.'

Roman shook his head.

'It's not that easy, Dad. She had the whole package – looks, personality, intelligence. We just gelled.'

'I know, son. But she's gone. Someone out there decided her time had come. She'd obviously put someone's nose out of joint.'

'You don't think it was anything to do with me, do you, Dad?'

'What? That someone knocked her off? No. I can't think why you'd have been a factor in that. Just someone with a screw loose. Maybe some frustrated asshole who wanted her himself and couldn't have her.'

Roman rolled his eyes.

'But that's just my point. It might have been someone who believed they should have been with her on Valentine's Day, saw me with her and was full of resentment.'

'No. You've got to put those sorts of thoughts right out of your head or you won't be able to move on. Just put it down to experience. It's the way life turns out sometimes. You think you're on a roll. Then something kicks you in the teeth and you're on the floor. The guys with grit like us get back up, dust ourselves down and get on with life. That's what you've got to do.'

'All right. I'll try,' said Roman.

'Look, maybe this will help take your mind off things,' said Makepeace, resuming his seat. 'I've got a small problem and I'd like you to sort it out for me.'

Roman shrugged his shoulders.

'It's been a few weeks since I last helped with one of your money-making ventures,' said Roman.

'It's someone who's owed me money for a while. You know I don't like it when someone owes me money.'

'Yes, Dad.'

'None of the other lads are free at the moment. We've got a big shipment coming in from Europe and they're all tied up with preparing for that. I just wondered if you could sort this person out for me?'

'Would I be doing this on my own?'

'No. I thought I'd send Chester with you.'

'All right, Dad. What does it involve?'

'Right,' said Makepeace, leaning forward on the settee. 'There's a woman down in Queensbridge who owes us ten grand. I won't get into the ins and outs of why it built up so much. I want half the money in cash immediately and a payment plan set in place for the other half. How does that sound?'

'Pretty straightforward. I suppose you want me to get a little heavy with her.'

'You'll have to decide that. You're a big lad now. I'll let you take any executive decision like that. I'll just get some paper.'

Axel Makepeace stepped across the room to a writing bureau, tore a paper sheet off a pad and walked back, handing it to his son.

'You've helped me with a few other unpleasant jobs. But consider this your introduction to the world of debt collection,' he said. 'Have you got a pen?'

Roman nodded but before he could write any details down, the door opened and in walked his mother, Klara, carrying a tea tray. She put the tray down on a coffee table stationed between the settees and kissed her husband on the cheek.

'Good day, dear?' she asked.

'Not too bad,' Makepeace replied.

Klara, who was middle-aged, slightly overweight and had her blonde hair tied in a bun behind her head, said, 'I won't interrupt you two. I can tell you're talking business. I'll leave the tea and scones here.' Then she swept out of the room.

'Thanks, love,' yelled Makepeace.

Roman searched in his trouser pocket for his pen.

'So what's the name of this woman you want me to see?' he asked.

'She's someone who used to live with one of our dealers, a guy called Styler, but I don't think she's with him anymore.'

After writing down her current address for him, his father added, 'Her name's Jackie Perrins.'

Chapter 19

After pinning photographs of their main murder suspects on the CID whiteboard on Monday morning, Sunita Roy stepped back and studied them. She tapped two of them with the end of her pen.

'You've spelt Makepeace wrong,' she told DC Dawson. 'There's no *Y* in it. Otherwise everything's fine.'

The rueful young detective grabbed his marker pen and a cloth and amended the spelling.

'What's the problem?' asked the chief inspector, emerging from his nearby room.

'Sorry, sir. Nothing important,' she replied.

'All right,' said Roscoe as Sunita and Dawson found themselves chairs. 'I think we need to start the meeting.'

He clapped his hands and bellowed, 'Time to gather round.'

DC Omar Khalid and DC Wendy Hopkirk came forward from the back of the office. Moments later, the detectives were joined by Dr Ling and John Hepworth from forensics and by PCs Kaur and McDonald.

As his audience sat down on chairs and, in some cases, desks, Roscoe revealed that Bina Patel, Lydia Squires' landlady, had confirmed the previous evening that the knife found in the hedge was the missing kitchen knife. 'It's a steak knife made in Switzerland with a twelve-inch blade and a wooden handle which had been left in the house by a previous tenant. A lethal weapon found in many kitchens across the land,' he said.

'However, we've had bad news from the forensics team. No DNA has been retrieved, apart from the victim's,' he announced. 'The handle had been wiped clean. There is suspiciously little information on Lydia's phone or tablet. Dr Ling has said they're hoping to get results shortly on the traces of human saliva found in the kitchen.'

Murmurs of disappointment rippled round the room.

'Yes, it's frustrating but we've got to move on,' he continued, stepping towards the board. He pointed towards the five images on display. Names, ages and occupations had been scrawled beneath each one.

'Let's go through them,' he announced, tapping on the first photograph with a pen. 'This first mugshot belongs to Vernon Bainbridge, the customer service assistant who was stalking Lydia Squires. There's a question mark over whether he would have had enough time to break into the house and lie in wait. He claims he tried to follow the boyfriend home but lost him after a few miles. There's no CCTV of his car in Balmoral Gardens. There's probably a blind spot the CCTV can't reach.'

'He's no longer in custody, is he?' said Sunita.

'That's right,' Roscoe replied. 'Bainbridge has been released under investigation but he's not completely ruled out.'

He tapped the second picture.

'This smartly groomed young man is Roman Makepeace, Miss Squires' boyfriend of a few weeks. He's the only son of Axel Makepeace. We know that, on Valentine's Day, he bought her dinner at the Five Bells. He claims he left her at the gate to her home at around ten thirty, walked to his silver Porsche, which he'd parked nearby, and drove back to his flat in Coleshill. But the question is: did he leave Balmoral Gardens at the time he claims he did?

'Although his car's registration was picked up by ANPR on the M42 just before 11 p.m., you'd have expected him to have reached the motorway earlier than that. So why the delay? When Bainbridge claims he lost sight of the Porsche, did Makepeace double back and kill his girlfriend? We know that, with the pendulum of human emotions, feelings can quickly swing from fervent love to virulent hate. The annals of crime are full of cases in which folk kill their lover in a fit of rage — often to rue the day later when it's too late.'

Sunita nodded. 'Yes, you're right, sir.'

'His father is also a suspect,' Roscoe continued. 'We've spoken to Axel Makepeace and he's promising to help the police in any way. He claims to have found Miss Squires charming but if you see this man's criminal record, you'll understand why he must be considered a person of interest.'

DC Dawson broke into a smile. 'They call him The Magician, don't they?' he declared. 'He's mastered the art of making people vanish.'

Roscoe nodded. 'I've heard that nickname used,' he admitted. 'There are past murders his name's been linked to. But gathering evidence against him that will stick, that's proved challenging.'

Khalid, who was sitting on a desk behind Dawson, raised his hand. 'What could Axel Makepeace's motive be in this case, sir?' he asked.

'We clearly don't know at this stage,' said Roscoe, 'but since his son features in the case, we'd be foolish to overlook him. He represents a sinister force and we simply can't afford to rule him out. At some point, by the way, we're going to have to ask ourselves, was it significant that this murder happened on Valentine's Day? Or was that just a coincidence?'

There was muttering among his audience as he turned his attention back to the board.

'Now we finally come to the ex-partners,' he said, 'Sophie Bishop and Dominic Jenks. DS Roy has spoken to them both and they both appear to have strong alibis for the night of the murder.'

'Yes, sir,' said Sunita. 'Miss Bishop was performing on stage. Mr Jenks says he was at a vet's in Coventry.'

'We all know,' said Khalid, 'that alibis have to be verified and there've been times when so-called firm alibis have turned out to be not so firm.'

'Agreed,' said Roscoe. 'They've often turned out to be a pack of lies.'

Chapter 20

The moment the chief inspector arrived in the CID office the following morning, he was informed that the chief superintendent wanted to see him.

With some degree of trepidation, he climbed the stairs to the second floor, concerned that his superior had found fault with some aspect of his performance and he was about to be reprimanded.

But Chief Superintendent Norris seemed good-humoured as he knocked and entered her office. She was engrossed in a conversation with DI Vickers, who also seemed in an affable mood.

Roscoe greeted them both with a cheery 'Good morning.'

'I'm guessing that Tom's had some success?' he remarked.

'Yes,' said Norris, peering towards him over the top of her reading glasses.

'The first results have come back on the human remains we found in Jakeman's Wood last week,' said Vickers. 'It's definitely the skeleton of Councillor Portman. We're very pleased that Flint came up trumps after all this time, although, of course, it's distressing news for family and friends.'

'Where exactly were the victim's remains found?' asked Roscoe.

'There's a narrow lane halfway along the Bedivere Road, not far from the school. You go along there a short distance and there's a public car park. The clearing where the body was found was less than a hundred metres from there.'

'That dog, Flint, has done a magnificent job,' said Roscoe, as he selected a chair and sat down beside his colleague. 'I take it the family have all been informed?'

'Yes. I went round to see the husband, Ben Portman, last night,' said Vickers. 'Their son, Tim, was there and I broke the news to them both.'

'Tim's a councillor like his mother, isn't he?'

'Yes.'

'How did they take it?'

'They're absolutely devastated, guv. As you know, they mounted a vigorous campaign to keep the councillor's disappearance in the public mind. I imagine, as time passed, they were starting to come to terms with the prospect of never seeing her again, but it was still a terrible shock.'

'I feel sorry for them,' admitted Roscoe, 'but at least they can move on with their lives now.'

'They can't hold a funeral yet – not till the coroner gives the go-ahead,' said Vickers.

'What about the press?' asked Roscoe.

'I thought it wouldn't be long before news got out,' said Vickers, 'so I've had a word with the media team and they're going to release a statement.'

'I'm going to hold a press conference, Gavin,' said Norris, 'and I'd like you to be there. This was a high-profile case eight years ago and we need to make the public aware that, even though it was challenging at the time, technology and resources have moved forward and we've made huge strides. The case was never formally closed and we've found the victim's remains thanks to the determination of our police teams.'

'Dogged determination, ma'am,' said Roscoe.

'Yes,' she said with a smile. 'Dogged determination.'

'The other news, which I'm quite excited about, is that we found a mobile phone with the remains,' said Vickers.

'The councillor's phone?' asked Roscoe.

'No,' said Vickers. 'Forensics have had a good look at it. It's Todd Styler's phone.'

'Case closed,' said Roscoe. 'We know Styler had money problems. We know more than eight hundred pounds in cash was stolen from the Portmans' house at the time she vanished and Styler was later flush with funds. Now you tell me Styler's phone was actually buried with the victim. What more do we need?'

Vickers nodded in agreement.

'The only sticking point,' said the inspector, 'was that Styler's girlfriend at the time, Jackie Perrins, swore blind he was with her the whole night.'

'Nonetheless,' said Norris, 'the chief inspector is right. We've got a wealth of evidence against Styler. Up until now, we'd no human remains and it would have been challenging to frame a murder charge. But now that's changed, we're in a good position to move forward. We need to arrest him and confront him with all this evidence.'

Roscoe leaned back in his chair. 'By the way, was the mobile phone lying loose beside the victim?' he asked.

'Yes,' said Vickers.

'Has it been checked for prints?'

'Yes, guv. There were prints from three different people on the handset – Councillor Portman, Todd Styler and an unidentified print.'

'Were there any other suspects at the time the councillor disappeared?'

'Not really. Styler and his workmate, Zak Bridges, had had a minor disagreement with her over the fee for the job but that wasn't thought of as being anything significant. Bridges was at his lodgings in Stratford on the night she vanished.'

Roscoe stroked his chin as he mulled over the facts of the case.

'Where's Styler now?' he asked.

'He runs a business in Queensbridge laying patios and drives. He still lives on the Troutbeck estate,' said Vickers.

'Before we arrest him, I think we should track down Jackie Perrins and have one last crack at her,' said Roscoe. 'Once we've explained what we've found and repeat the known facts of the case, she might have a change of heart. We also need to ask her again about Styler's sudden financial windfall. To move forward, we just need to build the strongest case against him that we can. Does she still live on the Troutbeck?'

'No. I've been making inquiries. She's got a flat over a pub in Queensbridge High Street.'

'Good. So you've got her current address?'

'Yes, guv. I agree with what you're saying about Miss Perrins,' said Vickers. 'I was wondering if I could take DS Roy along with me to meet her. I find women are sometimes reluctant to cooperate with a male officer. She might be more forthcoming if there's a lady asking the questions.'

Chapter 21

It was a cold, overcast morning when Brett Dawson set off from his Birmingham home for his appointment with Bina Patel in Worcester. Bina Patel, the owner of 67 Balmoral Gardens, had suggested they meet at the house.

He drew up in his car shortly after half past nine and was relieved to find she was waiting for him on the pavement outside.

The young detective had heeded his sergeant's advice and was less flamboyantly dressed in a plain winter coat.

'Mrs Patel,' he said as he leaped from his car and hurried over to shake her hand. 'This is good of you to come.'

'It's the least I can do in the circumstances,' she said. Her demeanour was nearly as sombre as the dark clouds overhead.

She strode up the path, took a huge bunch of keys from her handbag and opened the front door.

Bina Patel was a short, austere woman in a grey trouser suit. A plait of dark hair flowed over her left shoulder as she led him into the front room. Stepping across to the bay window, she flung the curtains open, flooding the room with light.

'I was so shocked when I found out Miss Squires was dead,' she said. 'I was at the hairdressers when customers were talking about it and I quickly realised they were talking about someone dying at my house. Of course, it's made things very difficult for us. We can't relet the house until the police have totally finished with it.'

As they sat down facing each other, Dawson slipped a small notebook from his trouser pocket.

'So what can you tell us about Miss Squires?' asked Dawson. 'When did you first meet her?'

'My husband took a call from her back at the start of August last year, inquiring about houses or flats to let,' she said. 'We told her we'd several properties available and invited her to visit our office in Worcester.'

She took a document from her handbag and referred to it.

'That's right,' she said. 'She came to the city on 14 September with her brother-in-law. He was a nice guy. We showed them three houses and two flats but this was the one she preferred. She paid a holding deposit. Her references were all fine, so she moved in in October. We sorted out the contract and the finances and I handed her the keys. Her mother was meant to be living here as well but I found out from the neighbour she's been in hospital.'

'What sort of references did she provide?' Dawson asked.

'She had a work reference from a firm in Staffordshire and one from a previous landlord in Staffordshire.'

'Could I see them?'

'I haven't got them with me but I could email them over to you,' she said.

'That would be cool,' he said.

'The references were full of praise for her, so we decided she'd make an excellent tenant,' she added.

Dawson, who had been taking notes, glanced up. 'Have you got a date of birth for her?' he asked.

'Yes, here it is,' she said, pulling out another document and perusing it. 'It's 23 June 1994 in Tamworth.'

'What were things like after she moved in?' he said.

'No problems. She was a good tenant. Always paid the rent on time.'

'No strange incidents?'

'No. Nothing.'

'You weren't aware she was being stalked by an admirer from her factory?'

'Well, Clare, the neighbour, said something about that. She mentioned a man with a ponytail, but before then I'd no knowledge of anyone troubling her.'

* * *

The CID office was nearly deserted when Dawson returned from meeting the landlady. Only Sunita Roy was hard at work behind her computer screen with her desk phone pressed firmly into her ear.

'Where is everyone, Sarge?' he asked.

Sunita, who was holding on the line for somebody, said, 'There's a presentation in Norris's office for Superintendent John Williams, who's retiring.'

Then, she began speaking into the mouthpiece of her phone.

'And you definitely don't have anyone by the name of Judith Squires in any of your wards?' she said. 'All right. Thank you for your time.'

After ending the call, she gazed across at her colleague, who was sitting a few metres away.

'I've phoned all the local hospitals,' she told Dawson. 'None of them has any record of a woman named Judith Squires being admitted. It's really strange. I can't get hold of her daughter Allison either.'

'Well, it's funny you should say that,' said Dawson, turning round to face her. 'I've just come back from seeing Bina Patel.'

'Oh, yes. How did that go?'

'Fine. Nothing out of the ordinary, except she's never met Lydia's mother, who was meant to be moving in with her daughter. Don't you think that's odd?'

'Very odd.'

'Mrs Patel learned from the neighbour that the mother had been taken into hospital,' he added.

'Do me a favour, Brett,' said Sunita. 'Can you email our family history guy and get him to look into the Squires family?'

'Yes, of course. No problem.'

'There's one other thing I've found out that's a bit strange. Weren't you telling me that Aiden Pagett claimed not to know who owned the house?'

'That's right.'

'Well, according to Mrs Patel he came along to view the house with Miss Squires.'

'That *is* strange,' she agreed.

Sunita rose to her feet and collected her fawn jacket from a coat stand.

'Where are you off to, Sarge?' Dawson asked.

'I'm going over to the Pagetts' place,' she said. 'It's time I had another little chat with him. Hopefully, we can find out what's happened to Miss Squires' mother. It would also be useful to have a word with his wife, Allison. She works nights and, as it's coming up to midday, this might be a good time to catch her.'

* * *

On arriving at the Pagetts' ground-floor apartment, Sunita initially thought the office manager might be out. No car was in the driveway. But after a wait of several minutes during which she pressed the bell three times, she noticed a dark figure appear behind the partly glazed door.

'Who is it?' asked a quiet male voice.

'DS Roy from Heart of England CID,' she replied.

'You can't be too careful,' Pagett said as he drew back the door and invited her in.

As she stepped in, he asked, 'Have you any news for the family?'

'Not yet,' she said. 'Aiden, I need to ask you a few questions.'

'Fire away.'

'First of all, is Allison here?'

'No. You've just missed her. She's gone into town.'

'I've been calling her number constantly and have left countless messages. I still haven't heard from her.'

He shrugged. 'I'm sorry. I gave her the message. She must have forgotten.'

'Right. Give her the message again, please. Now the other thing is that none of the hospitals in this part of the West Midlands have admitted a woman called Judith Squires. Is that her full name?'

'Yes.'

'Judith isn't her middle name?'

'Not as far as I know.'

'Anyway, the hospital staff were all very helpful when I explained it was a police matter connected with a murder,' said Sunita. 'They carefully checked for any patient with the surname Squire or Squires and I've totally drawn a blank.'

'You're probably wasting your time talking to me,' he said.

Sunita had already begun thinking along the same lines.

'You need to speak to Allison,' he continued. 'I'm pretty certain she'd like to talk to you as well.'

Sunita took her notebook from her jacket pocket.

'Can you give me her work address?' she asked him.

'I'm not sure you'll have any joy at the biscuit factory,' he said. 'It would probably be hard to find her among all the staff working there and, more importantly, I don't think her bosses would like it. You're better off calling back here tomorrow lunchtime to see her.'

'No. I'll give her work address a try,' Sunita insisted.

'All right,' he said. 'Give me your pen and paper, and I'll write it down for you.'

He wrote down an address in Lickey Road in the south Birmingham suburb of Longbridge.

'That's really helpful,' Sunita said. 'What sort of time do you think she'd be there?'

'Any time after five o'clock, I would think,' he replied, 'but don't say I didn't try to warn you. I don't think her bosses will be all that delighted by her being disturbed at work. The wheels of industry and all that.'

'You're forgetting this is a murder inquiry and it's in everybody's interests to assist the police – especially yours, Mr Pagett,' she said. 'By the way, we still haven't seen your firearms certificate.'

'Don't worry. It's all in hand,' he insisted. 'Anyway, good luck, Sergeant.'

After a journey of fourteen miles, Sunita found the address in Lickey Road she'd been given. She got out of the car and checked the street numbers of neighbouring buildings. No, she was certain now. The address Aiden Pagett had provided was… a derelict warehouse.

Chapter 22

As soon as Sunita Roy woke on Wednesday morning, her mind darted back to that moment the day before when she realised the three-storey building in Longbridge was not a working factory. It was the same moment she totally grasped that Aiden Pagett was not to be trusted.

He had failed to get Allison to phone her. He had tried to dissuade her from approaching Allison at her workplace and then he had given a bogus address. Before long, she would have to confront Pagett over his web of lies. What was he trying to hide?

She drew back the bedroom curtains and gazed out at the lawn, which would soon need to be mown, and the flower beds brimming with daffodils quivering in the gentle spring breeze.

Could he be involved in some way in Lydia Squires' death?

She would not know the answers to all these questions until she had a chance to question him again.

After taking a shower, getting dressed and eating a quick breakfast, she heard the sound of a car trundling over the gravel in her front drive and realised Tom Vickers had arrived from his home in Halesowen.

'You all right?' he called out as he got out and strode over to her open front door.

'I'm always all right after seeing you,' she said, planting a kiss firmly on his cheek. 'Leave your car here and we'll go in mine. I want to hear your opinion on something.'

Five minutes later, they set off on the four-mile journey to Queensbridge police station, where they were due to question Todd Styler's ex-girlfriend, Jackie Perrins, at half past nine.

'So what's this problem you want my views on?' asked Vickers.

'It's not a problem exactly. Well, all right. It's a problem,' she said. 'There's something strange about Lydia Squires' family. I haven't spoken to anyone yet who's ever met Lydia's mother, Judith. I'm beginning to wonder if she exists. I've called all the main hospitals and she's not listed.'

'Maybe she's in a private hospital,' he suggested.

'I suppose that's a possibility, although I'm not sure they'd have the money. The other thing is I've been trying to speak to Lydia's older sister, Allison. Maybe she's trying to avoid me. Allison's husband, Aiden Pagett, is absolutely no help. He seems to be blocking me. He gave me an address in Longbridge which was meant to be where she works. When I turned up, the place was a disused warehouse.'

'So he's giving you the runaround?' said Vickers.

'Yes.'

'You need to be tougher with him and remind him there's a charge of wasting police time. Do you want me to come along with you to see him?'

'No, Tom. That's kind of you, but I don't need anyone with me. I'll go back to Pagett in a day or so and give him a grilling. Somehow I'll get to the bottom of this mystery.'

'Look, Sunita, I'd better quickly mention today's business,' said Vickers. 'I think there's a chance the Perrins woman will be more open with us if you take the lead. Is that all right?'

'Yes. Fine. I've read the files. I think I'll be OK. And if I'm not, I'll have you to back me up, won't I, Tom?'

* * *

Jackie Perrins was in a ground-floor interview room when the pair arrived at the police station. She was a tall, pale-skinned woman with childlike eyes and long, silky hair. She was sitting at a table close to the front window, which overlooked the town's high street.

She smiled when Sunita knocked and entered, followed by the inspector.

'I'm sorry if we're a few minutes late,' said Vickers. 'I'm DI Vickers and I'm in charge of this inquiry. This is my colleague, DS Roy. Are you OK for us to chat in here?'

'Yes. This is fine,' she said. 'But I don't know how much I'm going to be able to help you.'

'Well, we'll see,' said Vickers, who was holding a large memo pad.

He and the sergeant seated themselves on the opposite side of the table. Sunita opened her small notebook and at once took charge of proceedings.

'You're here because, as you'll have seen in the press, police have reopened the inquiry into the disappearance of Councillor Debbie Portman eight years ago,' she said. 'You'll also have seen that human remains identified as those of the councillor have been found in Jakeman's Wood.'

'Yes, I know,' said Perrins.

'One of the last people to be seen in the presence of Mrs Portman was your former boyfriend, Todd Styler, and for that reason, we need you to make a statement.'

'I'm happy to do that.'

'All right. Before we write anything down, we need to go through the events leading up to the night of Mrs Portman's disappearance, 25 April. Where were you living at that time?'

Perrins wrote down an address on the Troutbeck estate on a piece of paper for them.

'And you were living there with Mr Styler?' asked Sunita.

'That's right. The tenancy was in my name. I'd been living there for thirteen years.'

'When did he move in?'

'Some time in the summer of the year before.'

'And you were cohabiting?'

'Yes, we weren't married, if that's what you mean.'

Sunita made a note of this in her book.

'And how was your relationship with Styler?' she asked.

'I'll have to be honest,' Perrins said. 'It was up and down. When he was sober, he could be Prince Charming. But when he'd had a drink, he could be a charmless bastard. He beat me up several times.'

Vickers interrupted to say, 'You're no longer living with him?'

'No. I've got a flat above the Red Lion in Queensbridge, where I'm a barmaid. He's still living on the Troutbeck somewhere. I had to move out. I couldn't stand being with him anymore.'

Sunita leaned back in her chair.

'At some point, Mr Styler got to know the Portman family. How exactly did that happen?' she asked.

'Todd got a phone call from Ben Portman, the councillor's husband, asking for a quote for a new patio outside their living room. They accepted his quote and he and Zak spent a week up there, installing some new block paving.'

'Who is Zak?' asked Sunita.

'Zak is Todd's assistant.'

'OK. So when was the job finished?'

'It was done about two days before the woman vanished.'

Sunita leaned across the table. 'Turning to the night of the councillor's disappearance, police believe someone broke into the Portmans' house between 6 p.m. and 8 p.m. There was a violent incident in which a vase was smashed. Where were you at that time?'

Perrins shrugged. 'That's a long time ago, but I've gone through it in my mind so many times. I was at my flat.'

'And where was Todd?'

'He was with me. We watched *Pointless Celebrities* at seven o'clock and, at eight o'clock, there was an old episode of *Father Ted.*'

Sunita thought to herself that almost anyone could come up with a couple of television programmes at the drop of a hat.

'I tell you what,' she told Perrins. 'Can you name any of the contestants on *Pointless?*'

'Kate Garraway and Fern Britton.'

'Very good,' said Sunita, making a note to verify the information later.

At that moment, Vickers received a call on his mobile phone and left the room.

'Thank you for listening to me,' Perrins said as soon as they were alone. 'I have the impression you believe me. A lot of the cops who've talked to me over the years haven't been as understanding.'

'That's all right,' said Sunita. 'I have to be honest. I've met a few men and women over the years who've lied to me through their teeth. But your comments sound credible and ring true.'

Vickers re-entered the room. 'Sorry about that,' he muttered. 'I'll turn my phone off now. Where were we? Oh yes. You were telling us about the television programmes you and Todd were watching. What I'd like to know is: how can you be so sure about these programmes? This was eight years ago.'

'I was asked about this at the time the woman went missing and those two programmes have been ingrained in my memory ever since.'

'Phone records show your then boyfriend was in the Bedivere Road area and at Jakeman's Wood around eight o'clock,' he continued.

'No. He was by my side, watching TV,' Perrins insisted. 'Look, I know he's not the Archangel Gabriel. He's done a lot of things he shouldn't have done. Like I said, he beat me up several times. I lost a baby because of him. I've got no reason to try to protect him. But my old dad always told us girls to tell the truth. And I can honestly say he was with me the whole evening.'

Vickers tutted.

'All right,' he said. 'How do you account for the phone records showing otherwise?'

'I can only tell you what I know,' she insisted.

'Tell me something else,' Vickers went on. 'Friends of Todd's told us eight years ago he was broke when the councillor went missing. How come he was able to clear some of his debts around that time?'

Perrins nodded. 'I remember being asked about this back then,' she said. 'I didn't know the answer at the time and I later asked Todd the same question. He said one of his paving customers had paid for materials in advance.'

Vickers shrugged.

'We'd need to check his bank statements again,' he muttered.

With help from the two detectives, Jackie Perrins spent the next forty minutes writing out her statement and signing it before leaving the station.

After she went, Vickers took Sunita to a nearby cafe in the high street so they could mull over what they had learnt from the witness.

Vickers was dispirited since Perrins was standing by her original account of what had happened eight years before. He looked across the table at Sunita after they had ordered two hot drinks.

'That hasn't really helped me at all,' he said. 'I'm going to find it much harder now to convince the CPS.'

'Tom, I have to be frank with you,' said Sunita. 'I found Jackie's words extremely compelling. Your case has been blown out of the ocean.'

At that moment, Sunita noticed she had been left a voicemail on her mobile phone.

'Excuse me, Tom,' she said as she put the phone to her ear.

'Sergeant Roy,' the message began. 'It's Jackie Perrins. I've been thinking about what I told you. I need to talk to you again urgently.'

Chapter 23

A gentle rain was falling as the chief inspector drew his bedroom curtains apart early on Thursday. He gazed out across the rear lawn and noticed, for the first time, the encouraging signs of nature's silent handiwork. Lime-green leaves were appearing on beech trees while snowdrops were huddled in one of the flower beds, heralding the advent of spring.

His mind entered a period of tranquil reflection as he set off for St James Street. But this ended abruptly when he arrived at half past ten. He had only just unlocked his door when Sunita Roy leaped from her desk and rushed forward.

'Good morning, Sergeant,' he said as she eased the door open. 'You must give me a chance to take my coat off.'

'Yes, sir. Sorry, sir,' she said.

'What is it, anyway?' he asked.

She came in and closed the door. 'Sir, I've got a feeling someone's trying to pull the wool over our eyes as regards Lydia Squires' family,' she said.

'How do you mean, Sergeant?' he asked as he settled into the chair behind his desk.

'Well, Miss Squires is meant to have moved into the house in Balmoral Gardens with her mother, but no one's ever seen the mother – not even the landlady or the next-door neighbour. What's more, she's meant to be in hospital but none of the local hospitals have any record of her being admitted.'

'Maybe she's in a specialist hospital further away or a private hospital.'

'Aiden Pagett, Miss Squires' brother-in-law, believed she was in either the Worcestershire Royal Hospital or Queensbridge General, but I've checked thoroughly. She's not in either.'

'What's she being treated for?'

'Cancer.'

'All right. So where does that take us?'

Sunita gazed at him across the desk.

'There's a lot more,' she said. 'Miss Squires is meant to have a sister, Allison Pagett. But I've been unable to speak to her. Pagett gave me a false work address for her.'

'Mr Pagett is clearly giving us the runaround,' said Roscoe, staring out of the window at the park across the street. 'I wonder why?'

'There's a bit more,' she said. 'I've just heard back from our family researcher. He can't find birth records for any members of the family. Not even for Lydia Squires herself. Nothing's come up matching the date and place of birth we have for her. On top of that, our man can't find a marriage between an Aiden Pagett and an Allison Squires. It's as if the whole family is a work of fiction.'

Roscoe glanced back at her and swung his chair round.

'Go on,' he said.

'When I've spoken to Aiden Pagett, he's been unable to provide certain material information – such as Lydia's previous job and previous address,' she said.

Roscoe paused while he assimilated this. Then he glanced across at her.

'It's starting to look now as though the lives of the Pagetts and Miss Squires have been partly based on lies and that these may not even be their real names. With Judith and Allison, I think we have to work on the assumption that they definitely don't exist and never have existed – unless someone can prove the contrary.'

Sunita nodded in agreement. 'Yes, sir.'

'You've done well, Sergeant,' he said. 'This discovery of yours is clearly central to our investigation. It appears the murder victim was trying to conceal her identity for some reason and we need to find out what that reason was. It could be key to resolving the whole case. It seems to me the quickest way to sort this out is for the two of us to go over to Aiden Pagett's flat in West Bromwich and confront him. I think, with both of us challenging him, it will be hard for him to wriggle out of it and he'll be forced to come clean.'

* * *

As soon as they arrived outside in Roscoe's car, Sunita knew it had been a wasted journey. Some of the venetian blinds were open and they could see directly into the flat from the driveway.

After walking up to the door and pressing the bell, Sunita peered through the front window. The Warwickshire landscapes still embellished the walls, but there were no dirty dishes on the table; no television; no books on the bookcase; no coats hanging by the door; no rugs on the floor; and no motoring magazines scattered around the room. Some of the furniture was missing. All that remained was an exercise bike, two blue towels and a pile of mail on the mat.

She pressed the bell again but it was pointless. The sound simply echoed round the deserted flat.

Chapter 24

Concerned about Aiden Pagett's sudden departure, the chief inspector began pacing up and down on the pavement in Trinity Drive like a prospective father in a maternity ward.

'This has just made our chances of finding the killer so much harder,' he told his sergeant as he came to a halt and stared across at the flat.

'I expect you're right, sir,' she replied. 'But we need to track him down straight away, if we can. Shall I have a word with the neighbours? There's a light on in the upstairs flat and some of them might be around. Pagett was certainly still living here on Tuesday. So it looks as though he either moved out yesterday or early today.'

'Good idea,' he replied. 'While you're doing that, I'll call some of the lettings agents around here. If we can find the agent or landlord, they might have a forwarding address.'

Sunita stepped round to the left of Pagett's flat and found a side door. She pressed the bell and waited. After a short time, she noticed through the glazed door a man descending the stairs and approaching her.

'Yes?' said the occupier, an elderly, studious-looking man with grey hair and glasses. He was holding a recipe book in his hand.

'Sorry to bother you,' she said, holding out her warrant card. 'DS Roy, Heart of England CID. Were you around when your downstairs neighbours moved out?'

'Yes. It was very late last night. The noise woke me up.'

'Could you be more precise about the time?'

'Let me think. It would have been about eleven o'clock. I'd only just gone to sleep.'

'Did you know Mr and Mrs Pagett?'

'I only ever saw Mr Pagett. Don't know about any wife. I just used to say hello to him sometimes. I keep myself to myself. But I was surprised to see him move out. He'd only been here five minutes.'

'You know for a fact he moved out? How do you know that?'

'I peered through the curtains and saw them loading a white van.'

'How many people did you see out there?'

'Well, there was Mr Pagett and two men. Stocky men, they were. I believe most of the gear in the flat belongs to the landlord, but they must have had a few sticks of furniture, a load of bedding, a television and other personal things.'

'Do you think he was going willingly?' she asked. 'I mean, it didn't look as though he was being abducted?'

'Good God, no. He seemed to be shifting most of the stuff himself. I'd say he was leaving of his own accord.'

Sunita wrote some of these details down in her notebook. Then she glanced towards him.

'Did any strange events happen while he was here? Was there any trouble at all?'

'No, he was as good as gold. What's happened then? Why all these questions?'

Sunita smiled. 'Nothing for you to worry about, sir. We're investigating his relative's death. We need to track him down so we can ask him a few more questions.'

'And him doing a moonlight flit like that might point to him being a suspect?' said the man.

'Not really. We just need to trace him. Do you have the name of the landlord or letting agent?'

'I'm not sure who the landlord is. It's changed. I can tell you the letting agents are Sillwood and Burns in the High Street.'

Sunita tried two other neighbours' doors but found no one at home. She was about to join Roscoe when a blonde woman in her twenties hurried out of the building next door. Sunita explained who she was and asked about Pagett.

'The guy with the beard?' the woman asked.

'Yes,' said Sunita.

'I was coming home last night when he and two mates were loading a van,' she said. 'He said the place didn't really suit him after all.'

'He was meant to be living there with his wife,' said Sunita.

'Never saw anyone else there, apart from him.'

'Was there a name on the van?'

The woman thought for a moment. 'Not that I recall,' she added before walking away.

Roscoe was leaning across the passenger seat, trying to attract Sunita's attention.

'Pagett's been into the agents' office and paid everything up to date but they haven't got a new address for him,' said Roscoe. 'I think it's time to go back to St James Street.'

'Can you give me the agents' number?' Sunita asked. 'If I find time, I'll give them a call myself this afternoon.'

* * *

Sunita found her partner had arrived home a few minutes before her that evening. After he greeted her with a kiss and they had exchanged details about their day, they began preparing a supper of fish, rice and vegetables together.

'It's all right, Tom,' she said after ten minutes. 'We've only got to wait for the rice now. You go and watch the news, if you like.'

But moments later, after he had begun watching the Midlands TV news, she heard him calling from the living room.

'Come and look at this, Sunita,' he was shouting.

She put the pan of rice down on the hob and rushed in to find images of Aiden Pagett's flat on the TV screen. A constable was standing guard outside and police tape had been wound round the entrance.

She watched in shock while the news reader revealed he had some 'breaking news'.

> Armed police have been called to Trinity Drive in West Bromwich after reports of a drive-by shooting. It's been reported a man arriving home at his ground-floor flat has been critically injured after a gunman peppered the building with bullets.

West Midlands Police say patrols have been stepped up in the area. We'll bring you more when we get it.

Chapter 25

'Tom, I've got to get up there,' Sunita told her companion after learning Aiden Pagett's flat had been targeted by gunmen.

'What about your meal?' he said.

'I'm suddenly not very hungry.'

They at once set off in Sunita's car for Trinity Drive.

The street had been sealed off by police by the time the two detectives arrived. A crowd of journalists had gathered behind a police tape, set up more than a hundred metres from the targeted building. A plain white Ford Transit van was parked nearby.

Sunita thrust her warrant card in front of a stern-faced constable standing behind the cordon. 'DS Roy, Heart of England CID,' she said. 'Do you know who's the SIO here?'

'That would be DI McLachlan,' he replied. 'She's just over there, speaking to one of the SOCOs.'

They observed a tall, slim woman in a blue-quilted jacket standing halfway along the front path outside Pagett's home. A white tent covered the front doorway and porch.

As soon as she saw them approaching, McLachlan ended her conversation and turned towards them. 'Can I help you?' she asked with a vague smile.

'We're from Heart of England,' Sunita explained, showing her warrant card again. 'DS Roy and DI Vickers. I was here just a few hours ago in connection with one of our cases.'

'Really?' replied the inspector, shaking both their hands. 'DI Laura McLachlan, West Midlands Homicide Unit.'

'We're looking into the Lydia Squires murder in Worcester.'

'I've heard about the case, obviously,' said McLachlan with a nod.

'The victim's brother-in-law has been living here,' Sunita explained.

'What details have you got?' asked McLachlan as Sunita outlined what she knew about Pagett.

'We've found out the flat was rented by a company in the name of MQZ Properties (Wolverhampton) Limited,' said the West Midlands officer.

'What's actually happened, Inspector?' asked Vickers.

'Eyewitnesses say the victim arrived in that white van and walked up the path,' said McLachlan. 'Just as he unlocked the front door, two men in a black Range Rover Evoque drove past in a southerly direction. The vehicle slowed down and a hail of bullets was discharged. The car then drove off at speed with the sound of screeching tyres. We've tried to trace it, but it looks as though it had false plates which have no doubt since been changed.'

'Who was actually shot? Aiden Pagett?' asked Sunita.

'We haven't identified the dead man yet,' said McLachlan.

'He's dead?' said Sunita, open-mouthed.

'Yes. He passed away shortly after the shooting, which was about half past five this evening.'

'Has the dead man got a beard?'

'Yes.'

Sunita and Vickers exchanged anxious glances.

'It said on the news he was critically injured,' said Vickers.

'That's probably because when the press first called our media office, we refused to confirm he had actually died,' said McLachlan.

Grey-haired Home Office pathologist Dr Silas Reynolds overheard their raised voices from inside the tent, where he had been inspecting the body. He emerged in his white overalls.

'Sunita!' he cried. 'An unexpected pleasure. And you've brought that old rogue Tom with you. I expect you'd like to know what's happened to this poor fellow, wouldn't you?'

'Yes,' said Sunita. 'Have you finished your initial examination?'

'More or less,' he replied. 'The victim has suffered from at least six gunshot wounds to the head, chest, liver and left hand. It's impossible to give the precise cause of death at this stage, but the chest wound alone would have been fatal within a few seconds.'

'So the victim would have died quickly?' Sunita suggested.

'Almost instantaneously,' Reynolds replied. 'If the weapon used was on automatic or semi-automatic fire, these injuries could have been sustained very quickly in a burst of gunfire or a number of short bursts. The poor blighter wouldn't have stood a chance. He will be taken to the Sandwell Mortuary shortly so I can carry out a full examination.'

'Could I have a look?' said Sunita. 'I want to see if I can recognise him.'

'Is that all right with you, Dr Reynolds?' asked McLachlan.

'Feel free,' said the pathologist. 'The poor fellow's fairly presentable and I've got most of what I need.'

While the pathologist stepped away to speak to McLachlan, Sunita braced herself, unsure whether her eyes were about to gaze down on the solemn face and dark hair of office manager Aiden Pagett.

She peered round the tent flap at the blood-splattered body of a man in his mid-thirties lying on his back in the doorway. He was wearing a blue shirt and dark trousers. There was no doubt at all in her mind that, beneath the glow of the arc light, it was not Pagett. Like Lydia's brother-in-law, this man had receding dark hair and a small beard. But, unlike Pagett, he was short in height. His face was rounder. His skin tone was darker.

She felt relief in a way from a selfish standpoint. She needed Pagett to be alive. She needed to find him. She needed to find out why he had been playing games with the police. But she also felt huge sympathy for the family of the dead man.

Sunita shuddered before withdrawing from the makeshift shelter.

'It's not Aiden Pagett,' she announced.

'That's a blow,' Vickers suggested. 'Could take a while to work out who this guy really is.'

'Oh, I know who it is,' said Sunita as Vickers, McLachlan and Reynolds looked in amazement.

Chapter 26

Detective Inspector Laura McLachlan walked briskly up the path towards Sunita Roy, who had just emerged from the police tent shielding the murder victim's body.

'What do you mean – you know who the man is?' she demanded.

'Let me explain,' said Sunita. 'This afternoon I was chatting to someone at Sillwood and Burns, the lettings agents. I was asking them about the whole process they follow when a tenant moves out. They mentioned that, although Aiden Pagett moved out on Wednesday evening, he was paid up until this coming Saturday. That's when he was due to hand the keys in. So that meant he was free to leave some of his belongings behind for a few days and come and collect post. Pagett had also agreed that their cleaning contractors could come in and spruce the place up.'

'So I'm guessing this guy is one of the cleaners?' said McLachlan, writing details down in her notebook.

'That's right,' said the sergeant, removing her own notebook from her coat. 'The guy's called Marius Nicolescu, born on 3 June 1988 in Bucharest,' she said, reading her scribbled notes from earlier. 'He's Romanian. Single, as far as I know. He lives in a flat in Rectory Drive, Oldbury. Number eighty-seven.'

Vickers looked astonished.

'But how do you know all that?' he asked as a black van arrived to collect the body and Dr Reynolds went to speak to the driver.

'I just downloaded the cleaning firm's brochure earlier on and made a few quick calls,' said Sunita. 'I recognised his face from the centre pages. He's one of two supervisors who are featured. They get sent round to price up jobs.'

'That's very helpful. Thank you,' said McLachlan before adding tetchily, 'We had an idea he might work for a cleaning company. He's got some business cards in his pocket with the firm's name. We just needed it confirming.'

'This looks very much like a case of mistaken identity,' Sunita remarked.

'We'd already reached that conclusion,' said McLachlan, petulantly. 'One of the neighbours thinks they saw a black Range Rover parked in the street twice in the past week or so with two men in it. There's every chance they were lying in wait for the guy that lived here. It seems highly unlikely that someone coming to clean the property was the intended victim.'

'That makes sense,' said Sunita. 'It certainly looks as though he's been killed by accident. He was probably in the wrong place at the wrong time. Not that the ruthless men who did this will have any regrets when they find out.'

Vickers nodded.

'They're just callous bastards,' he said. 'They'll probably laugh when the identity of their victim becomes known on TV and in the press. Criminals like that dismiss this sort of thing as collateral damage.'

He turned towards McLachlan. 'I imagine, Inspector, you've already considered who may be behind this attack and, like us, there's one person heading the list of likely suspects?'

She mouthed to him the words 'Axel Makepeace' as though reluctant to speak the gangster's name out loud. He nodded.

'Yes,' he said. 'Doesn't take too much working out.'

After making a note of McLachlan's personal phone number, Sunita followed Vickers back to their car. The victim's body had been driven away now. Dr Reynolds had also left.

The street had fully reopened, although a cordon still remained around Pagett's flat and a constable stood on duty outside. Reporters and camera crews were busy trying to interview neighbours.

Sunita was about to start the engine when there was a knock on the window. Startled by the unexpected distraction, Sunita glanced round and saw the scholarly man from the flat above Pagett's standing by the driver's door.

As she lowered the window, he said, 'It's DS Roy, isn't it?'

'Yes. A nasty incident here this evening, sir.'

'Yes,' said the neighbour. 'I've been advised to move out by the local police. I'm being forced to stay with a friend for a couple of days. I see there's just the one cop on guard now.'

Vickers shouted across from the passenger seat, 'West Midlands are keeping an officer here twenty-four hours a day for the next few days and there are going to be regular patrols.'

'That's some comfort,' said the man. 'I thought I'd mention I found some shredded paper Mr Pagett left behind. It had spilled out of his grey bin. It was all social services reports about drugs.'

'I can't explain that,' said DS Roy. 'Perhaps you could pass that to the officer by the front door.'

The pair watched as Pagett's neighbour wandered off down the street.

'That's interesting, isn't it?' said Vickers as Sunita started the car. 'It suggests that perhaps our Mr Pagett wasn't the paragon of virtue we'd previously thought him to be. Why would he have social services reports?'

'I don't know what to think,' Sunita admitted as they drove away. 'I've never considered him a paragon of anything. He had a shotgun by his front door, remember. But, the more I think about it, I am beginning to wonder whether Pagett was the intended target of the gunman.'

'I would have thought it was as clear as a cloudless morning that he was the target,' said Vickers.

'Tom,' said Sunita, 'I've learnt since joining Heart of England that there's always room for doubt. There's always the possibility that Marius Nicolescu bought drugs and upset the West Side Gang in some way. You know how sensitive the bad guys can get if someone fails to pay for their purchases.'

'That's true,' he said.

'I'll phone the boss in the morning,' she said. 'He might want to get a member of the team to check out Nicolescu's background.'

'I think that's wise,' said Vickers. 'We've got to cover our backs.'

'There's something else worrying me,' she said.

'What's that?'

'If we assume the cleaner was shot because he was mistaken for Pagett, did the same gunman kill Lydia?' she said. 'And are the whole family under threat? Is that the reason I can't find Allison and Judith?'

Chapter 27

'You should take more precautions,' said the ginger-haired man as he leaned back on Jackie Perrins' single bed.

Perrins was so shocked to see the man lying there as she entered her flat that, for several seconds, she was unable to speak.

She stood trembling in the doorway in her dark-green coat on Friday morning. Her heart was pounding.

She finally found the strength to demand, 'Who the hell are you? What do you want?'

'Just need to have a little chat with you, Jackie,' he said.

'Is your name Roman?' she asked.

'Well thought out,' he replied.

'How the hell did you get in here?'

'There's not a very secure lock on your street door, is there?' said Roman. 'My mate had no problem getting past it.'

His eyes turned towards the nearby kitchen doorway, where his companion was standing. 'He knows a whole range of techniques, don't you, mate?'

Perrins was disturbed to see Roman's well-built accomplice, heavily tattooed and with short dark hair, emerging from her kitchen. She was inclined to run back down the stairs, dash into the street and call the police. Roman must have noticed signs of her intentions flickering across her face. He leaped up, darted across the room and slammed the stair door shut behind her.

'You need to find some funds to cover what you owe,' said Roman.

'I haven't got any,' Perrins insisted, turning to face him as he remained by the door. 'Come back on Saturday. I'll have had my wages by then.'

Roman shook his head. 'Sorry, darling. You've owed this money for too long. We can't wait any longer. We want at least five thousand pounds now and a thousand a month for the next five months.'

'Where am I expected to find that kind of money?' she asked. 'I'm a barmaid.'

The second man, Chester Crane, said in a deep, croaky voice, 'You should have thought of that before you bought the drugs.'

Crane charged at her, knocking her onto the top of a mahogany table. Perrins lay sprawled out for several seconds with Crane's hand pressing hard against her back, holding her down. He produced a knife from his trouser pocket and, while maintaining his pressure on her, thrust the blade forward and plunged it into the table with a thud. The weapon narrowly missed her hand.

He retrieved the knife, grabbed her round the throat and hauled her into a standing position. Then he held the blade beneath her chin.

'Thanks, mate,' said Roman, who walked back to the bed and sat down on it. 'I'm going to say this just once more, Jackie. We want at least five grand now.'

'I'll see what I've got,' she said meekly as Crane gradually released his grip on her throat.

She scurried about the room, rummaging in drawers and a double wardrobe. She ferreted about in a series of handbags on a low-level sideboard and squinted inside her purse.

'Right now, I can give you the princely sum of forty-nine pounds thirty-four pence,' she said, her eyes reddening and wavering in desperation.

'That's a pitiful amount,' Roman said. 'Didn't you realise this day of reckoning was going to come?'

'No. I suppose the drugs deadened me to reality.'

'Who do you bank with, Jackie?'

'Lloyds.'

'That's good. They still have a branch in town. I want you to go there now and withdraw five grand.'

'I'm not sure I've got that much. Can't I pay you at a rate of a thousand a month, beginning next month?'

Roman folded his arms.

'You're starting to annoy me,' he said. 'I've been sent to collect five grand and that's what I'm going to be leaving with. I don't care how you do it, but I suggest the best way is for you to go to the bank and withdraw it. Even if it means you go overdrawn.'

Perrins nodded.

'Off you go,' he said before turning his attention to his associate. 'Can you go along with her to make sure she takes our advice and doesn't do anything stupid?'

Crane nodded. 'Sure thing,' he said, moving towards the door.

Perrins followed Roman's stocky companion down the stairs and into the street.

When they returned forty minutes later, the barmaid had a sullen expression. She opened her handbag and pulled out an envelope, which she handed to Roman. He was still sitting on her bed.

'It's all there,' she said.

'What took you so long?' he asked.

'There was a long queue, mate, and then the cashier asked her loads of questions,' Crane explained.

Roman stood up and walked across the room to the sideboard. He swept the handbags and costume jewellery to the side with his hand. Then he conscientiously counted out the money, which was in fifty-pound notes. He returned the notes to the envelope and placed it in a pocket inside his jacket.

'You see, Jackie?' said Roman. 'You put on all that performance when we first arrived here. You gave us all the reasons you could think of as to why you couldn't pay us. But now you've settled half your bill and, because of that, you only need to pay a thousand a month. My friend here will call on you round about this time next month for your first monthly instalment. Is that clear?'

She nodded. 'Yes.'

Roman stepped towards the door.

'I can give you some advice, Jackie, for a happy and peaceful life,' he said. 'Always pay on time.'

The two men were minutes later walking down the high street towards the supermarket, where they had parked their car. Shops that a week ago had been showing displays of Valentine's hearts were now enlivening their windows with hearts promoting Mother's Day.

'I must remember to get something nice for my mother,' Roman muttered to himself as they entered the car park.

'I tell you what,' he continued as they climbed into the front of Crane's red Audi A3, 'I'm not sure I'm cut out for this kind of caper, Chester, putting the squeeze on a neurotic junkie who can't properly organise her money. It might suit my old man and his mates, but I've always looked for an easy life.'

'Don't worry about it, mate,' said Crane. 'You did good. I personally thought we could have been a bit tougher on the woman. You know, if you hadn't told me different, I'd have probably roughed her up a bit. But we got the money and your old man couldn't ask for more.'

Chapter 28

The chief inspector's car gathered speed as he and his sergeant travelled onto the M5 motorway on Friday.

'This looks like quite a strong lead from DC Hopkirk, doesn't it?' he remarked as he overtook a lorry.

Sunita nodded.

'Yes, sir,' she said.

The pair were heading towards an industrial estate of warehouses and logistics buildings in the market town of Oldbury. Information DC Hopkirk had collected from an ANPR camera suggested the removal van used by Aiden Pagett was owned by Central Van Hire and had been booked there. The depot was just two miles from the Trinity Drive flat.

Roscoe parked next to a line of rental vans before leading the way to the entrance door. A man in blue overalls was studying some vehicle documents behind the counter of a small office. He glanced up as the pair came in.

'DCI Roscoe, Heart of England Police,' said the chief inspector. 'We need to know about a van that was hired to move someone from a flat in Trinity Drive, West Brom, two nights ago.'

The man – sporting a label on his blue tunic saying 'Steve, Manager' – seemed unsure.

'When would it have been signed for?' he asked.

'No idea,' Roscoe replied. 'I've got the registration, if that will help.' He drew out his notebook and read out the van's number.

'Oh, this might prove a problem,' said Steve.

'Why's that?' asked Roscoe.

'I've been told not to talk about it,' said Steve. 'Hold on a minute.'

The manager sat down at a desk behind him and tapped a few words on a computer keyboard. He jotted down a name and phone number on the back of a blank invoice and handed it to the chief inspector.

Roscoe glanced at it. 'Oh, this might explain a lot,' he said before thanking the manager and leading his sergeant out of the building.

'What is it, sir?' Sunita asked.

'It looks as though we might be treading on somebody's toes,' said Roscoe.

There was a pause before he added, 'There's a guy called Quinton Taylor whom I've known since we were constables together, back in my West Midlands days. Somehow he must be linked up with all this.'

Sunita was feeling bewildered as she followed the chief inspector to his car.

'What on earth is going on, sir?' she asked him.

Roscoe slipped his phone from his pocket and dialled the number that the firm's manager had just given him.

'It looks as though another team of officers has been involved in moving Aiden Pagett out of his flat,' he said. 'But if I can reach my old friend, Quinton Taylor, I think everything will become a lot clearer.'

The call was answered brusquely by a deep, gravelly voice saying, 'Taylor.'

'Quinton, a voice from your shady past here. Gavin Roscoe,' he said.

'Gavin, you old devil,' Taylor replied enthusiastically. 'I've been trying to get hold of you. How've you been? Are you still down among the country bumpkins?'

'Yes. I'm pleased to say we don't have to put up with the hectic pace of life of you urban dwellers, among the smoke and fumes.'

'I sometimes envy you country boys, with your stolen tractors and missing sheep,' said Taylor. 'I hear you've risen through the ranks, Gavin.'

'Yes. You probably know I'm a DCI with Heart of England now and it gets much more exciting than missing sheep.'

'I'm sure it does. Listen, as you probably know, I'm the detective chief superintendent with West Midlands ROCU. Gavin, I'm delighted to hear from you but I sense this isn't just a social call?' said Taylor.

'No. We're investigating the murder of a glamorous young lady by the name of Lydia Squires, and our paths seem to have crossed. We've been trying to trace a man called Aiden Pagett.'

'Oh, right,' said Taylor. 'I'm glad you called because an apology is overdue. Pagett is one of ours, Gavin. He's mentioned both your names to us. The problem is he's been involved in a special operation. This is all a bit awkward over the phone. Where exactly are you right now?'

'We're sitting on a trading estate in Oldbury.'

'What rotten luck,' said Taylor.

'But we're about to head back to St James Street.'

'That's quite good for me,' said Taylor. 'I'm at the airport right now. What time do you reckon you'll be back at your base?'

'It's now nearly two o'clock and we haven't had lunch. Shall we say four o'clock?'

'Perfect. I'll see you at St James Street at four,' said Taylor, ending the call.

Sunita, who had been listening intently to the conversation, was bristling with questions.

As Roscoe returned his phone to his pocket, she asked, 'So your friend is a chief super with the Regional Organised Crime Unit?'

'He's the boss,' said Roscoe.

'That's the body set up to tackle cross-border organised crime?'

'That's the one. Aiden Pagett – if that's his real name – is one of his operatives.'

'That explains why the man kept a firearm by the front door,' she said.

'Yes. It will probably explain a lot of things but there's no sense speculating. We'll have to wait till four o'clock now and see what Taylor's got to say for himself.'

* * *

Promptly at four o'clock, a gleaming, grey Jaguar drew up outside St James Street police headquarters. Detective Chief Superintendent Quinton Taylor, a tall officer of medium build with thick-framed glasses, climbed out of the back seat and walked through the main doors.

After the constable at reception had notified the chief inspector of Taylor's arrival, the visitor was escorted up to the first floor. When he reached Roscoe's room, he knocked and peered round the door.

'Gavin!' he said as his old colleague swiftly ended a phone call. 'How great to see you.'

Roscoe rose from his seat and warmly shook Taylor's hand after the door had swung shut.

'I'd like my sergeant, DS Roy, to be present,' said Roscoe. 'She's heavily involved with the Squires case.'

'Very well,' he said, taking off his black gloves and sitting down. 'You know, you've hardly changed. Perhaps a little more weight around the middle.' He tapped his own stomach.

'I think we're both enjoying life too much,' said Roscoe, opening the door and summoning Sunita.

'Ah, so you're DS Roy,' said Taylor as the sergeant entered the room and shook his hand. 'Pleased to meet you. Did you know your boss and I used to patrol the streets round Bordesley and Digbeth back in the eighties?

As a young constable, he single-handedly tackled an affray in Birmingham city centre before back-up arrived.'

'I've heard the story, sir. He's a legend.'

Roscoe was becoming embarrassed. 'Come on. That's enough of that,' he said. 'Let's hear about your Mr Pagett.'

Taylor leaned back on his chair. 'Your murder victim – I think she was calling herself Lydia Squires – was, like Pagett, one of our operatives. I must swear the pair of you to secrecy over this. A lot of people's lives could be at stake if a word about this got out. That includes CID colleagues.'

'No problem,' said Roscoe. 'My team are all extremely trustworthy.'

'You have our word,' said Sunita.

'They'd been working together on a special operation to infiltrate an OCG known as the West Side Gang. We'd been finding it extremely difficult to obtain intelligence about the gang, run by a guy you've probably heard of called Axel Makepeace. So one of our people had the bright idea of bringing in a woman and encouraging her to build a relationship with the son, Roman. I was pleased to find that that seemed to be working well.'

'A honeytrap?' Sunita suggested.

'That's not the expression I'd use,' said Taylor.

'But why didn't you get one of your officers to go undercover as a member of the gang itself?' she asked.

'Don't worry. We've tried that as well and our efforts are continuing.'

'So can we assume that both Lydia's and Aiden's names were fictitious and that Judith and Allison Squires don't exist?' Sunita asked.

'I'm afraid that's all correct,' he said. 'The mother and sister were created so there was a bit of a back story.'

'Quinton,' said Roscoe, 'why didn't you tell us about all this before? One of your own people has been brutally put to death and it's only now – more than a week afterwards – that we're having this conversation.'

Taylor shrugged. 'Look, I'm sorry. I tried to call you a couple of times towards the end of last week.'

'I wondered what those missed calls were,' Roscoe muttered. 'You should have left a message. It's only now we're finding out the real facts about this young woman's life.'

'I know,' Taylor continued. 'To be honest, Gavin, this woman's death threw us into chaos. We've been genuinely up to our eyes with our own inquiries. At first, we couldn't work out what had happened. I'm sorry. In hindsight, I should have put one of my inspectors in touch with you about this sooner.'

'You should have,' said Roscoe. 'Have you given any thought to the officers on the case, like DS Roy? What a state this has left us in? We're trying to investigate a murder. We don't even know the victim's real identity.'

'Her real name's PC Lizzie Hope.'

'Lizzie Hope?' said Roscoe. 'We'll have to issue this name to the media as well and simply explain she went under two names. Her real name is bound to come out eventually, knowing the perseverance of the press.'

'Look, as I say,' said Taylor, 'I regret not keeping you guys in the loop. One reason is that losing that girl was a hammer blow and it created a real crisis for us. She was a wonderful operator and so courageous. Her death is a huge loss. Not only to her family – I've had her mother on the phone constantly – but also to her friends and force colleagues. We're all devastated.'

'We can appreciate that,' said Roscoe.

Sunita turned towards the chief superintendent.

'Can I ask what Aiden Pagett's real name is?' she asked.

'Alan Pargeter. He's a detective inspector and a senior member of the team. He felt he had to move out of the place where he'd been set up in Trinity Drive. He didn't feel safe. I suppose he didn't want to come home and find a stranger in the kitchen.'

'We can understand his concern,' Sunita agreed. 'If he'd been around last night in Trinity Drive, he could have died in a hail of bullets – like the poor Romanian cleaner did.'

'Point well made,' said Taylor. 'We're actually going to have to remove him from the entire operation since his cover's clearly been blown.'

'You can't give us Mr Pargeter's new address?' said Sunita.

'I'm afraid I can't. However, on his behalf, I'd like to apologise for all the wasted time that's been expended on trying to trace him and also on inquiries into the other two relatives.'

'This news about your special operation obviously makes our investigation more difficult,' said Roscoe.

'Well, I deeply regret that,' said Taylor. 'However, from now on, I can pledge you all my help because ROCU are just as keen as Heart of England to ensure justice is done for poor Lizzie.'

'We have a number of suspects for PC Hope's murder and Axel Makepeace was some way down the list until now,' said Sunita. 'He's suddenly risen to the top. So, naturally, we're going to need to speak to Mr Pargeter.'

'I'll arrange something.'

'And, with respect, sir,' she added, 'when I speak to him next, we'll need his full cooperation.'

'Of course. I'll speak to him and sort something out. But could you both keep me informed of any progress you make on Makepeace and his activities? If you interview him or arrest him, let me know because it could impact our work.'

'That's fair enough,' said Roscoe as he nodded his head.

'Chief Superintendent, it would also be very helpful if we could have access to any reports PC Hope filed while she was undercover,' said Sunita.

'That may be a little tricky,' he said.

'Regarding Axel Makepeace,' she continued, 'I interviewed him a week ago and I was a bit concerned when he boasted about having close friends in the police.'

'I'm afraid Makepeace may well have some good police contacts, and at a senior level, too,' said Taylor.

'This revelation from you is going to force us to look at this case in an entirely fresh light,' said Roscoe. 'I mean, it must be in your mind that, somehow or other, Axel Makepeace might have discovered Hope's true role.'

Taylor turned his gaze towards his old friend.

'Gavin,' he said, 'we believe it's quite possible Makepeace might have discovered what Lizzie's game was and, despite the heartache this may have caused his son, might well have arranged for her life to be terminated.'

Sunita looked the chief superintendent in the eye.

'Equally, isn't it possible the son, in a fit of anger on realising his new girlfriend's true intentions, may have carried out the deed himself?' she suggested.

Taylor shrugged his shoulders.

'We can't rule that out either,' he said.

Chapter 29

Sunita Roy had an exasperating time on Saturday morning. She spent two hours trying to set up a meeting with the ever-elusive ROCU officer Alan Pargeter. She left voicemail messages and sent him a text, urging him to call her. But, it seemed, he was continuing to avoid her.

Sunita was also trying to make contact with Jackie Perrins, whom she had been trying to reach for days. Again, messages had been left but no response had been forthcoming.

The last words Perrins had spoken to Sunita had been, 'I need to talk to you again urgently.'

The barmaid was clearly desperate to speak to the sergeant. Perhaps she wanted to change her statement. Perhaps Todd Styler had *not* been with her, after all, on the night Councillor Portman disappeared. Perhaps her entire testimony had been a pack of lies.

Finally, as she watched her colleagues arriving in the office one by one, she decided to phone the Red Lion in Queensbridge. If Perrins wasn't currently at the pub, her employers might know where she was and how to get in touch with her. Her call was answered by the genial voice of landlord David Wainwright, who had assisted the CID team in a previous murder inquiry.

'I'm trying to get hold of Jackie Perrins,' Sunita explained.

'Oh, haven't you heard?' said Mr Wainwright. 'She has just been rushed into Queensbridge General after a drugs overdose.'

Concerned for Jackie Perrins' welfare, Sunita hurried across to the chief inspector's room and knocked on his door.

'Sorry to disturb you, sir,' she told Roscoe as she peered inside. She explained what she'd just learned.

'Do we know any more?'

'I've just been speaking to her boss at the Red Lion pub.'

'Dave Wainwright?'

'Yes. He and his wife found her beside an empty bottle of tablets on her bedroom floor this morning. They called an ambulance but it's not looking good. Wainwright says it's touch and go.'

'You'd better get down there and see if she'll speak to you. You don't have any idea what it was she wanted to talk about?'

'No, but it sounded important.'

'Get down there, but be as quick as you can.'

Sunita collected her coat and scurried out of CID before making her way down the stairs. She had only reached the half landing when she heard a voice she knew well.

'You're off in a hurry, Sunita,' said Tom Vickers as he waited for her at the foot of the stairway with a broad smile. 'Going anywhere exciting?'

'Jackie Perrins is fighting for her life in hospital,' she gasped. 'I'm off to see her now.'

'I'd better join you,' said Vickers. 'She's a key witness.'

* * *

They found a space in the visitors' car park and hurried to the main entrance.

'We're looking for a lady named Jackie Perrins, who was brought in sometime earlier,' Sunita told a man at the main reception desk.

'She's been moved out of intensive care. She's now in Cofton Ward,' he said. 'It's on the first floor.'

When they reached the ward's reception desk, Sunita showed a young nurse her warrant card and explained they were police. They were pleased to hear that Jackie Perrins had made a good recovery. The nurse immediately left to inquire whether the patient was well enough to receive visitors.

'We should have brought something – flowers or grapes or something,' Sunita remarked.

'She'll have to settle for the pleasure of our smiling faces,' Vickers replied.

The nurse returned, nodding her head.

'You go along the corridor and it's the first room on the right,' she explained.

Jackie Perrins was lying on her side with her head on the pillow when the two detectives stepped into the room she was sharing with three other patients who were away from their beds. She appeared to be watching passing clouds.

'Hi! How are you?' said Sunita.

Perrins seemed to struggle to raise herself into a sitting position.

'Here, let me help you,' said Sunita, lifting one of the pillows and taking hold of the patient's arm.

'That's better,' said Perrins while Vickers fetched two chairs. 'You heard what happened to me then?' Perrins asked.

'We heard you took an overdose,' said Vickers.

'I didn't want to be here,' she said.

'Now that's just silly, isn't it?' said Sunita. 'You've got a lot to be thankful for.'

'I know. But I've had all sorts of problems with men.'

'What kind of problems?' asked Sunita.

'I'd rather just tell you,' said Perrins, peering suspiciously across at the inspector.

'It's all right. I'll make myself scarce,' said Vickers. He then turned to Sunita, saying, 'I'll see you back at reception.'

While they were waiting for Vickers to gather his coat and leave, Sunita glanced at the cards on Perrins' bedside cabinet. One stood out to her – a shiny greetings card with pink and yellow flowers and a 'Get Well Soon' message, from someone whose name she recognised.

As soon as they were alone, Perrins whispered, 'I like you, dear, but I wasn't really comfortable with your friend being in on the interview. I find him a little pushy.'

'He's fine when you get to know him,' said Sunita with a smile.

'I'm sure he is. It's just that I've had a terrible time at the hands of men. I seem to attract the wrong type and there aren't many I feel I can trust.'

'Anyway, it's just the two of us now.'

'All right. Well, I'll tell you what's happened to me. Two men broke into my flat in Queensbridge,' Perrins explained. 'They forced me to withdraw £5,000 from my bank and I've had to borrow money from my father.'

'Did you owe the money?' asked Sunita.

'Well, I did, but they wouldn't give me time to pay.'

'What did you owe the money for?'

'Do you really want me to say?'

'Was it drugs?' Sunita whispered.

She nodded.

'Give us the names,' said Sunita. 'We'll see what we can do.'

'I only know one of them,' she said. 'But I don't like to say his name out loud.' She pointed to the other three beds.

'His sidekick stabbed his knife into my tabletop, just missing my fingers,' she added.

'Here you are,' said Sunita, handing her a pen together with her notebook, which she had opened at a blank page. 'Jot the name down for me.'

Although weak, Perrins managed to scribble a name into the sergeant's book. Sunita was surprised when the book came back and she saw the name 'Roman Makepeace'.

'We'll try to make sure he doesn't bother you again,' said Sunita. 'Can you describe the other man?'

'Big build. Short, dark hair. Lots of tattoos.'

'That doesn't mean anything to me,' said Sunita. 'You didn't catch his name?'

'His name wasn't mentioned. But he was horrible to me. As we walked to the bank, he told me, "The boss always uses me for jobs like this because he trusts me, Jackie. He has to. I'm too valuable to him. I know where the bodies are." And then he said something really scary. He said, "Todd Styler's brother, for example. I know where he is. He went to landfill."'

'Jackie, I'll pass all that on. But he may well have said that simply to scare you. Listen, you were trying to reach me on Wednesday shortly after you left the police station.'

Perrins nodded.

'Yes. I'm afraid I wasn't totally honest with you at the station and I felt guilty about it afterwards. I didn't want you to think I'd misled you. It's about Todd.'

One of the nurses interrupted them to ask if Perrins wanted a drink of water. The patient nodded and the nurse poured some into a glass, then left.

Perrins continued, 'You know we were talking about Todd and Zak laying the patio at the Portmans' house?'

Sunita nodded.

'Well, that was the Thursday, two days before the councillor went missing. On the Friday, Todd couldn't find his phone. We searched everywhere. He decided, in the end, he must have left it at the Portmans' house. He called Councillor Portman on his other handset and she confirmed she had his phone. She said she was planning to come into Queensbridge at some point over the next few days and she'd bring it round to our house. But that never happened.'

'Wasn't Todd stuck without his phone?' said Sunita.

'He had his second one as back-up,' Perrins explained. 'The next thing that happened was the police came round and arrested Todd, demanding to know what he'd done to Councillor Portman. But he'd had no real axe to grind with her. She'd paid him in cash for the work and he was definitely with me all night on the Saturday she disappeared.'

Sunita wrote this information down in her notebook and then stared across the bed at the barmaid.

'I've been told it wasn't long after that that you and Todd finished,' said Sunita.

'That's right,' said Perrins.

'Do you know the precise date?'

'I think it was 1 May. It was the day he went to Zak's flat to view his new car and he came home drunk. My dad made sure he left.'

Sunita remembered her interest in the shiny 'Get Well Soon' card with a distinctive floral design just before she left. She nudged it off the bedside table onto the floor while Perrins was sipping from her glass of water. Then she reached down and slipped it into her bag without the patient noticing.

'Jackie, I must go now,' said Sunita, rising to her feet. 'Take good care of yourself.'

A few minutes later, she rejoined her boyfriend by the reception desk and she drove him back to St James Street.

'Why was that woman so touchy with me?' he asked as they set off towards the M42 motorway.

'Maybe she thinks you look shady,' said Sunita with a grin.

'Shut up,' he said.

'Don't worry about Jackie,' she insisted. 'She's got a problem with men but seems to trust me and I got some vital information from her.'

'She's a funny woman, if you ask me,' Vickers moaned.

Sunita revealed details of her conversation with Perrins. Then, she surprised him. 'Forget about Todd Styler being responsible for the murder of Councillor Portman,' she said. 'I've got an idea of another suspect – a much more likely suspect. It's my belief that this second person carried out the killing and then left Styler's phone with the body to cast blame on him.'

Chapter 30

Believing she was close to a breakthrough in the Portman murder case, Sunita Roy walked with a bounce in her step when she returned to St James Street just after lunch. She paid a visit to a colleague in forensics and asked her to carry out some research for her following certain discoveries she had made. She needed the results of some tests before she could share her conclusions with anyone.

However, after walking back from the forensic department, which was at the rear of the headquarters building, she headed straight for the chief inspector's room. Some of Jackie Perrins' disclosures at the hospital related to the Lydia Squires… the Lizzie Hope case, and she was eager to share them with her boss.

'Come in!' Roscoe bellowed as she reached his door.

She opened it a fraction.

'You'll be interested to know, Sergeant, that Khalid has visited Roman Makepeace's flat in Coleshill,' said Roscoe. 'The landlord found him a "decent, hard-working young man" who split from his girlfriend last year after a series of rows. He arrived home at around 11.15 p.m. on Valentine's Day. He remembers because *Newsnight* had just finished. Khalid's also spoken to relatives and work colleagues of Marius Nicolescu. There's no suggestion of any involvement in drugs and he's got no form. So the hit men almost certainly mistook him for Pargeter.'

'Oh well,' said Sunita, 'it was worth a punt.'

'How did you get on with Jackie Perrins?' he asked.

'Fine, sir,' she replied. 'I've got a few things to tell you.'

'Good. I've got a few minutes,' he said. 'Take a seat.'

She came in and closed the door.

'How was Jackie?' he asked, glancing up from his desk.

'She seems much better,' she said. She explained how Roman Makepeace and an associate had forced her to pay them five thousand pounds.

'Did he? That's useful to know. With a knife?'

'Yes.'

'Interesting – in view of the attack in Balmoral Gardens.'

'Yes, sir. The accomplice was a burly, heavily tattooed guy with short, dark hair.'

'No name?'

'No, sir.'

'I'll have a word with Tapper and see if he knows who that could be.'

Sunita looked blank. 'Tapper, sir?'

'Oh, sorry. DCS Taylor. Just our old nickname for him,' he said without elaborating.

'He's given the investigation a new lease of life,' she said.

'That's right. It's looking likely now that, somehow or other, Axel Makepeace and his gang found out about Lydia… Lizzie's clandestine role and decided to have her eliminated. So we've got to talk to Pargeter. It's essential we learn all we can from him, and don't take any nonsense. If he doesn't play ball, let me know at once and I'll have a word with Taylor.'

'I think he's avoiding me. I've left messages all over the place for him.'

'Keep trying, Sergeant. I'll give Taylor a call if you don't hear from him. I tell you what. At some point, we're also going to have to send someone down to the smoke to speak to the murdered woman's real family and look into her early life. Anyway, we'll worry about that later. Right now, I've sent Omar over to Sutton Coldfield to see if we can verify Axel Makepeace's alibi for Valentine's Day.'

* * *

That evening, after making himself comfortable on his girlfriend's leather armchair, Tom Vickers picked up the glass of lager she had poured him. He took a sip before placing it on the small table beside him.

'I was shocked when you told me Roman Makepeace threatened that Perrins woman and took a big payment,' he said.

'Yes,' said Sunita. 'He turned up with a brawny guy who was plastered in tattoos.'

'Sounds to me like Chester Crane, one of the heavies used by Axel Makepeace,' he said. 'So come on. You've called me over here, claiming to have solved my case in a matter of days. What have you found?'

Sunita Roy stepped across her living room, clutching a glass of chilled orange juice. She settled herself on a settee.

'I know for certain who killed Councillor Portman,' she said.

'So do I,' said Vickers. 'Todd Styler. I've just found his new address on the Troutbeck estate and we're going to arrest him later this week.'

'Well, you'd be making a big mistake,' she said. 'What are your main reasons for pointing the finger at Styler?'

Vickers took a large swig of lager from his glass.

'Cell data analysis of the night the councillor disappeared placed Styler's phone in the area around the councillor's house and nearby Jakeman's Wood,' he said. 'Then, when we found the human remains, Styler's phone was lying beside them. On top of that, although previously short of funds, a week after the death he was suddenly able to pay off a load of bills. He'd also been to the house a lot and was familiar with the layout. I'm fairly sure he'd seen the antique vase on one of his visits and used it to batter the councillor to death. I didn't tell you, did I? Dr Reynolds has given the cause of death as blunt force trauma.'

Sunita shrugged her shoulders.

'Do you remember the explanation Jackie Perrins gave us about Styler's finances?' asked Sunita. 'She told us one of his customers had paid for materials in advance. Did you study Styler's bank account?'

'I did and I couldn't find any sizeable incoming payment,' he said.

'Well, whoever it was probably paid in cash,' she said. 'Paying cash in hand is quite common. Listen, Tom, I found Jackie Perrins very plausible. She insisted Styler had been with her on the night of Portman's disappearance and nothing you say will make me shift my opinion.'

'All right,' said Vickers, stepping across the room to fetch himself a second can of lager. 'So what have you found out over the past few days?'

'Well, Jackie told me something interesting at the hospital, while you were banned from the room…'

'I knew you were going to bring that up,' he said.

She smiled. 'Listen. This is important. She said Todd realised he must have left his phone at the Portmans' house. The councillor called and said she'd drop it round to his flat.'

After sipping her orange juice, Sunita continued, 'Now this is what I believe happened. The real murderer discovers Styler's phone around the time the councillor was killed. Perhaps it was in her handbag, along with the money that was stolen. Then he makes use of the phone – perhaps sending out some harmless, anonymous texts. This ties Styler in with the location. Finally, while burying the body in the nearby woods, the killer places the phone in the grave – further implicating Styler.'

Vickers drank more lager.

'So come on. Who do you suspect of killing Councillor Portman?' he said.

'Zak Bridges, Styler's workmate,' she said.

'Bridges? Are you serious?'

'At the hospital, Jackie mentioned that, on the day she and Styler split up, Styler had been to view the new car Bridges had just bought. That was the first clue that Bridges might have been behind the murder. He wasn't earning much working for Styler. How come he suddenly had money? But what clinched it was the "Get Well Soon" card Bridges gave Jackie when he visited her at the hospital this week.'

'A get-well card?'

'Yes. You know there were three fingerprints on the screen of the phone found in the woodland grave, don't you?'

He nodded.

'Yes,' he said. 'Councillor Portman's, Todd Styler's, and an unidentified print.'

'Jackie let me borrow the greetings card and I passed it onto Dr Ling. The front of the card had a glossy surface – good enough for fingerprint evidence – and, sure enough, Ling found a print of Bridges' index finger on it. It matched the third print found on the handset.'

'That's brilliant work, Sunita,' said Vickers, jumping out of his seat and nearly knocking over his lager.

'I've also checked out Bridges' alibi,' she went on. 'Bridges wasn't at his digs in Stratford on the evening of the murder, as he claimed in his statement at the time. I spoke to his landlady. She recalls being annoyed because she'd wanted to speak with him about the rent.'

He stepped across to the settee and sat down next to her.

'You've saved me a lot of time,' he said. 'As I told you, I was planning to arrest Styler this week. Now it looks as though I'll be arresting his workmate instead. Sunita, I don't know how you do it.'

'My father always used to say that advice sharpens a rusty opinion,' she said. 'I have only added to what you had already achieved.'

'You've helped me enormously,' Vickers insisted.

'If you remember, Styler and Bridges had a disagreement with Councillor Portman over the money she paid them for their work on her patio,' she continued. 'I put in a call to Ben Portman, the widower, who confirmed that Bridges was the main complainant. It looks to me as though he went over to see the councillor on the Saturday evening – maybe to have it out with her over what he felt was an underpayment. She probably refused to increase their fee and that, ultimately, led to him losing his temper and striking her with the vase.'

'That all seems to fit in with the facts,' Vickers admitted. 'So your belief that the killer was Bridges and not Styler was triggered by a chance remark about a new car?'

'Yes, it was partly that. Together with the statement from Jackie Perrins. Styler had treated her badly and beat her up several times, according to her. Do you remember she'd even lost a baby because of him? She'd no reason to protect him but her father had impressed on her always to tell the truth. That was the moment I realised Todd Styler was innocent.'

Chapter 31

Omar Khalid was in high spirits early on Monday as he made his way through the CID department and knocked on the chief inspector's door. After being invited in, he was pleased to inform his boss that his visit to the Santos Cocktail Bar in Sutton Coldfield on Saturday had been successful.

'As soon as I mentioned the name Axel Makepeace, no one would talk to me,' he told Roscoe while drawing up a chair. 'But after buying the barmaid a drink, she got a little talkative. She said a hulking great guy with tattoos brought Axel some kind of message at a few minutes past eleven on the 14th.'

'Great work, Omar,' said Roscoe. 'Remind me to let you have an extra day off sometime.'

Khalid smiled. 'Thank you, sir.'

'What you've told me fits in with what I know,' said Roscoe. 'We're receiving intelligence from another police unit about the activities of the West Side Gang. They've mentioned a large fellow with tattoos who works for the Makepeace family and the thinking is that it's a man called Chester Crane. He's a guy that Axel Makepeace uses as his muscle. If the late-night caller was Crane, you've no idea what the message was that he gave his boss?'

Khalid shook his head.

'Sorry, sir,' he said. 'I asked the barmaid several times about it, but she didn't have a clue.'

'Why do you think Crane made that journey and didn't phone Makepeace?'

'I've been wondering about that as well,' said Khalid. 'All I can think is that, because he was taking his wife out, Makepeace may have turned his mobile off.'

'That makes sense.'

'Or, possibly, Crane didn't simply have a message. Maybe he needed to hand something to his boss.'

'How do you mean?'

'I don't know. Maybe, if he'd just killed Miss Squires, he'd stolen something from her that Makepeace wanted.'

'But it didn't look like anything was stolen from her home or from her person.'

'Maybe Crane passed something else to his boss.'

'Maybe.'

Roscoe leaned forward and rested his head in his hands.

'Let me see,' he said. 'It's nearly forty miles from Worcester city centre to the centre of Sutton Coldfield. Generally, it takes about an hour to make that journey via the motorways. But if you're travelling between ten and eleven at night, the journey could be quicker.'

'You're wondering if Chester Crane would have had time to carry out the murder before his arrival at the bar?' said Khalid.

'Precisely,' said Roscoe. 'According to the advice I've been given, there's no way Axel Makepeace would have carried out the task himself. He always steers clear of the action. He delegates his dirty work to others and, at present, Crane's his errand boy. Until he tires of him. So I want you to go and speak to Crane.'

'Certainly, sir. The trouble I had on Saturday was that I didn't have any kind of address for him. I thought today I'd go to Tribune Coaches and see if I could find him there.'

'He doesn't work for the coach firm,' said Roscoe, picking up a scrap of paper from his desk and handing it to his colleague. 'I've managed to wangle this address from one of my contacts. Go over to his place in Handsworth and see what he's got to say for himself. If you need to mention the murder victim, continue using the name Lydia Squires.'

Khalid raised an eyebrow.

'I was going to ask you about that, sir,' he said. 'It's a little confusing that the victim's got two names. It could cause problems.'

'I can't tell you the full story but suffice it to say the lady's security would have been at risk if she'd used her real identity on moving to Worcestershire. So while I'm going to be asking DS Roy to trace the woman's family using her real identity, for everyday inquiries about the murder we'll continue using the name Lydia Squires. In any case, the news media are going with that name and it's taken root in the public mind.'

'All right, sir,' said Khalid.

'Challenge Crane about his trip to the cocktail bar. See how he reacts and what his explanation is, if any.'

* * *

Heavy metal music was blaring out from the building when DC Omar Khalid reached the Handsworth address he had been given for Chester Crane.

The house was a dilapidated, mid-terrace with a small front garden crowded with overflowing refuse bins. One of two panes of glass in the front door had been broken and partly covered by board. Timber round the sash windows had been allowed to rot, while some of the brickwork was crumbling. A red Audi which he recognised from police records as being registered to Chester Crane was parked outside.

The detective found a parking space and approached the front door. It was answered by a scruffily dressed young man with straggly hair, wearing a T-shirt carrying the slogan 'Resist'.

'Yeah, mate?' he said.

'Looking for Chester,' said Khalid.

'Who wants him?'

'Just need to ask him a few questions.'

'Yeah, but who wants him?'

'My name's Omar.'

'Not Omar Khayyam?'

'No. Can you tell Chester I'm here?'

'Where are you from, mate? Are you a copper?'

'Yes.'

'He won't talk to you.'

Khalid was beginning to lose his temper.

'Put it this way,' he told the man in the doorway. 'If he refuses to come to the door in the next thirty seconds, I'll leave and come back with a whole army of people and he'll be arrested – and probably you as well.'

'I'll see if he's here,' said the man, retreating into the dingy hall.

After a brief outburst of shouting between the man in the T-shirt and someone at the rear of the house, a burly man with tattoos on his hands, arms and neck came to the door.

'Yeah, what do you want, mate?' he asked.

'Are you Chester Crane?'

'Yes. Who are you, mate?'

'DC Omar Khalid, Heart of England CID,' said the detective, producing his warrant card. 'Is there somewhere we can talk in private?'

'We can talk here, mate,' said Crane, although he was wearing just a sweatshirt and jeans and appeared to be shivering.

Khalid glowered. He never relished attempting to interview a suspect while standing in a doorway – especially when outdoor temperatures were only just above freezing.

'I need to ask where you were on Valentine's night?' said Khalid.

'What's all this about?'

'Just answer the question.'

'I was probably here or down the pub,' Crane replied. 'My memory's not too good.'

'So you didn't go out with your girlfriend?'

'I don't have one at the moment, mate.'

'I see. You work for the Makepeace family, don't you?'

'I'm not saying nothing. Is that why you're here?'

'No. The reason I'm here is that a young woman about your age was murdered in Worcester on Valentine's Day.'

Crane's face bore a blank expression.

'She'd been dating Roman Makepeace,' Khalid continued. 'I'm surprised you haven't heard about it.'

'Oh, I know what you're on about now, mate,' said Crane.

'Look, I know it's a pain having to answer questions like this,' said Khalid, trying a softer approach. 'It's just that we're talking to everyone who might have had something to do with the woman, Lydia Squires. We're trying to work out who might have seen her on the night she died. We know your boss's son saw her that night.'

'I haven't got a boss.'

'I thought you worked for Axel Makepeace?'

'I've just done a few jobs, driving for him.'

'Did anyone ask you to go to Worcester that evening and keep an eye on Roman?'

'You're joking,' said Crane. 'He can look after himself.'

'You weren't in the city for social reasons?'

'I wasn't there at all. Like I said, I was either here or down the pub.'

Khalid sighed.

'I want you to think carefully,' he said. 'Which was it?'

'The trouble is, since I ain't got no girlfriend, that evening was just like any other, which doesn't help when

I'm trying to remember. I'm pretty certain I was here for the whole evening, mate.'

'Can anyone else vouch for that?'

'Vouch? Oh, you mean can anyone back me up? Only Chico, the guy who opened the door.'

'I've been told you went to Sutton Coldfield that night and called in at a place in Birmingham Road called the Santos Cocktail Bar,' said the detective.

'You can sod off now,' said Crane, suddenly becoming belligerent. 'I ain't talking to you no more. Just get the hell out of here and leave me alone.'

Chapter 32

'Someone called Alan Pargeter has left a message for you, Sarge,' Brett Dawson announced when Sunita Roy arrived in the CID office on Tuesday. 'He's apologised for being out of reach. He's been down in London.'

'He's someone I need to speak to urgently,' she said.

'He said he could meet you today for lunch if you don't mind heading into Brum. He's left a new number for you.'

Dawson stepped across from his desk to present her with a slip of paper.

'Thanks, Brett,' she said, glancing at the number he'd written down. 'I'll call him.'

A few minutes later, she finally managed to speak to Pargeter and it was agreed the pair would meet at one o'clock on the concourse at Birmingham's Moor Street Station.

Sunita took a train from Solihull, which arrived in the city centre a few minutes before the meeting time.

Once she had alighted from the train, she walked into the centre of the low-roofed, red-brick station, which had been sensitively restored to the style of the 1930s. She sat down on a bench seat and waited until she saw a bearded, smartly dressed man ambling towards her.

'DS Roy,' Pargeter said awkwardly. 'Pleased to see you again.'

Sunita stood up and shook his hand.

'Pleased to see you as well,' she said. 'But I hope you're not going to waste my time like you did last week by sending me to a derelict building.'

'I really must apologise for all that deception,' he said, looking chastened.

'You and your colleague's supposed family were more elusive than a cat at bath time,' she said.

'We felt it necessary to say those things at the time to protect our investigation team,' he replied.

'Yes,' Sunita agreed, 'but I was involved in a murder inquiry and we were trying to find out, as it transpired, who killed one of your own people.'

'A thousand apologies, Sergeant Roy. I'm also sorry that you've been unable to reach me for a few days. I've been dealing with Lizzie's distressed family. Shall we go and grab a sandwich and a coffee? This is on me.'

She nodded and they stepped across the concourse to a station cafe styled in a 1930s Great Western Railway theme. They sat at a table beneath a framed, vintage map of GWR routes and ordered two sandwiches, along with a coffee for Pargeter and a lemon tea for Sunita.

As the soothing tones of Glenn Miller music played in the background, Pargeter announced, 'I've been given permission to tell you anything you want to know, within reason.'

Sunita smiled to herself while sipping her tea, regarding that statement as tantamount to, 'I can't tell you much.'

'How long had you actually known Lydia Squires – or Lizzie Hope, as we'll have to call her now?' she asked.

'She first joined our team at ROCA six years ago.'

'She didn't come from Staffordshire and have a father in human resources?'

'No. She came from South London and her dad's an ex-police superintendent,' he admitted. 'But she's been singing with bands for a long time.'

'And Dominic Jenks was genuinely her previous boyfriend?'

'Yes, he's the genuine article. They met when she came up on stage in Queensbridge to sing with the band and he took a shine to her.'

'Don't you feel she played with his affections a little?' said Sunita.

'Not really. Neither of them was too serious about the relationship, which suited us. If she'd been totally single, it might have seemed odd and aroused Roman's suspicions. After all, she was such an attractive, glamorous lady.'

Their lunch arrived and, after taking a bite from her egg-and-cress sandwich, Sunita began wondering how Roman and Lydia became acquainted. She brought out her pocketbook and began taking notes.

'You told me before that they met through online dating,' she said. 'Is that correct? Unfortunately, I can't check that with Allison.'

Pargeter, who was halfway through eating his food, pulled a face as her gibe hit home.

'Look, I've apologised, haven't I?' he said. 'No, they didn't meet through online dating. We discovered one of Roman's favourite pubs was the Crown and Sceptre in Queensbridge and he's often there when they have live bands. Lizzie spurred the band members into agreeing to perform there. I drove her over there and helped her identify Roman. Then, while the others were setting up the equipment, she made her way to the bar and queued up next to him. She got chatting and made it clear she was interested in him, and Roman took things from there.'

'Did she learn anything important about the OCG while in the relationship with Roman?' asked Sunita as she took another sip of her drink.

Pargeter nodded. 'She found out about a shipment of drugs coming in through Dover on a coach. Sadly, she died before the time and date were revealed to her. But all's not lost. There's a chance we may receive some intelligence from another source. I can't say more for fear of putting that person's life in peril.'

'Do you believe Axel Makepeace could be behind Lizzie's murder?'

He stared across the cafe as a young waitress served lunch to a man sitting in the corner. Then, he returned his gaze to his companion.

'You can never be totally sure,' he said after a pause. 'But it seems quite likely.'

'Do you think Axel had learnt of Lizzie's true role?' she asked as she nibbled her sandwich.

'Perhaps if Roman had had reason to be suspicious of her and found out something about her past, I suppose he might have passed on this knowledge to his father. I just don't know.'

Sunita took a pause from eating and picked up her pen from the table.

'Before I forget, could you tell me about Lizzie's family?'

He nodded. 'Her father's dead. Her mother's called Stella. She lives in Croydon. If you hand me your book, I'll write Stella's phone number down for you.'

After he had scribbled down the number for Sunita, she asked, 'So, if you were to hazard a guess, who do you think might have gone round to the house in Balmoral Gardens and killed your colleague?'

'One of the West Side Gang seems most likely.'

'Anyone in particular?'

'Can't think of anyone offhand,' he said as he finished his sandwich.

'There's a stocky guy with tattoos called Chester Crane. Have you considered him?'

'I can't comment on that. What I can tell you, though, is that the chief super and I were becoming suspicious that Lizzie had gone off message.'

'How do you mean?'

'We suspected her relationship with Roman was changing.'

Sunita frowned.

'I don't follow,' she said, while taking a bite from her sandwich.

'Lizzie was becoming genuinely infatuated with Roman and at risk of putting the whole operation in jeopardy.'

Sunita was puzzled by this revelation.

'What sort of signs suggested this to you?'

'Oh, I don't know,' he said. 'Probably the way she smiled mysteriously every time I mentioned his name. But more than that – she changed plans several times in order to be with him. When I asked about that, she simply insisted she needed to spend more time with him so that he could learn to trust her totally.'

Sunita shook her head. 'I suppose that's the risk you take with these seduction techniques. The huntress becoming ensnared,' she said.

'Do you have any other questions?' Pargeter asked.

'Well, aren't you worried about your own safety? You obviously know a man got shot dead outside your flat, don't you?'

'Yes, I was upset about that. Guy from Romania, wasn't it?'

She nodded. 'That was a bullet intended for you.'

'I heard he worked for a cleaning company with a gimmicky name. Squeaky Shiners?'

She nodded again, this time giving a faint smile.

'And you left some social services reports at the flat,' she said.

'Yes, well, our address leaked out, so I left in a hurry, didn't I? I tried to shred some documents about one of my cases. I should have put it through proper police channels but didn't. I was in a rush.'

Sunita shrugged her shoulders. She had realised by now that Pargeter was the kind of officer who always trod a fine line and sometimes crossed it.

'Are you heading back to St James Street now?' he asked as he stood up, ready to leave.

'To be honest,' she said, 'since we're so close to the Bullring, I thought I'd spend half an hour going round River Island and H&M.'

'Why not?' he said.

She nodded. The pair left the cafe at 1.45 p.m., crossed the concourse and made their way out of the station. Not a word was spoken as they walked together to the pedestrian crossing outside. Sunita glanced up at the sign for the Bullring Shopping Centre on a building immediately in front of her.

Although the traffic lights were showing green for motorists, Pargeter took a few steps off the pavement and then turned back.

'Before I go, I wanted to say that I hope there's no bad feeling between us,' he said while standing in the gutter, close to the kerb.

Neither of them was watching as a car began hurtling towards them along Moor Street Queensway.

'I'm really sorry about the deception, but I can assure you it was necessary because–'

His last words were cut short. Both he and Sunita had failed to see the black BMW approaching. Perhaps its driver had failed to see the man by the kerb. The vehicle struck Pargeter and Sunita watched in horror as he was flung into the air, before the car continued on its way.

Chapter 33

Sunita Roy and other onlookers dashed forward to help as Alan Pargeter, shaking and moaning, lay in a crumpled heap in the street. The shocked detective had seen her police colleague hurled off the ground by the force of the collision. He had then crashed down onto the far pavement with blood dripping from his head.

'Are you all right, mate?' asked a male voice.

Pargeter simply lay there, whimpering.

'Has someone called an ambulance?' asked Sunita.

A man beside her nodded.

A woman behind Sunita called out, 'Don't let him go unconscious.'

'Did anyone see exactly what happened?' asked Sunita. 'I'm a police officer.'

'It was a BMW,' said a man in a grey jacket. 'The driver seemed to be going slow over the brow. Then he seemed to see matey boy and put his foot down.'

'No one took the number, did they?' she asked.

'It started with BP16,' the man replied.

Sunita stepped back and took the man's details.

Minutes later, an ambulance arrived and Sunita learned he was being taken to Queen Elizabeth Hospital, just over three miles away.

* * *

An hour later, Sunita was sitting in the waiting area inside Ward B at the hospital in Edgbaston, waiting to receive any news about the critically injured Alan Pargeter. A nurse at the reception desk on the second floor warned her that she might have a long wait before hearing about his condition.

Eventually, she heard some heavy footsteps in the corridor leading to the Critical Care Unit and recognised DCS Taylor heading towards her in his police uniform.

'DS Roy, isn't it?' he said with a smile as he noticed her among a group of visitors waiting for news of patients.

'Yes, sir.'

'I gather you were with Alan when he was rushed in and came with him in the ambulance.'

'That's right, sir.'

'Well, thank you very much for doing that. What exactly happened? I've only heard a garbled account from a colleague.'

He sat down beside her in the waiting area.

In a low voice, she explained how Pargeter had been struck by a car and thrown in the air by the force of the collision. The paramedic in the ambulance had said the patient might need major facial surgery.

'God. Poor Alan,' said Taylor. 'Did anyone get the car number?'

'All we know at this stage is that it was a black, three-litre BMW. I think it was what they call a sport saloon. I'm guessing from the registration, which begins "BP16", that it was registered in 2016.'

'You seem rather knowledgeable about BMWs,' he said. 'You weren't in car sales before?'

'No, but I recently bought a car,' she explained, 'and spent some time looking at BMWs.'

'I see.'

'I found a witness, a guy called Harry, who gave me the first part of the registration. Unfortunately, he didn't get the three letters at the end.'

'CCTV?'

'Yes, there's a good chance the car will be on camera.'

'And you were right with him as the accident happened?'

'That's right, sir. We were about to cross at the crossing. For some reason, Mr Pargeter stepped into the road.'

'Not good. Not good,' said Taylor. 'I don't suppose you got a look at the driver?'

'I was looking the other way at the time,' she admitted. 'But I asked Harry, who took the number. He said the driver had dark hair and glasses.'

'Maybe he needed a stronger pair,' said Taylor. 'Listen, are we going to get a chance to speak to someone?'

'The woman on reception said she'd try to get someone to come out and talk to me, but she warned of a long wait.'

'Maybe I can hurry things up,' he said.

The chief superintendent strode up to the desk. Sunita could not hear what was being said, but almost at once, the receptionist left her post and hurried away down a corridor.

'She's going to try and fetch someone,' said Taylor as he returned to his seat.

Five minutes later, a grey-haired man in a white coat and glasses appeared at the desk and spoke to the receptionist. Then he made his way towards the pair.

'I'm Ian Frobisher, one of the senior consultants. I can't tell you very much,' he said. 'We've just carried out some emergency surgery because Mr Pargeter has some fractures – particularly on the face – that needed immediate attention. But ultimately he's going to need some fairly major reconstructive surgery. His jaw has been shattered. His right eye has been displaced and he has a broken nose.'

'Thank you so much for coming to tell us,' said Taylor. 'My name's Taylor. I'm the patient's boss. Could you pass on our best wishes? Tell him I'll be informing his wife and family of his condition and they'll no doubt be coming in to see him shortly.'

'Yes, of course,' said Frobisher.

'This is the lady who was with Mr Pargeter when the accident happened. Miss Roy,' said Taylor.

The doctor nodded towards her.

'Hit and run, I hear?' he said.

'Yes,' said Sunita.

'Terrible business,' said Frobisher. 'I hope they catch him.'

'All efforts are being made on that front,' Taylor said.

'You know, the human face is a complicated area of medicine,' the doctor continued. 'It contains so many bones, blood vessels, nerves, muscles and sensory organs. If there's any delay in treatment after an act of trauma like this, there's a risk of loss of function – vision, chewing, speaking, swallowing, not to mention disfigurement. I think in this case, there's every chance we'll need to reset the jaw and wire it up while it's healing. There's also a risk the patient could develop double vision.'

'So Mr Pargeter could well be off work for quite some time?' said Taylor.

'Unfortunately, that is the case,' said Frobisher. 'Anyway, I'm needed in theatre, so I'll have to leave you. Try not to worry too much. He's in safe hands.'

After the consultant had left, Taylor suggested they go to the restaurant for some hot drinks.

As they walked there, Taylor turned to Sunita. 'Sergeant Roy,' he said, 'do you believe what's happened to poor Alan was an accident? Or do you think he was targeted?'

She paused to contemplate her answer.

'I've been thinking long and hard about this while waiting to hear about Alan's condition,' she replied. 'The eye witness who took down the car number, Harry Lovesey, claimed the car was being driven slowly on the approach to the station. Then the driver seemed to recognise Alan and accelerated. So the answer to your question is I think it might have been attempted murder.'

Chapter 34

It was a cold, overcast night as Sunita Roy stood in the doorway of her house in Shawley Green, listening out for the sound of her boyfriend's car. Finally, just after seven o'clock, Tom Vickers' Audi swept through the gates and stopped on the gravel drive.

She slammed her front door and jumped into the passenger seat.

'Oh Tom,' she said, reaching across and giving him a peck on the cheek. 'I've had such an horrendous day.'

'Sorry to hear that,' he said. 'I thought we'd go to the Wheatsheaf. Is that all right with you?'

'That's brilliant.'

'Tell me what's happened,' he insisted as they drove out onto Old School Lane and then joined the main road leading to Queensbridge.

She explained how she met Alan Pargeter at Moor Street Station for lunch and how he was afterwards involved in a hit-and-run collision outside.

'I feel so sorry for him,' she said. 'There's a good chance he'll need a metal plate fitted in his face.'

'Poor guy,' said Vickers. 'You didn't get a look at the driver?'

She shook her head.

'No. I was looking across at the Bullring at the time. One of the witnesses says the driver had dark hair and glasses.'

'Not much to go on.'

'I got part of the car number from a witness. West Midlands Traffic are dealing with it.'

'Do you think it was deliberate?' he asked.

She shrugged.

'Hard to say. I think it might have been. The driver slowed down by the taxi ranks and then sped up. Quinton Taylor also thinks it may have been deliberate.'

'Is that old Tapper Taylor from ROCU?'

'Yes. Why's he called Tapper?'

'When he was a young constable, he was continually borrowing money from people,' he explained. 'That was a long time ago.'

'I'm not sure about him,' she admitted.

'Oh, he's full of blarney and bluster, but when you get to know him, you realise he's at the top of his game. So do you think Lizzie Hope's killer has struck again? I mean, she and Pargeter worked together.'

'Of course, it's a possibility,' she said. 'I'm waiting to hear back from the officer in the case, but it looks as though the car was stolen.'

They arrived at the quiet roadside pub north of Studley. The inspector parked and then accompanied Sunita through the main door of the stone-built inn, which was surrounded by rolling countryside.

Sunita had always admired its flagstone floors, dark oak beams and wood panelling. A roaring log fire greeted them before one of the waiters – a slim, amiable man with short, dark hair – escorted them to a table in the corner. He handed them menus before lighting a candle in the centre of the table.

'You still haven't explained why you wanted to take me out tonight,' she said as she made herself comfortable in her chair.

'The reason is we've got something to celebrate,' he said.

'What's that?' she asked.

'We've arrested and charged Zak Bridges,' he said. 'He's appearing in court tomorrow.'

'Congratulations, Tom.'

'Niggler Norris is delighted about it, so I'm looking forward to a great night.'

The inspector ordered roast chicken when the waiter returned to their table, while Sunita opted for grilled salmon.

'And what drinks would you like?' the waiter asked.

Sunita was about to ask for an orange juice.

'A bottle of your finest champagne. We're celebrating,' said Vickers.

'You're really splashing out, Tom,' she remarked as the waiter left them.

'And why not? We need to live it up now and then.'

A few minutes later, the waiter brought a bottle of Moët & Chandon to their table. He opened it and poured the couple two glasses.

'Here's a toast to you, Sunita,' said Vickers. 'You played such a key role in solving the Portman case. I couldn't have done it without you.'

'I'm sure you'd have reached the same conclusions as me. It just might have taken a little longer,' she said modestly.

While they waited for their meals to be served, Vickers explained how Bridges had at first been indignant when he and three constables from Queensbridge called at his home on the Troutbeck estate the previous evening.

'As soon as I mentioned Councillor Portman, he became edgy and suddenly ran out of the back door and down the garden path, like he was Usain Bolt. He tore down an alley, but one of the lads was a cross-country runner and caught up with him. We took him over to Queensbridge nick and, after the DCI arrived, the two of us gave him a grilling.'

'I suppose he denied everything?' she said.

'To begin with,' said Vickers. 'He claimed it was Styler who'd lost his rag with the councillor for refusing to pay them in full. She'd been due to pay three thousand two hundred pounds for their week's work, he said, but she only paid two grand because she wasn't totally happy. Bridges claimed Styler must have returned to the Portmans' house, killed her in a rage and buried her body in the woods.

'The guvnor asked him where his proof was that Styler had done the murder and Bridges lost his temper. He said it was obvious Styler had killed the woman. For one thing, it had been all over the press that Styler was the main suspect and that his phone was found with the body.

'But gradually his denials of his personal involvement were exposed as a tissue of lies. Bridges had insisted he was at his home in Stratford, but, as you discovered, his landlady didn't support his story. He couldn't offer any proper explanation as to why he was flush with funds after the patio job and how he was able to stump up one thousand five hundred pounds for a six-year-old Ford Focus. We looked at his bank statements. He only had six hundred pounds from Styler for the work on the patio, so all the indications are he stole the eight hundred pounds that went missing from the councillor's house and used that.'

'Did he try to explain how he came by the money for the car?' Sunita asked.

'He made an effort. He claimed his parents helped him. But we know they're both in a nursing home and don't have much money. He broke down when we mentioned his fingerprint being on the screen of Styler's phone. It took him by surprise and he totally lost it. He called Councillor Portman a "stupid woman" who refused to pay them the full amount they'd been expecting for the patio. His solicitor tried to calm him down, but he ranted on and on about her. Then he said, "I didn't mean to kill her. I just lost my temper because of the things she was saying and hit her with the first thing that came to hand, an old vase. I couldn't believe it when I realised she was dead."'

Chapter 35

As soon as the chief inspector reached his office on Wednesday morning, he was informed Chief Superintendent Norris wished to see him. He found her sitting behind her office desk with the door open.

'Come in, Gavin,' she said, glancing up from her computer screen. 'I'm really pleased with the efforts Tom Vickers and Sunita Roy made on the Portman case. I gather this man Bridges is up before the bench this morning?'

'That's right.'

'Let's hope he gets a good, long sentence when his trial comes up,' she said. 'Anyway, the assistant chief constable was asking about the Worcester murder. How are you getting on with that?'

Roscoe had guessed she would be wanting to know about the progress of their investigation. But nonetheless, when the question came, he struggled to find the right words.

'You heard about our initial suspect, Vernon Bainbridge, being released, didn't you, ma'am?' he said.

She nodded.

'You're obviously aware of ROCU's involvement now?'

'Indeed. I've had a call from Quinton Taylor, who's filled me in.'

'So you'll be aware that the victim in Worcester, Lizzie Hope, was an undercover operative investigating the West Side Gang?'

She nodded.

'We believe, ma'am, it's possible the gang learned of her identity and may have targeted her as a result.'

She nodded again.

'Please let me know if they become at all obstructive and I'll have a stiff word with Taylor,' she said.

'Thank you, ma'am. That would be appreciated. On top of that, of course, Lizzie Hope's colleague, Alan Pargeter, was the victim of a hit-and-run in Brum yesterday,' he said. 'We're trying to work out whether there's a connection with the Worcester murder.'

'I can see you've got your work cut out,' she said.

* * *

When the chief inspector returned to CID, he noticed the office was quieter than normal.

'Where's DS Roy?' he asked Dawson, who was sitting with his eyes fixed firmly on his computer screen.

'She's gone up to the Queen Elizabeth to meet up with DCS Taylor, sir,' Dawson explained. 'She said she's going to call you later this morning.'

Roscoe strode over to his sergeant's desk and leaned on the back of her chair while he was speaking.

'How are you getting on with checking the alibis, Dawson?' he asked.

Dawson spun round in his chair to face him.

'The victim's ex-boyfriend, Dominic Jenks, claimed he was visiting a vet's in Coventry,' he replied. 'The firm have confirmed he was there. His grandmother's pet dog needed urgent attention.'

'What time do they say he was there?'

'He left their premises just after 9 p.m.'

'It would take around an hour to get from there to Worcester,' said Roscoe, sitting down at a nearby desk. 'So he could have made it over there by ten. Doesn't rule him out. What about Sophie Bishop, Roman's ex? She was meant to be at the theatre in Tewkesbury, wasn't she?'

Dawson turned back to his desk and picked up his notebook.

'I've spoken to a girl in the ticket office,' he replied. 'She says there were eight performers in the orchestra on Valentine's Day – two keyboard players; a guitarist; a drummer; two musicians playing reed instruments; and two string players.'

'And the Bishop woman was one of the keyboard players?'

'Yes. Apparently the musicians played throughout the performance, which finished at around ten thirty.'

'She'd have had no time to get over to Worcester,' said Roscoe, 'and, in any case, all the roads north of Tewkesbury were clogged with traffic after an incident on the M5. So she's out of the picture.'

They were disturbed by the sight of a figure with curly, black hair scurrying across the office towards them as if he had hot coals in his shoes.

'What's the matter, Omar?' asked Roscoe.

The detective constable paused for a few seconds to catch his breath.

'I've just been chatting to the manager of a service station near Worcester,' he said. 'He remembers seeing a red Audi A3, driven by a guy with lots of tattoos, at a quarter to eleven on the 14th. He paid for forty pounds' worth of petrol. Their camera shows it was Chester Crane.'

'Didn't Crane swear blind he wasn't anywhere near the city that night?' said Roscoe.

Khalid nodded.

'That's right, sir.'

'He's told us a blatant lie,' said Roscoe. 'We'd better bring him in.'

Chapter 36

After finding a space in the multi-storey car park on Wednesday morning, Sunita Roy walked towards the main entrance of the Queen Elizabeth Hospital, which is based around three nine-storey, elliptical towers.

As she approached the revolving doors, a grey Jaguar drew up and Detective Chief Superintendent Taylor stepped out in full uniform. He immediately recognised her, greeting her with the words, 'DS Roy! They can't keep you away.'

'Morning, sir,' she said with a broad smile. 'I feel a slight responsibility for Mr Pargeter's unfortunate accident. I was beside him and should have paid more attention.'

'Nonsense,' he said as he followed her into the foyer. 'There's no need for you to feel guilty at all. Anyway, let's get up to the second floor and see how he's faring.'

A few minutes later, they approached the reception desk at Ward B, where they found a young, dark-haired nurse.

'We're hoping to see Mr Pargeter, if that's possible,' said Taylor.

'Would you wait there?' she asked.

While they stood waiting by the counter, Sunita's phone began to ring.

'Would you excuse me, sir?' she asked before stepping outside the ward and taking the call in the corridor.

'DS Roy?' asked a gruff male voice.

'Yes,' she said.

'Sergeant Peter Stevens, West Midlands Traffic,' he said. 'I thought you should know the black BMW involved in the hit-and-run with your friend was found burnt-out last night.'

'Really? Where?'

'Smethwick. But you'll be pleased to know we found a fingerprint on the rear-view mirror that somehow evaded the fire.'

'That's brilliant,' she said.

'That's led us to a guy by the name of Ritchie Deakin,' he continued, 'one of our local petty villains. But I'm afraid the trail's gone cold for the moment. He's not at his home or any or his known haunts.'

'What about the BMW's number plate? Did that take you anywhere?'

'The engine and chassis numbers led us to a family in Edgbaston whose vehicle was stolen a couple of days ago.'

'That's very helpful. Thank you, Sergeant. Do you have an address for this Mr Deakin?'

After taking down the address, Sunita returned to the reception area. She found Taylor was standing by the nurse's desk, beckoning her furiously.

'Come on, Sergeant,' he said. 'Alan's ready to see us. We've probably only got a few minutes. We'd better make the most of it.'

A middle-aged nurse with a plastic tag saying 'Nadine' on her blue tunic led the pair to a side room where Pargeter was being treated.

As they stepped inside, they found he was sitting up in his bed with his head partly encased in bandages. He tipped his head towards them slightly and gave a weak smile when his visitors appeared.

'How are you, Alan?' asked Taylor with a concerned expression.

The patient reached for a notepad on his overbed table and scribbled a few words. Then he handed the pad to his boss.

Taylor read the words out loud. 'What do you think?'

Pargeter took the pad back. 'Can't eat properly. Hard to talk. Ache all over. Having time of my life. Expect to go dancing with nurse later,' he added.

Taylor smiled on reading his inspector's comments. After fetching two chairs from the other side of the room, he remarked, 'Good to see you haven't lost your sense of humour. Alan, I'm really sorry about what happened. I've brought DS Roy with me.'

The patient nodded.

'Hello, Alan,' Sunita said as the two visitors sat down by the bed.

'She stayed beside you after the collision and accompanied you here to the hospital,' said Taylor. 'She's also helped the accident investigator.'

Pargeter grabbed the pad back and wrote, 'Sorry if I'm a bit crotchety. Thanks for your help, DS Roy.'

'Alan, what do you remember of the accident?' Sunita asked.

'Not much,' the patient wrote. 'I remember chatting in the station and then we starting to cross the road.'

'The car that struck you was a black BMW,' she said. 'Do you remember seeing a car like that in the past week or so? You know, I was wondering if the guy might have been spying on you or following you.'

Pargeter shook his head.

'You didn't see the driver's face during the collision?' Taylor asked.

'No,' came the reply. 'Just waiting by the road, then nothing.'

'I've actually got some news,' said Sunita.

She glanced at the chief superintendent. 'The car has been found burnt out in Smethwick. They're hunting for a guy called Ritchie Deakin.'

'Thanks, Sergeant,' said Taylor. 'That's very helpful but I did know about that.'

Pargeter spent more than two minutes writing a response, which said, 'Deakin? We saw his file the other day. He's low life. Brum. Maybe linked to West Side.'

'Years ago, that was,' said Taylor. 'He's hardly a big-time villain. The major operators and the professionals don't have time for him. To them, he's a joke.'

'But if he's had links with Makepeace in the past,' said Sunita, 'maybe he was drafted in to target Alan.'

'It's possible that, after the shooting in Trinity Drive, he's been targeted for a second time,' said Taylor, peering at her over the top of his glasses. 'But we shouldn't get ahead of ourselves. We should wait and see what Sergeant Stevens makes of it all.'

Pargeter looked agitated and scribbled away furiously on the pad before handing it to Taylor. The chief superintendent read Pargeter's words. 'Bloody obvious I was targeted. Deakin must have followed me to the station. Bloody lucky I wasn't killed. Protection?'

'We'll look into the possibility of some protection,' Taylor told him, 'but it's not easy for an outsider to come all the way up here and find you – especially since you're in this room on your own. There are doctors and nurses around all the time. You'll be fine.'

Pargeter scowled before writing, 'I wish I had your faith in the staff. I was dying for a glass of water last night. The nurse took more than ten minutes.'

There was a knock. The middle-aged nurse, Nadine, who had brought them to see Pargeter, poked her head round the door.

'How are you feeling, dear?' she asked the patient.

He wrote the word 'tired' on his pad and showed it to her.

'I can imagine,' said Nadine. 'You were in theatre for a quite a while yesterday. Now I'm afraid I'm going to have to ask your visitors to go. You need your rest.'

Taylor immediately stood up as though glad of an excuse to leave.

'That's all right,' he said. 'We've had a little chat. Alan, I'm so glad you're in safe hands. You concentrate now on getting better.'

'Thank you for coming,' the patient wrote.

'Yes,' said Sunita, walking to the door with the chief superintendent. 'We can see you're being well looked after in here. Just focus on your recovery.'

'I will,' he wrote.

The pair walked back down the corridor and took the lift to the ground floor.

'Can I be honest with you, DS Roy?' Taylor told her as they made their way towards the main exit. 'I'm more concerned about Alan than I let on just now. I fear his life could be in danger and, although I didn't mention it before in order not to worry him, it's in my mind to get him some protection. There's something I haven't told you. While he was staying in Trinity Drive, before the drive-by shooting, he had a couple of strange visitors.'

'Really?' said Sunita.

'Yes. People trying to make parcel deliveries when he'd not placed any orders. That's why I told him to move out. As for the hit-and-run, we don't really know if that was a genuine attempt on his life or just the result of some atrocious driving.'

Chapter 37

The chief inspector cast his eyes up and down the street as soon as he arrived outside Chester Crane's shabby terraced house accompanied by DC Khalid.

'Can you see his car?' he asked his colleague. 'A red Audi, isn't it?'

'Yes, sir,' replied Khalid. 'I don't think it's here.'

'Damn,' said Roscoe. 'I suppose we'll just have to wait for him.'

'He could be hours.'

'Well, let's give him a bit of time anyway,' said Roscoe.

It had been raining throughout their journey from St James Street. Now, after parking his car, Roscoe could see the drizzle had subsided and the pair got out to stretch their legs.

'I tell you what,' he said while gazing towards the house. 'Have a walk to the end of the road – just in case he's parked away from here for some reason.'

A few minutes later, Khalid returned.

'No sign of the car,' the constable announced.

Roscoe frowned.

'I don't want to knock the door,' he said. 'Someone inside might call our man and warn him off. We'll just have to sit tight.'

Nearly an hour passed, in which the pair discussed their football teams – Roscoe followed Birmingham City while Khalid was a Wolves supporter – until their patience was finally rewarded. Chester Crane pulled up outside the house in his car.

'You go and see him, Omar,' said Roscoe. 'I'll give it a minute or two. We don't want to crowd him.'

Khalid stepped out of the car and made his way along the pavement towards Crane, who was locking the driver's door. As soon as Crane recognised the detective, he swore, took to his heels and sprinted away up the long, terraced street. Khalid raced after him and, as Crane approached a parade of shops at the far end, he began to gain on him.

Crane turned left into a similar street of high-density housing and careered along the pavement as though a pack of hounds was on his tail. But, although the pair were both in their late twenties, Khalid was fitter as he was a rugby player and often trained at the gym. He caught up with Crane and managed to grab the left arm of his green sweatshirt.

The stocky man spun round.

'Leave me alone, you bastard,' he snarled and punched Khalid on the jaw, sending the constable reeling.

Khalid managed to leap forward again and struck his opponent back with his fist, landing a far more powerful blow to his chin. This led Crane to overbalance and tumble to the ground. He then lay dazed on the pavement for a short time, panting.

Roscoe, who had been hurrying behind the pair at his own pace, marched up to the suspect and hauled him up from the ground.

'Have you got your cuffs, Khalid?' he asked.

The constable nodded. He secured Crane's hands behind his back while Roscoe announced he was arresting him on suspicion of the murder in Worcester and recited the police caution.

'What? You're having a laugh,' was all Crane had to say in response.

The two detectives then marched him back to Roscoe's car.

* * *

Two hours later, the chief inspector and Khalid watched through the one-way glass as Chester Crane held a discussion with the duty solicitor, Roger Sims.

'This won't be easy,' said Roscoe. 'If he carried out the murder on behalf of Makepeace, he's going to make no admissions. Everyone is scared witless of the man, including his cronies like this guy.'

'We can only give it our best shot, sir,' said Khalid.

'Come on then,' said Roscoe, as he led the way into the interview room.

While Khalid sat down at the small table opposite the tall, bespectacled lawyer, Roscoe made sure the radiator was turned on and shut the fanlight window. Then he switched on the digital recorder and made the introductions.

'Right, you know why you're here,' said Roscoe, staring directly into Crane's cold eyes, leaving him in no doubt that he was in charge.

'Not really,' said the suspect.

'We believe you're involved in the murder of Lydia Squires on Valentine's Day,' said Roscoe.

'How do you work that out?'

'Well, you told us an outright lie about your movements that evening. You told DC Khalid here you were at home all the time, but he's discovered you bought fuel from a filling station near Worcester at a quarter to eleven. The lady who was murdered is thought to have met her death just before that time.'

Crane shrugged his shoulders. 'Well, I never had nothing to do with it,' he said. 'I don't know who the woman is.'

'Well, you've behaved as if you have something to hide,' said Roscoe. 'First, you couldn't remember where you were, then recalled you were at home. You insisted you'd not been in the city. Then, lo and behold – we find a filling station boss who remembers you calling in for fuel.'

'We've also got your red Audi on camera, entering and leaving the garage,' said Khalid.

'That's right,' said Roscoe. 'So it's time for an explanation.'

Crane glared at the detectives before replying, 'No comment.'

'We believe you must have had some involvement in the death of the woman, who was killed in the heart of the city.'

'No comment,' said Crane with a blank expression.

'We know that, once you'd filled up with fuel, you drove to Sutton Coldfield, which is about an hour's drive away. We have a witness who identified you when you appeared at the Santos Cocktail Bar, where you had words with Axel Makepeace. You've really been rather busy for someone who spoke of having a quiet night in.'

'No comment,' he replied.

'You're not doing yourself any favours by continuing to reply in this vein,' said Roscoe. 'You've got yourself into a tricky situation and the best way you can deal with it is to be frank with us and explain what's been going on.'

Roger Sims interrupted. 'Chief Inspector,' he said. 'Are these the full details of the evidence you have involving my client?'

'It's enough, isn't it?' snapped Roscoe. 'We've further inquiries to make but Mr Crane's now become a leading suspect in our investigation.'

'I can't understand what possible motive my client might have for murdering a woman that he insists he did not know,' said Sims.

'It's our contention, Mr Sims, that Mr Crane went to Worcestershire that night on the instructions of his boss, the businessman Axel Makepeace. His boss is a man that, we believe, had a personal motive for wishing to see Miss Squires disposed of.'

'My client's told me repeatedly prior to this interview that he has no knowledge of this lady,' said Sims.

'If that's the case, I'd have thought it was in Mr Crane's interests to help us by speaking frankly about what he knows,' said Roscoe. 'Because, from where I'm sitting, he's suspected of breaking into the house where Miss Squires lived in Balmoral Gardens and stabbing her to death. It then appears he bought fuel and drove off to give his employer a job report.'

Chapter 38

Brett Dawson answered the phone in CID just before lunch on Wednesday to find himself speaking to his sergeant.

'What are you up to, Brett?' Sunita Roy asked.

'Nothing too important, Sarge,' he replied.

'Good,' she said. 'I want you to come and meet me in Smethwick. I've got an address for the hit-and-run driver that nearly killed Alan Pargeter.'

It took nearly an hour for Dawson to reach Exmouth Road, a street of modest, terraced houses close to the town's railway station. Each home had a ground-floor bow window overlooking a compact front garden. It was such a narrow thoroughfare that drivers were obliged to park partly on the pavement.

The constable found a space for his car and got out, scanning the street for a glimpse of his sergeant. Within seconds, he had spotted her car – further up the street and on the opposite side – and began walking towards her. She stepped out to greet him.

'It's good you're here,' she said. 'I didn't fancy going to see him on my own. He's already committed one serious act of violence.'

'Too right, Sarge,' he said.

She nodded.

'What's this guy's name again?' he asked.

'Ritchie Deakin. There's four guys listed as living at the address, so it looks like a house-share. He's going to be very surprised to see us.'

She crossed the road and pushed open the black iron gate leading to number twenty-three. Then she pressed the bell, which was on the wall beside a white, double-glazed front door.

After nearly a minute, a man in his forties appeared. He had a pale, thin face with glazed eyes and large, round, horn-rimmed spectacles. The earthy scent of cannabis wafted out from the dingy hallway behind him.

'What do you want?' he asked, sounding as welcoming as a clap of thunder in a rainstorm.

'Heart of England Police,' said Sunita. 'Are you Ritchie Deakin?'

'I might be.'

'We wanted to have a chat with you about an accident you were involved in yesterday.'

'What accident?'

'A colleague and I were about to cross the road outside Moor Street Station. You were in a black BMW which struck him.'

'Nothing to do with me,' he insisted as he began to shut the door.

Dawson instinctively put his foot across the threshold to stop it closing. For several seconds, the man continually tried to shut the door, thumping it against the constable's shoe. Eventually, Deakin realised his efforts were pointless and opened the door fully again.

'Why've you come here?' asked Deakin. 'I wasn't involved in any accident.'

'Your fingerprint was found on the rear-view mirror of a car after it was set alight last night,' she said.

'Maybe that's because I took a ride in a friend's car and adjusted the mirror for him,' he suggested.

'Come on,' she said. 'There are witnesses who can testify you were driving the car and it's appeared on CCTV with you driving it. Why did you speed off after the accident?'

'All right. You got me in a corner. I'll tell you what happened. I'll tell you the same as I told the West Midlands Traffic cops.'

'Sergeant Stevens?' asked Sunita.

'I'm not sure. So how come you're involved as well?'

Trying to be helpful, Dawson said, 'Sergeant Stevens is a traffic officer who's investigating the accident. We're involved in a separate inquiry which concerns the pedestrian.'

'I don't really understand what you mean, but anyway I hold my hands up,' said Deakin with a stern expression. 'Here's what happened. I was driving past the station. It must have been about quarter past two.'

'It was a quarter *to* two,' said Sunita. 'I was there, so I know.'

'Well, as I approached, this guy with a beard suddenly appears in the middle of the road. He must have had a death wish. I didn't have a chance to put my brakes on and unfortunately I hit him. I thought to myself, "Oh, my God. What have I done now?" I stopped up the road and walked back to make sure the guy was all right.'

'No, you didn't,' Sunita insisted.

'I spoke to a couple of shoppers. They told me he was OK, so I went back to my car and drove off.'

'That's not how it happened,' said Sunita. 'I told you – I was there. You put your foot down and sped away without a second thought for my friend, who was seriously hurt.'

Deakin adopted a solemn expression.

'I was going to ask. How is he?'

'Well, he's out of critical care now,' she said, 'but he's had an operation and he's going to have several more.'

'I'm sorry to hear about your friend Mr Pargeter, but I can't be blamed. The guy stepped out into the road and didn't give me a chance.'

Puzzled, Sunita glanced towards Dawson before her gaze returned to Deakin.

'How did you know his name was Pargeter?' she asked.

'Oh, um. It's been on the news,' he said.

'I don't think his name's been released to the media.'

'Maybe I got it from Sergeant Stevens.'

'Let me take you back to before the accident,' said Sunita. 'You'd stolen the vehicle, hadn't you?'

'It's a misunderstanding. It was a friend's car. He sometimes lets me drive it and he forgot I'd planned to take it into the city centre.'

'Your friend couldn't have been too happy when it ended up burnt out,' said Sunita.

'No. He's not too happy. But what can I do? Happens from time to time – electrical faults causing fires.'

'Why did you leave it in Smethwick?' asked Dawson.

He shrugged his shoulders. 'That's where I was driving when the fault came up.'

'You set fire to it to try to destroy evidence, didn't you?' said Dawson.

Deakin shook his head vigorously.

'No,' he insisted.

'Where had you been in the BMW just before the accident?' the constable asked.

'I met a mate at Wetherspoons in Corporation Street.'

'Oh yeah?' said Dawson.

'Hang on,' said Deakin. 'I only had a pint because I was driving.'

'So what happened when you left the pub?' asked Sunita.

'I picked up my car from the multi-storey and set off towards Moor Street.'

'Listen,' said Sunita. 'One of the witnesses says you came to a halt or slowed down near the taxi rank on the approach to the station.'

Deakin shook his head.

'No, I didn't stop. I might have gone a bit slower because I was looking at the satnav. Look, let me go and get that card,' he said. 'I'm not sure if the copper's name was Stevens.'

Deakin stepped back inside the house. Sunita took the opportunity to take a few steps back towards the gate and gaze around the street while her colleague leaned against the doorpost.

'At least he's admitted to being the driver, Sarge,' Dawson told her in a low voice.

'Yes, but he hasn't shown much in the way of remorse,' she replied.

Her eyes were drawn to a small, red advertising banner in the front window. It said, 'Tribune Coaches – Take a break and let us drive.'

She turned to Dawson. 'Have you seen this?' she asked.

Her colleague took a step towards her just as Deakin emerged in the doorway.

'Yes, you're right. Sergeant Stevens,' he said, brandishing the visitor's card. 'I'll probably phone him in a minute.'

'I notice you've got a Tribune Coaches sticker in your front window, Mr Deakin,' Sunita said.

'Yes, I'm a part-time driver for them,' he said.

'So you know Axel Makepeace?' she continued.

'Yes. I've known him for years. I went to school with his son, Roman.'

Chapter 39

Axel Makepeace hobbled over to his office window early on Thursday morning with the aid of his walking stick. The sun was beginning to break through from behind the clouds and its rays were flickering over the slate roofs of surrounding houses. He cast his eyes down and his mood changed. One of the coaches on the forecourt below had come to a halt and was blocking the entrance.

'Why the hell hasn't that coach bound for Windsor gone out yet?' he grunted.

He strode back to his desk and pressed the button on his intercom.

'Sajid!' his voice boomed down his handset. 'What's holding up the Windsor coach?'

'The engine warning light keeps coming on, boss,' Sajid replied. 'We're getting it sorted out now.'

'Make sure you do it pronto,' shouted the boss.

'Right away,' said Sajid. 'And Chester's coming up.'

He replaced the handset on its cradle and swept some of his straggly grey hair out of his eyes.

'As if I haven't got enough to worry about,' he moaned to himself.

He heard the sound of footsteps pounding up the stairs and along the corridor. There was a knock on the door.

'Who is it?' he demanded.

'Chester.'

'Come in, Chester,' yelled Makepeace.

'You took your time,' said the businessman as his burly associate lumbered through the door, panting like a veteran athlete.

'You've been in a spot of bother with the Old Bill, I hear,' said Makepeace. 'What's been going on?'

Crane slumped down in a leather armchair.

'They pulled me in to ask me about the murder in Worcester,' he said.

'Was this Heart of England Police?'

'That's right.'

'Why did they do that?' asked Makepeace, leaning forward across his desk.

'I don't fully understand it myself,' said Crane. 'They had me in for a few hours and asked me all sorts of ridiculous questions. They suggested I'd driven over on Valentine's night to kill the woman on your instructions.'

'Did they?' said Makepeace.

'They reckon you had some kind of personal reason for wanting rid of her.'

'How did they work that out?'

'I don't know.'

'That's interesting. That ties in with something I've been told. Who interviewed you? Was it that Asian woman who came here the other day? I think her surname was Roy.'

'No. It was a chief inspector called Roscoe and an Asian guy called Khalid.'

Crane explained to Makepeace about the CCTV at the petrol station. 'They also know I met you at Santos,' he said.

'What did you tell them?' asked Makepeace, who was stroking his chin.

'I refused to comment after a word from my brief. Of course, they weren't too happy, but the brief said it was all circumstantial and they'd got nothing on me.'

'Good. That sounds about right. We know from Sergio that a nosy cop was around the other day asking questions. He must have found out about your visit.'

'Yes.'

'So they don't know anything about the key to the lock-up you passed onto me?'

'No, boss.'

'God. I don't know. You can't scratch your arse these days without some bloody copper breathing down your neck. So how's it been left?'

'They've let me go for the moment. They call it "released under investigation".'

'That must mean they're still suspicious but they've got nothing to back it up.'

'That's right. As I say, my brief's convinced they've got nothing.'

Makepeace sat upright in his chair. 'By the way, did you hear about poor old Ritchie Deakin?' he asked.

'Yes, I saw it on the TV news.'

'Stupid prat has been charged with causing serious injury by dangerous driving and failing to stop after an accident.'

'More points on his licence then?'

'Yeah. Anyway, Chester, the reason I called you in here is we know for definite now that someone's passing on information about us to the cops. It's been confirmed by one of my police contacts. The cops and Border Force know all about the coach we took to the Netherlands on the pretext it needed the air conditioning fixed. So we're bringing the coach back on Friday but we're not hiding the gear in the fake waste-water tank. We've switched the cargo. So when it's stopped by the border guards, they're going to be so disappointed. I wish I could be there to see their stupid faces!'

'So how's the gear coming over?' asked Crane.

'This is where you come in,' said Makepeace. 'I want you and Roman to get over to Calais in one of the minibuses and you're going to be doing the run instead.'

'OK.'

'All the arrangements have been made. The bus will be loaded up overnight and you'll meet up with a guy called Gervais in a car park. He'll give you the keys. You're going to be driving the bus back to Dover and dropping the load off at the shop you found. The cops might be watching you, but we'll have to forget that. There's no one else available. You'll just have to watch your back.'

'Great. OK. Does Roman know about this?'

'Not yet, but I'll be seeing him later and I'll tell him then. It'll mean an early start for you both, mind, and don't forget to bring your passport.'

'Lucky the cops didn't seize it yesterday, although they've got my phone.'

'The same thought was running through my mind,' Makepeace admitted.

'So, you've no idea who the mole is?'

'No. Could be one of the new street pushers. But I've got it confirmed by a guy who's high up in the West Midlands force, so we know it's kosher.'

'How are you going to flush them out?'

'The cops are trying to be clever bastards, so we'll have to play them at their own game and become clever bastards too. We'll have to set some kind of trap.'

'What kind of trap?'

Makepeace shook his head. 'I'm not sure yet.'

'Do you think this person, whoever they are, has tipped off the Old Bill about anything else? You know, anything apart from the Dover delivery?'

'Doesn't look like it at the moment. That's why I'm pleased about the shop you found. It's in a quiet country town. Brum's too hot right now. Our Vietnamese friend, Pham Nguyen, is going to sleep over there and I want you to visit the place daily till we get the boxes moved again.'

'All right, boss,' said Crane. 'That suits me fine.'

'But don't take your usual motor, just to be on the safe side.'

Crane stood up and moved towards the door as he sensed their meeting was winding up.

'Oh, by the way,' said Makepeace, 'my lad's still full of doom and gloom about that Lydia. So it's best you don't let on to him that you went round her place on Valentine's night.'

Chapter 40

By the time the chief inspector arrived in CID on Thursday morning, Sunita Roy had pinned two more images to the whiteboard – photographs of Chester Crane and Ritchie Deakin. She diligently used a black marker pen to add their names in capital letters beneath each picture before standing back to inspect her handiwork.

'Nice job,' remarked Roscoe.

He unlocked his door and stepped inside. Then, he took off his coat, hung it in a cupboard and returned to the doorway.

'Sir, as you know, the hit-and-run threw us a little off-course,' Sunita pointed out. 'But, before he ended up in hospital, Pargeter was telling me that Lizzie Hope's mother is called Stella. He gave me her address in south London.'

Roscoe nodded.

'The victim's family is our next priority,' he said.

'I've spoken to Mrs Hope on the phone,' Sunita continued. 'She's free later today.'

'Splendid,' said Roscoe. 'I don't know. It comes to something when, more than two weeks into a murder investigation, we still haven't spoken to any member of the victim's real family.'

Sunita shrugged.

'It just a sign of how different this case has been, compared with most, sir,' she said.

Roscoe said the interview with the mother could prove crucial to the investigation. 'You heard about our brush with Chester Crane yesterday, did you?' he asked as he stepped into his office and took a seat behind his desk.

Sunita nodded.

'Yes. I hear he was very difficult,' she said, taking a chair by the door.

'Yes. By the way, I received a call from John Hepworth in forensics this morning. He's retrieved deleted pictures of Lizzie Hope's car, a blue Mini Hatch, from Crane's phone – two of which he'd sent to a mobile number, a contact listed as AM.'

'Axel Makepeace?'

'Almost certainly,' said Roscoe with a nod. 'The message was sent on Valentine's Day, informing the recipient that the car was once registered to someone in the police. There are six images of the Mini Hatch taken under a streetlight and they're time-stamped for 10.35 on 14 February.'

Sunita looked aghast.

'But surely that's round about the time of the murder?' she said.

He nodded.

'The evidence against Crane and Makepeace is mounting up, isn't it?' he said.

Fresh thoughts were swirling through her mind.

After a pause, she said, 'Sir, maybe Crane travelled to the Santos Cocktail Bar because Makepeace wanted to see all the photos on his phone.'

'That's possible. Anyway, this now raises the question of whether Crane went to Balmoral Gardens with the sole intention of taking those pictures. We certainly know Makepeace was becoming suspicious of Hope.'

'I can see the point you're making,' Sunita admitted.

'We've had to let Crane go for the moment,' Roscoe continued. 'By the way, I was amazed when you called and explained how the hit-and-run driver works for Makepeace's coach firm.'

'It could just be an astonishing coincidence that Deakin works as a part-time driver,' she said. 'I'm not sure.'

'We'll have to see how the two charges laid against him by Sergeant Peter Stevens at Traffic pan out,' said Roscoe.

'It isn't clear that Deakin was deliberately targeting Alan Pargeter,' said Sunita.

'No,' said Roscoe. 'Listen, we have to bear in mind Makepeace isn't a man to play games. If he'd wanted Pargeter out of the way, there's an obvious argument that he'd have had him killed in a clean, clinical, calculated way. Running a guy down in the street with all the attendant risks probably isn't his style.'

He paused, then added, 'We've been instructed to tread carefully to avoid messing up the undercover operation Quinton is working on. We have to be extra careful here and only bring people in for the murder charge where we have absolutely irrefutable evidence that nails them properly. We can't just go on circumstantial evidence or their suspicions will be raised and the Organised Crime Unit's operation undermined.'

'You've made some good points there, sir,' said Sunita. 'Oh, I also asked Deakin about 14 February. He claimed he was at home all night with his three housemates.'

'Very flimsy alibi,' muttered Roscoe, stepping towards his room at the side of the office.

'The only thing is,' said Sunita, 'the Traffic officer who first informed me about Deakin described him as "one of our local petty villains" and having met him myself, I can see why he used those words. Deakin somehow doesn't have the stamp of a man who'd break into a house, lie in wait and stab a woman to death.'

'The problem is: who does, Sergeant?' said Roscoe. 'The only one of the suspects listed on this board that I'd have no hesitation in accusing of the offence is Crane and the only really strong evidence against him is the images on his phone. So I think our strategy from now on should be to focus on Crane, his friends and family, and see if we can't find stronger evidence to link him to this murder. I asked DC Hopkirk and one of her colleagues earlier this week to try to tail him and see how he spends his time.'

* * *

Stella Hope's home was a three-storey townhouse in a quiet street just a short distance from Croydon civic centre. Its compact front garden contained a small lawn, some shrubs and a parking space for a small, silver Toyota car. Across the street lay a communal garden.

The sun came out as the chief inspector stepped out of his car and glanced up and down the street.

'It's turning into quite a nice day, sir,' his sergeant remarked as she got out of the passenger side.

'The sun's doing its bit. Now let's go and do ours,' he said as he walked up the concrete path to the front door and pressed the doorbell.

Lizzie Hope's mother must have noticed their car arriving. The door flew open almost immediately.

'DCI Roscoe,' the detective announced, displaying his warrant card. 'This is my colleague, DS Roy.'

'Please come in, Chief Inspector,' replied Stella with an anxious expression. 'Did you have a good journey?'

'Not brilliant,' he admitted as he entered her bright, airy hallway. 'Long hold-ups on the M25.'

'No surprise there,' she said.

The pair followed her into a small, contemporary living room with a light-oak floor and a wall-mounted television.

Family portraits and photographs of police presentations were showcased on one of the walls.

'First of all, can we say how sorry we are to have to visit you at a time like this,' said Roscoe. 'You have our deepest sympathies over the loss of your daughter.'

'Thank you, Chief Inspector,' she said. 'That's very thoughtful. Everyone's been so kind – especially Alan. Would you both like to take a seat?'

Sunita and Roscoe sat down on a cream-coloured three-seater sofa while Stella remained standing.

'I've been one of the main detectives working on this case,' said Sunita, 'and everyone I've spoken to had only the highest praise for Lizzie.'

'Thank you,' said Stella with the hint of a smile. 'These last two weeks have been a nightmare. When Alan came and told me my daughter was dead, it just didn't sink in to start with. He explained that she'd been working undercover using the name Lydia Squires, and that was the name in all the press reports and on TV. Then the press found out her real name and that's just added to the upset.'

Roscoe nodded. 'We were obliged to confirm her two names after being contacted by the press about it,' he went on. 'I'm afraid it was necessary for your daughter to hide her identity as part of a police operation. It was for her protection.'

'It didn't give her much protection, did it?' Stella said curtly. 'So you mean to tell me her life was put at risk and she paid the price?'

'We're still investigating what happened,' he said. 'We don't know if her death can be linked to her undercover police work. Listen, Stella, I think it might help if you gave us a brief account of your daughter's life, if that's not too painful.'

'Of course,' she replied. 'My daughter was an only child; she was born in Croydon on 23 April 1995. Her father, Tim, was a superintendent with the Met. You can see him in photographs here on the wall. Sadly, he's no longer with us. After grammar school, all Lizzie wanted was to join the police and, after two years at Hendon, she worked as a constable in Enfield for a while. She spent a year in CID before managing to gain a place with the regional crime team in the Midlands.'

'A very gifted young lady,' said Roscoe. 'I'd have loved to have had her on my team. We gather she was also a talented singer.'

'Yes, Lizzie had singing lessons at school and was in the school choir,' said Stella as tears began forming in her eyes. 'She had a brilliant voice.'

She picked two tissues from a box on a low-level oak sideboard and wiped her eyes before settling down in an armchair.

'I'm sorry. Just give me a moment,' she said.

'Take as much time as you like,' said Roscoe reassuringly.

'I'll be all right in a second. Everything keeps flooding back.'

After pausing to let her collect her thoughts, Roscoe asked, 'When did you last see your daughter, Stella?'

'Christmas.'

'And when did you last speak to her?'

'It must have been round about the start of February. She'd just met this new guy in Warwickshire, a man called Roman. I never discovered his surname. She was absolutely besotted with him. She'd had men in her life but she told me she'd never had a relationship like this. The girl was in love and I'd never found her so happy. During her call, she revealed that Roman had proposed to her and that she'd agreed to marry him. They decided to keep their engagement quiet for the time being.'

Sunita and her boss looked at each other in surprise.

'Engaged?' said Sunita. 'We didn't realise she was his fiancée. There was no ring on her finger when she died.'

'No. They'd sent it away to be adjusted,' said Stella. 'The young man bought her a one-carat diamond engagement ring and she said she couldn't wait to show it to me. You know, she really loved this man and couldn't wait to introduce him to me. I remember her saying something like, "I've never met anyone like Roman before. I'd travel to the ends of the earth for him. I want to spend the rest of my life with him." But she told me there was a minor problem and she was in a quandary. She'd have to consider giving up the police service because this Roman had a relative who had been in some sort of trouble with the law. She didn't say any more than that.'

'I see,' said Roscoe. 'This is making sense to us, Stella.'

'Well, Chief Inspector, it's devastating to have lost Lizzie but it brings a little comfort to know she was working to serve the police and her community.'

'That's exactly the way to look back at her life,' said Roscoe. 'She was a commendable woman who died while doing her utmost to help others and uphold the rule of law. You can take a great deal of comfort from that.'

'Alongside the loss of my poor husband, who died through illness, the loss of Lizzie has been the most devastating blow to me, Chief Inspector,' she said. 'Have you had to cope with unbearable grief?'

He shrugged. 'I've lost both my parents,' he admitted. 'So I can certainly begin to understand what you've been going through.'

'It would help if we could arrange a funeral,' said Stella. 'You don't know when we might be able to do that, do you?'

'I'm afraid not. That's down to the coroner,' he said. 'But I don't suppose it will be too long now.'

Stella folded her arms. 'You knew she was married, didn't you?' she asked.

For the second time in the course of a few minutes, Roscoe and his sergeant stared at each other in surprise.

'We'd no idea,' said Sunita. 'Who was she married to?'

'Her husband's called Jason Wright. He lives down the road from here, in Purley.'

'So how come she had the surname Hope?' asked Sunita.

'Their break-up was very acrimonious. Afterwards, she quickly reverted to her maiden name.'

'Could you tell us a little about the husband?' asked Sunita.

'Yes, of course,' said Stella. 'She met him in her early twenties when they were both working as constables in Enfield. They married after dating for six months, but the marriage didn't work out and they separated after a year. She asked for a divorce, but Jason has been very awkward about it and I don't think it was ever properly sorted out.'

'We're so grateful to you for giving us this information, Stella,' said Roscoe. 'You couldn't help us with an address for him, could you?'

'No problem,' she said. 'Is it all right if I write it down on a scrap of paper?'

'That would be fine,' said Roscoe.

She rose, stepped across the floor to the sideboard and tore a piece of paper from a writing pad with a sweep of her hand. She jotted down an address and passed it to the chief inspector.

'There. I hope he's civil to you,' she said. 'He can be quite offensive sometimes. In fact, when he's talking about Lizzie, I'm told he can be quite spiteful.'

Chapter 41

A dog began to bark as soon as the chief inspector pressed the doorbell at the home of PC Jason Wright later on Thursday afternoon.

The thirty-one-year-old enjoyed far less salubrious surroundings than his mother-in-law. He lived in a first-floor studio flat in a tired, somewhat neglected apartment block in Swallowtail Lane, Purley, close to the main railway line between London and Brighton.

As the constable opened his front door to the two detectives, he was forced to grab the collar of his excitable German shepherd, which whined and growled at the visitors.

'Stop it, Casper,' he yelled before turning his attention to the visitors. 'What d'you want, mate?' asked Wright angrily, while straining to control his pet.

'Heart of England CID,' said Roscoe, brandishing his warrant card. 'Can we have a word?'

'Hang on. I'll put the dog in the kitchen,' he said.

A minute later, Wright returned to the open doorway with a more respectful tone to his voice. 'What's it about, sir?'

'Are you Jason Wright, stationed at Enfield?' asked Roscoe sternly.

The constable nodded.

'We understand you were married to Lizzie Hope and we wanted to talk to you about that,' he explained. 'I'm DCI Roscoe. This is DS Roy.'

'You'd better both come in,' he said. 'You'll have to excuse the mess. I don't get many visitors.'

He led them into a large room which contained a line of maple wood wardrobes along one wall. A king-sized bed stood in the far corner beside a three-seater settee and a television. An unpleasant dog odour lingered in the air. Items of clothing were scattered across the wooden floor.

Their host gathered some of the clothes and placed them in a single pile on the bed.

'When did you last see your wife?' Roscoe asked.

'I haven't seen her for years, sir,' he continued. 'I'm aware of her death, obviously. I'm very sorry she died and in such a brutal way but I'm not going to be much help to you, I'm afraid. Would you like to sit down?'

The visitors seated themselves on the settee while Wright tried to make himself comfortable on a multi-coloured beanbag covered with dog hairs. He positioned himself so that his back rested against the wall.

'Do you recall when you last spoke to her?' Roscoe asked.

'Now you've got me. About six years ago? As soon as she went to Birmingham. I didn't hear a word from her. Then, about two years ago, I got a letter demanding a divorce. We've been keeping in contact through solicitors since then. How did you get my address, by the way?'

'A family member gave it to us,' Roscoe explained.

'I know. Stella,' he said.

'I didn't say that,' said the detective.

'No, but it's obvious,' he said with a shrug. 'As I say, I was sorry to hear about Lizzie. Terrible thing to happen. I sent a letter of sympathy to Stella. Never expected to read about her being murdered.'

'You read about it in the press or on TV?' said Sunita.

'On TV. I didn't realise who it was to start with because they used the name Lydia. Then it was later revealed she also used the name Lizzie Hope. I wondered if she changed it to break the link with me.'

He paused for a moment – perhaps to reflect briefly on the once happy times he had shared with his ex-wife. Then his face brightened. 'I can't tell you much,' he said. 'Our lives have headed in different directions after she dumped me.'

'You could help us,' said Sunita, 'by telling us where you were on Tuesday, 14 February, the night she died.'

'Let me look at my diary,' he said with a frown. 'I think I left it over by my bed.'

The detectives glanced at each other as their host stepped past them and picked up a tiny black book from a bedside table.

'February, February, February,' Wright murmured to himself as he flicked through the pages. 'Here we are. I was on evenings that week, finishing at midnight. Valentine's Day, wasn't it? I seem to remember getting called out to an Italian restaurant where there was a row over a bill, but that could have been the following night. No, come to think of it. It must have been the 14th because the place was looking all fancy.'

'Were you on your own?' asked Sunita.

'No. I was with a colleague.'

'We'd need his or her name,' she continued. 'And we'd also need the name and address of the restaurant.'

'PC Ayesha Farooq was the officer with me,' the constable explained. 'In the end, we didn't need to arrest anyone, although it came very close. The restaurant was called La Bella Vita. It's in the centre of Enfield. Anyone will tell you where it is. But hold on. What's this all about? You don't seriously think I'd travel all the way up to Worcester and knock off my ex-wife, do you? And then make up a load of nonsense to explain where I'd been?'

'We're not making assumptions about anyone or anything,' said Sunita. 'We're simply trying to find out who killed your poor wife and we're asking everyone where they were at the time of her death. You say divorce lawyers had become involved?'

He nodded. 'Yes. And you know what they're like – or perhaps you don't. Money-grabbing buggers, excuse my French.'

'So can we assume you weren't in favour of the divorce, Constable Wright?' said Roscoe.

'Well, there was no life left in the marriage, so we had to end it,' said Wright, shrugging his shoulders. 'There was no doubt about that. It was just the way Lizzie was handling things I didn't agree with and the divorce has been taking a long time to go through.'

'You were making things difficult for her?' asked Sunita.

'No. Not really.'

After a pause, Wright added, 'I loved her. That was the problem. 'And if you'd met her, you might understand why.'

'I did meet her briefly,' said Sunita. 'It was just two days before she died. She was with another man and looked happy.'

This seemed to touch a raw nerve. She noticed Wright flinch as her words struck home. He seemed to struggle with himself before he regained his composure.

'That's good – I mean, if she was happy,' he said unconvincingly.

After taking their leave, they made their way out of the building and headed towards Roscoe's car.

Before opening the passenger door, Sunita happened to glance up at the building they had left. She was sure she could see Jason Wright's face peering through his bedroom window, like a lonely waif gazing from an orphanage.

'Do you know, I wonder if he was hoping to get back with his wife after all this time,' Roscoe said as he unlocked the vehicle and they got in.

'Yes,' said Sunita. 'Or maybe she finally found some way of serving the reluctant litigant with his divorce papers. Maybe he took exception, came to Worcester and killed her.'

Chapter 42

The porch light was shining brightly from the front of her house when Sunita Roy arrived back, tired and hungry after her journey to London with the chief inspector. She watched for a moment while Roscoe drove away. Then she stepped across the gravel to her door and searched for her house keys. As she did so, she noticed her boyfriend's car, parked by the living-room windows.

Before she could retrieve the keys from her pocket, the door swung open and Tom Vickers appeared, looking pleased to see her.

'Are you hungry?' he asked, kissing her on the cheek. 'I've put a vegetable lasagne in the oven.'

'Oh, Tom. You're a lifesaver,' she said following him in.

A few minutes later, they were sitting at the dining table, enjoying their meal and sipping from glasses of sauvignon blanc.

'How was your day?' he asked.

'This case is really getting me down,' she said between mouthfuls. 'The deeper we probe, the more testing it seems to become. That woman, Lizzie Hope, lived in such a complicated world. Charting her life is like following a winding maze of streets and alleyways which never seem to lead anywhere.' She revealed what Stella Hope and Jason Wright had told them in London.

Vickers shook his head.

'Don't tell me – he's one of those husbands who simply can't accept his marriage is over, despite all signs to the contrary,' he said.

'Exactly,' she said. 'And, while we were there, he made us feel as welcome as a polecat at a picnic.'

'So where does this leave the case?'

'We're at an impasse, Tom,' she said. 'We've got a slew of suspects who have a myriad of motives, but there's no clear pathway to reach the truth of what happened that night. If only… if only we could see our way through the maze.'

'Don't worry, Sunita,' he said as he finished his meal and pushed his plate away. 'Keep on probing like you always do. Eventually you'll make a breakthrough and everything will become clear.'

'I expect so,' she said. 'But it's all very frustrating at the moment. I've just spent several hours listening to the DCI. He's still convinced Axel Makepeace is behind the murder. He's planning a meeting with DCS Taylor.'

Sunita took another sip of her wine before she continued.

'Oh, did I tell you about Wendy Hopkirk? She managed to follow Chester Crane's car to a disused shop in Queensbridge which we believe is being used to store drugs. The boss has passed this information onto Taylor – so he thinks Taylor owes us a favour now.'

'But you don't share his view that Axel Makepeace is behind the murder of Lizzie Hope?'

'Not really. From what I've learnt about Makepeace, he's a professional. He wouldn't have sent someone round unarmed to Balmoral Gardens and, in all likelihood, they'd have used a gun. Cruel and brutal though it was, the murder of Lizzie Hope doesn't seem to have the mark of organised crime about it.'

* * *

Roscoe's wife Helen was waiting by the front door when the chief inspector's car trundled down the narrow, tree-lined lane that led to the Roscoes' home that evening.

'Gavin,' she called as he locked the car in the garage and walked past the leaded-light windows towards her. 'Amanda's gone in.'

He gazed at her with an expression reflecting at first bewilderment and then concern. Amanda was his daughter-in-law and expecting her first child.

'Already?' he asked. 'I thought the baby wasn't due for a few weeks.'

'That's right. Looks like there's a problem.'

He kissed her on the cheek and they both stepped into the house.

His eyes widened like those of a gourmet eyeing the cheese trolley in a hotel restaurant.

'Something smells good in the kitchen,' he said.

'I'm cooking a beef casserole,' said Helen, striding into the kitchen. 'It will be ready in a minute. Are you hungry?'

'Ravenous.'

'Good. Supper shouldn't be long,' she said.

Roscoe hung up his coat before moving into the dual-aspect living room and turning on the television. He had only just begun watching a *Midlands News* programme when he heard the faint sound of music. The thumping drum-and-bass track grew louder as their twenty-six-year-old daughter, Melody, descended the stairs.

'Hi Dad,' she said, instantly switching off her MP3 player. 'How's it going?'

'Fine,' he replied. 'Are you having supper with us?'

'You bet. Smells good, doesn't it? Did you hear about Amanda?'

'Yes. I hope she's going to be OK.'

'She'll be fine. Listen, Dad, I've got something important to tell you. You know we went to the Coach and Horses for my engagement party on Thursday?'

'Yes,' he said as she sat down beside him on the brown leather settee.

'I haven't had a chance to tell you but while she was at the bar, queuing to buy some drinks, Martha got talking to a guy.'

'That's Martha who runs the riding stables?'

'Yes, Dad. The guy turned out to be the bass player in the Urban Renegades. They were having a half-time break.'

'That's a man called Dominic Jenks,' said her father.

'That's right. Dominic,' she said. 'I never learned his surname. Anyway, they got talking and hit it off. Next thing, he's asked her out on a date.'

'Interesting.'

'Well, they couldn't go out on Friday night as the band had a booking. So they went out on Saturday.'

Roscoe frowned. 'I know Martha's been on her own for a while, so it's good she's met someone,' he said. 'But where's this leading?'

'Let me come to the point, Dad,' she said. 'Dominic sometimes uses his van to shift the band's gear. They decided to go for a quiet drink in a country pub for their first date and he asked if she minded travelling in the van.'

'That's not quite the level of comfort she'd be used to,' he remarked.

'No. Anyway, she said, "Why not?" And he picked her up at her place in Inkberrow.'

'So how did the date go?'

'It didn't go very well. On the way back to her place, she found a black glove with some blood on it tucked behind the driver's seat. He just said he'd cut himself while doing some DIY. She thought I should mention it to you.'

'Thank you for telling me,' said Roscoe.

Chapter 43

Chester Crane got off a bus in Smethwick and hurried through the coach depot's iron gates a few days later.

'Is your dad upstairs, mate?' he asked Roman Makepeace, who was vigorously tapping a computer keyboard in the front office.

'Yes. But I should be careful what you say. He's livid with you,' said Roman.

'He's not, is he? It was a nightmare yesterday,' said Crane, who was breathless and perspiring profusely.

'Yeah. I heard the cops raided your shop and picked up the gear we spent all that time bringing back from France.'

'You don't know the half of it, mate,' said Crane. 'I had to run out the back, scale a wall and run down an alley to get away.'

'Did they chase you?'

'Well, they were looking for me. I hid myself in a garage area for two hours until I was sure they'd stopped searching.'

'Bloody hell. So you went back to your car and drove home?' asked Roman.

'No, mate. There was a copper standing by the car, so I had to leave it there.'

'How did you get back to Brum then?'

'Bus and train. It took me two hours. Even then I couldn't go home. I'm having to stay round me mate's place because Chico at the house says there's a pair of cops parked there night and day.'

Roman shook his head. 'What a performance. Hold on a minute.'

He pressed an intercom button and his father answered with a brusque, 'Yeah?'

'Dad. Chester's here. Do you want him to come up?'

'Yeah. You'd better tell the bastard to come up,' came the response as Roman ended the call.

'You probably heard that,' said Roman.

'Yeah,' said Crane. 'Don't worry. I wasn't expecting him to put the flags out and skip round the room.'

'Not with his bad leg anyway,' said Roman.

'No. Not with his bad leg,' Crane said as he left the front office and began climbing the stairs.

Crane knocked on Axel Makepeace's door and opened it. His boss was sitting behind his desk, studying his mobile phone.

'You tell me your version of what happened and I'll give you my version,' said Makepeace.

'I'm really sorry, boss,' said Crane after shutting the door. 'It was just after half past one and the cops appeared from nowhere. They smashed their way in and I only just managed to get away.'

'All right. Now I'll give you my version, and I know it's correct because someone on the inside explained it to me. You steamed down there in your red Audi and I bet you didn't know a girl in a grey Fiesta was following you.'

'Was she?'

'Yes, she bloody was. You led the cops directly to our stash of the highest quality of cocaine it's been my pleasure to bring to the Midlands. Not only that. Poor old Pham Nguyen, who was staying down there full-time, has been arrested and I've had to get him a brief.'

'I'm really sorry, boss. I never thought I'd be followed. I guess they took an interest in me after that woman's murder.'

'Yes. When I got tipped off Lydia Squires might be up to no good, I probably shouldn't have used you to keep a regular watch on her place. After your motor was spotted at the service station, you should have got rid of it. I distinctly remember telling you to use a different motor on the Troutbeck in Queensbridge while watching the gear. You didn't take a blind bit of bloody notice of me, did you, you asshole?'

'Sorry, boss.'

'Get out of my sight. It makes me sick to look at you and don't ever come round here again.'

A blind rage swept over Crane like a fire. 'What about my unpaid wages?'

'You must be joking.'

Swaying in the grip of anger, the unwelcome guest took a step forward and Makepeace at once pressed the intercom button.

'Sajid,' he said, 'could you send Colin and Darren up?'

Crane at once had second thoughts about threatening Makepeace in pursuit of his missing wages. Instead, fuming and cursing, he rushed down the stairs.

'Everything all right?' Roman asked as he passed through the office.

'No, it bloody isn't,' Crane remarked across the counter. 'I've just been sacked. So I don't feel beholden to your old man no more and I'm going to tell you what's been on my mind. I was round at your Lydia's place on Valentine's night.'

'How do you mean?' Roman demanded, stepping up the counter and peering at Crane angrily.

'Your old man was suspicious of her and asked me to get some pictures of her motor.'

'Did you go inside the house? It wasn't you who…'

'Nah,' said Crane. 'Don't be a dickhead. I didn't see nothing, but your old man told me not to tell you. He didn't want you to know he'd got bad vibes about her. Suppose he didn't want to upset you.'

'Why was he suspicious of her?'

'You two seemed to be rushing into things and he was just being protective. He wanted to check her out.'

Roman raised a hatch at the counter and darted through, scowling and waving his fist at the taller man.

'That's bloody ridiculous. It wasn't you who killed Lydia, was it?' he demanded.

Crane raised his hands in a submissive gesture, trying to calm Roman down.

'Of course not. Your dad just asked me to take pictures of the car so he had the registration and could check it out properly. As it turns out, that Mini Hatch she had was bought off a copper and he reckoned she might have been undercover. Anyway, you probably won't see me again, mate. I'm off to find a job now.'

The response seemed to satisfy Roman, who backed away with a pensive expression.

Crane said nothing more. He marched through the doors and strode out through the gateway.

He had only taken a few steps along Tilehurst Street when a dark-blue Volvo came round a corner outside the coach depot and drew up in front of him. Two men in plain clothes jumped out.

'Chester Crane?' asked one of the men. 'We're from the Regional Organised Crime Unit. You're under arrest for possession of class A drugs with intent to supply.'

* * *

DC Omar Khalid paused for a moment outside the chief inspector's door on Tuesday afternoon and waited to hear whether his boss was engaged in conversation. Then he tapped lightly on the glazed panel.

'Come in!' called Roscoe.

'I thought DS Roy might be with you, sir,' said Khalid.

'No. I've sent her to interview the woman who runs the stables in Inkberrow,' Roscoe explained. 'This Martha went for a date with Dominic Jenks and found some bloodstained gloves in his van, so I want the sergeant to find those gloves and take them to Dr Ling. Anyway, you wanted to see me?'

'Yes. Could I have a quick word, sir?' asked the constable.

'Take a seat,' said his boss, who was eating a ham sandwich at his desk. 'What's happening, Omar?'

'I've heard from a contact in Brum that ROCU have arrested two men in connection with yesterday's drugs raid in Queensbridge,' he said.

'Is that right?' said Roscoe. 'That's news to me. I'll call my old pal Quinton Taylor and see what the score is. Give me five.'

While Khalid returned to his desk in the main office, Roscoe phoned his chief superintendent friend.

'Gavin, this isn't a good time,' was Taylor's response. 'Can you make it quick?'

'One of my lads has picked up a tip you've made another arrest,' said Roscoe.

'Yeah, we've pulled in Chester Crane,' said Taylor. 'By the way, thank you so much for your steer about the shop in Windermere Drive.'

'Glad it worked out for you,' said Roscoe.

'It's one of the largest seizures we've made in the Midlands in a while,' he said. 'Crane refused to answer any questions, as you might have expected, and both he and a man arrested at the scene have been released on conditional bail. We've seized two hundred and fifty kilograms of cocaine, which was being stored in wooden crates. It would have been worth up to twenty million if sold on the street.'

'What are your thoughts on Deakin now we know he's just facing two traffic offences?' Roscoe asked. 'Do you believe it should be left like that?'

'I'm still not sure, Gavin. Was it a clever attempt on Alan's life? I don't think we'll ever know, unless the driver confesses, which he's unlikely to do. So I'd say there's about as much chance of getting the CPS to accept a charge of attempted murder as of seeing a one-legged man winning a butt-kicking contest. Anyway, I'd better go. Someone's waving at me frantically from across the office about something important.'

'Very quickly,' said Roscoe. 'I know of someone who could be of great help to you as a witness. It's someone who bought drugs and then came under threat from the Makepeace gang. I'll get DS Roy, my sergeant, to have a word with her. If there's one person capable of getting her onside, it would be her.'

Chapter 44

Temperatures had plunged in the West Midlands overnight. Although it was now March, winter's frosty forces seemed to have mounted a vigorous rearguard action when Sunita Roy travelled into Worcestershire on Tuesday.

After passing the parish church and some thatched cottages at the end of her ten-mile journey, she reached the picturesque village of Inkberrow and found the country lane where Green Meadows Riding School was based. She had hardly had time to park in the potholed car park beside the stables when a stranger in wellington boots approached her. The jovial woman in her early forties was, like the sergeant, wrapped up warmly against the weather.

'Martha Unwin,' the woman announced, reaching out a gloved hand.

'DS Roy,' said Sunita, who smiled while clasping her hand. 'I just needed to ask you a little about your date with Dominic Jenks.'

'Well, the least said about the actual date the better,' said Martha. 'He seemed such a nice guy when we chatted in the pub. But first impressions can be deceptive, can't they?'

'So sparks didn't fly?' said the detective.

Martha shook her head. 'It's not that we weren't on the same page. We weren't even in the same book. Did Melody tell you what happened?'

'I haven't spoken to Melody,' Sunita admitted. 'Only her dad, my boss, but I gather you met at the Coach and Horses.'

'Yes. The guy was rather young for me, but I thought I'd give it a go. I've been on my own for a while. Well, he took me to a pub near Studley the other night and he spent most of the time telling me how badly Lydia had treated him last year.'

'Tell me about the gloves,' said Sunita with a nod.

'One of the amps was banging about in the back of the van when he brought me home. He pulled up and went round the back to investigate. I turned round to watch him and happened to notice some material protruding from behind the driver's seat. Out of curiosity, I tugged at it and two black leather gloves sprang out. One was stained with blood.'

'So what did you do – put them back where you'd found them?' asked Sunita.

'I should have done,' Martha replied, 'but he was too quick for me. He got back into the van and saw me holding the gloves. I said, "This one has got blood on it. You're not a serial killer, are you?" I meant it as a joke, but he got angry and stuffed the gloves back where I'd found them. He snapped at me, saying, "I cut my finger sawing some wood."'

'So you decided to inform DCI Roscoe?' said Sunita.

'Not immediately,' said Martha. 'I thought about it for a while and, in the end, I felt I ought to tell someone – just to be on the safe side. I've known Melody Roscoe for years. She's a good friend and I knew her dad was in the police, so I asked her to pass on what I've told you.'

'You did absolutely the right thing,' Sunita assured her. 'And don't worry. We'll be discreet about where we got our information.'

* * *

After obtaining details of Jenks' van from her, Sunita set off to the bass guitarist's home in Coventry, where she met up with DC Dawson. But when they both climbed the stairs to the first-floor flat and rang the bell, they were disheartened to receive no answer.

Sunita bent down and peered through the letter box. There were two unopened letters on the mat.

'Looks like he must have stayed somewhere overnight,' she told Dawson. 'Come on, Brett. Let's try the neighbours.'

A woman with a crying infant in her arms greeted them at the flat next door.

'DS Roy, Heart of England Police,' she told the startled woman. 'Have you seen the guy next door, Dominic, at all?'

'No. Hold on. I'll just take a look out of the back window.'

The woman retreated inside her flat and headed for her living room, which overlooked the car park. A minute later she returned.

'His van isn't where he normally parks it,' she said. 'Maybe he's gone to see his mother.'

'The van's a white Ford Transit, isn't it?' said Sunita.

'Well, I know it's white. Don't ask me what make.'

'This is the van he uses to transport all the band's equipment?'

'Yes. When it's loaded up, he parks it in a garage along the road.'

'Do you know where the garage is?'

'No.'

'Do you know where his mother lives?'

'Somewhere in Coventry. I'm sorry. I don't know the address.'

The pair got into the sergeant's car and prepared themselves mentally for a lengthy vigil. Sunita turned on her heater and pulled her scarf more tightly round her neck.

'I hate these jobs, where you're sitting and waiting for hours for something to happen,' she told Dawson, who was beside her in the passenger seat. 'I'd rather be kept busy.'

'I know what you mean, Sarge,' said Dawson.

After three hours, Sunita began to lose patience.

'We'd better call the DCI and see what he wants us to do,' she said.

The chief inspector was disappointed to hear they had been unable to find Jenks or his van.

'Sir, I've been looking at the Urban Renegades' Facebook page.' said Sunita. 'They're due to appear tomorrow evening at the Crown and Sceptre in Queensbridge. I think we should go down there and catch up with him then.'

'That's an excellent idea.'

* * *

As she set off back to her home in Shawley Green, Sunita switched on her car radio and searched for BBC Radio Birmingham.

A news bulletin was commencing with a row in Parliament. A report followed about a heatwave in Sydney. Then the presenter turned her attention to Midlands news. A man had been stabbed in a district of south Birmingham.

She was about to search for a music station when the announcer gave details of some breaking news.

'A man's been kidnapped in the street in broad daylight near the central police station in Snow Hill Queensway,' said the news reader. 'It happened just after two o'clock today. First reports say the man was forced into a car and driven away at high speed.'

'Oh my God,' thought Sunita. 'I'm sure that was the police station where DCS Taylor and his team were questioning Chester Crane. He must have been released around that time.'

Chapter 45

The Crown and Sceptre in Queensbridge High Street had once been a busy commercial hotel in the heart of the market town. But now its elegance was fading and its owners had been obliged to stage a string of weekly events to boost their business.

Sunita Roy and her colleague, Brett Dawson, arrived in their two cars at 7.30 p.m. on Wednesday evening – well before the band, Urban Renegades, were due to perform. They hoped to meet up with bass player Dominic Jenks while he was shifting sound equipment from his van before crowds of music-loving customers descended on them.

After more than half an hour, the pair, who were sitting in Sunita's car on the opposite side of the street, noticed Jenks' white van draw up. He parked partly on the pavement so that the back of the vehicle was directly outside the pub's entrance. Along with a male passenger, whom the detectives did not recognise, he got out, wearing a blue peaked cap, opened his rear doors and removed an amplifier. He then carried it into the pub.

The detectives waited for a break in the traffic before stepping across the road in the midst of a shower of rain.

As soon as Jenks returned to his van, Sunita confronted him.

'Mr Jenks,' she said, 'we came over to your flat recently. DS Roy. Do you remember?'

'Oh yes. You're investigating what happened to poor Lydia. How can I help?'

'I'm afraid we need to search your vehicle.'

Jenks frowned. 'Whatever for?'

'We've received an allegation from someone. It won't take long.'

The musician placed his hands on his hips and scowled.

'Have you got a warrant for this?' he demanded.

'We don't need one,' said Dawson, who was standing behind his sergeant. 'We've got the power to search a vehicle if we have reasonable grounds.'

'Please hand me your van keys,' said Sunita. 'This will only take a moment.'

As the furious musician paced up and down the pavement like an agitated animal, Sunita opened the driver's door and examined the cab. Within seconds, she located the gloves and called Dawson over so he could take photographs of them in place behind the top of the seat. Then she removed them both and carefully studied them.

'Do these belong to you, sir?' she asked Jenks.

'Let me see,' the bassist asked.

Sunita took a step back. After all their efforts, she was wary in case he tried to snatch them out of her hands. She held them up.

'Yes, they look like mine,' he said. 'Where did you find them?'

'Behind the driver's seat,' she replied. 'We're curious because it's quite clear the right glove is stained in blood.'

'Oh, it isn't that stupid bitch from the riding school who put you up to this, is it?' he asked. 'She's probably got a grudge. I didn't want a second date with her so she's been telling tales.'

Sunita ignored his remarks.

'How do you account for the blood on this glove, Mr Jenks?' she asked.

'I was doing some DIY and used the gloves to protect my hands,' he explained. 'I cut myself with a saw and the blood went everywhere.'

'So why did you hide them behind the driver's seat?' asked Dawson as the drizzle finally eased.

'They're not hidden. I keep them there for convenience. I use them for mucky jobs.'

'We're taking them away for testing,' said Sunita.

'That's ridiculous,' Jenks said while glaring at the sergeant.

'Don't worry – you'll get them back, provided we can be assured they weren't used in the pursuit of crime.'

After obtaining his van keys back from Sunita, Jenks, tutting and swearing, resumed his task of unloading the band's equipment.

The detectives returned to Sunita's car, where she placed the gloves in separate evidence bags and handed them to Dawson.

'Can you take them to forensics, Brett?' she said.

'Yes. No problem,' he said. 'Are you going straight home now, Sarge?'

'No,' she said. 'I'm going to hang on here for a while. I've just seen Roman Makepeace turn up. I'll think up some excuse to start a conversation with him. There's a few more questions I need to ask.'

After watching her colleague drive away, Sunita stepped into the pub's entrance hall and pushed open a glazed door that led to the bar. The room had high ceilings with elaborate covings and cornices. A range of dark-brown polished tables and upholstered chairs were arranged around the room, beneath brass chandeliers.

Dominic Jenks and other members of the band were setting up equipment on a stage at the far side. The guitarist, who was installing a microphone stand, glared towards her and then looked away. A colleague was calling 'one, two' into the microphone to test the sound quality.

Although always rather self-conscious when entering a pub on her own, Sunita stepped over to the bar, where she had spotted Roman waiting to be served.

'DS Roy, isn't it?' he said cautiously while reaching into his light-brown jacket for his wallet. 'Can I get you a drink?'

'Thank you,' she said. 'Just an orange juice.'

When a barman became free, he ordered a pint of lager for himself and a juice for her.

'On your own?' he asked.

'This is just a flying visit,' she replied. 'Listen, I need to ask you a few more questions. First of all, did you realise that Lydia wasn't using her real name? She used to be called Lizzie Hope.'

He nodded.

'I was reading a news report and it mentioned the name Lizzie Hope.'

'Was that the first you knew about it?' she asked.

'Yes. I must admit I was a bit puzzled to start with. Then I remembered she'd told me about her brief marriage and I just assumed she changed it in order to make a break from her past. Can we change the subject?' he said. 'It's still raw.'

'I'm sorry but we need more information to catch the killer. Who else knew Lydia's address in Balmoral Gardens apart from you?'

He handed a twenty-pound note to the barman and paused to think.

'All sorts of people, I suppose,' he said. 'People she worked with, probably. The neighbours, of course. The Urban Renegades and their hangers-on. Personal friends. Relatives. The list is endless.'

She shrugged her shoulders.

'Why do you want to know this, anyway?' he asked.

'To be honest, Roman, our team have so far interviewed up to a hundred people and we're still collecting information. But don't worry. We'll catch whoever it was.'

'I hope you find them quickly. But it's already been a few weeks and you don't seem to be making much headway.'

'You have to be patient,' said Sunita. 'We've got dozens of officers on the case. I'm sure it won't be long.'

'You haven't just come over here to see me, have you?' he asked. 'It's just that I'm meeting someone in a minute.'

'No. I had a job to do in the area. I just wandered in on the off-chance you might be here,' she said. 'Anyway I'd better go. My boyfriend will be wondering where I've got to.'

Sunita made her way towards the main door. More customers were arriving and the band launched into their first song, the Lionel Richie ballad *Easy (Like Sunday Morning)*. As she reached the high street, her phone bleeped to notify her of a text. She glanced at her handset and saw she'd received a message from Tom Vickers.

Still at the Crown? I've just finished work. On my way over as I fancy seeing the band.

She texted back, 'OK. I'll find some seats.'

Sunita was not totally surprised by him wishing to watch the band. When she informed him earlier they were performing at the popular venue, he had shown interest in joining her there – if work permitted.

She chose a small table in a corner at the far end of the room and sat down.

Half an hour later, just before ten o'clock, Tom Vickers appeared in the doorway while the sound of the Robbie Williams' hit *Let Me Entertain You* was drifting across the bar. He glanced round until he spotted Sunita and waved.

Then, after buying a second orange juice for her and a pint of lager for himself, he threaded his way through the crowd.

'They're not bad, are they?' he said before sitting beside her and kissing her cheek.

'No,' she said. 'I don't mind this kind of music. Easy on the ear. Is that the boss's daughter dancing down the front with her fiancé?'

Vickers nodded.

She explained about how the bloodstained glove was found in Jenks' van and then excused herself to go to the ladies.

Sunita walked into the foyer and followed signs for the toilets. But, as she made her way along the corridor, she noticed the pub's rear door was open. Beneath the light of the full moon, she could see a man and woman standing outside on the patio, holding hands and talking.

From his light-brown jacket, she could tell the man was Roman Makepeace. Then the woman stepped out of the shadows.

Sunita recognised her straight away.

Chapter 46

Just before seven o'clock the following morning, Sunita Roy got up and left her partner sleeping on the other side of the king-size bed.

She slipped on her white dressing gown and peered through the curtains. Temperatures had plunged to zero overnight and a flurry of snow was falling across her back garden.

After turning the heating on and making herself a cup of lemon tea in the kitchen downstairs, she made her way into the living room and settled herself down in front of her home computer.

That was where Vickers found her two hours later when he rushed downstairs with his shirt undone and panicking like a bargain hunter late for the high street sales. He knelt down by the living-room door, tying his shoe laces.

'Sunita, why didn't you wake me?' he demanded. 'It's nearly nine o'clock and I've got a meeting with Norris.'

She stood up sharply and strode towards him.

'I'm so sorry, Tom,' she said. 'I lost all track of time.'

'What have you been up to anyway?' he asked.

'You know those ideas I was tossing around last night? I thought I ought to do a bit of research.'

'Aren't you due to go into the office this morning?'

'I'm meant to be, but I think I'll call the DCI in a minute and see if he'll leave me to my own devices.'

He glanced across to the table where she had been sitting. A huge map of the Midlands was lying beside the computer, where she was logged into YouTube. She noticed his gaze.

'I've been watching a load of videos,' she explained. 'And I've put in a call to someone I need to speak to regarding the case. I really feel I'm getting somewhere now.'

'That's excellent, but I've really got to shoot off,' he said.

'Don't you want me to make you a coffee and a bit of breakfast?' she asked.

'There isn't time,' he said, giving her a peck on the cheek. 'I'll grab a bite in the canteen.'

He dashed out of the house, still fumbling with his shirt buttons. He jumped into his car and sped away.

Sunita glanced at her watch. It was a few minutes past nine. She hoped that the chief inspector would have arrived in CID by now and she called him.

She found he was in an ebullient mood and he spoke up first.

'I'm glad you called, Sergeant,' he said. 'DCS Taylor called me half an hour ago and has asked me to pass on his thanks to you. After you went round to see Jackie Perrins at the Red Lion, Jackie called his office and she's agreed to give evidence against Axel and Roman Makepeace. So your powers of persuasion have proved very effective.'

'I'm glad about that, sir. I suspected she might back out. She was concerned about how she could create a new life for herself away from the Midlands. She was talking about moving to Ireland to be near her sister.'

'Yes, Taylor is fully aware of all that and he'll be speaking to her about that in due course. Bear in mind she's far from being the only person prepared to give evidence against the Makepeaces. It won't be long before that guy Axel feels the firm hand of justice around his scrawny neck.'

Sunita waited before launching into her plea for time off.

'Sir, I've made some substantial progress on the Valentine's murder and I think I know who did it,' she said.

'That's excellent news. Who've you got in mind, Sergeant?'

'I'd rather not say just at the moment.'

'Oh, here we go,' he said.

'Well, sir, it's just that I don't want to bet on red and it comes up black.'

'I know what you mean,' he said. 'But with all my years of experience as a detective, I thought I might be able to guide you.'

'I appreciate that, of course,' she said.

He paused for a moment. 'I don't suppose you feel like sharing a little of your Archimedes moment with me, do you, Sergeant? Have you got Dominic Jenks in your sights? Dr Ling says it will be a while before they get the results back on the gloves.'

'No. It's not Dominic Jenks. It all came to me last night after I'd visited the Crown and Sceptre. I realised there was a possible explanation for how the murder was carried out that I'd overlooked before. But I'll need a few days to make some inquiries and see whether the facts support my theory. In particular, I want to make a couple of journeys away from our area to collect some information.'

'Sergeant, I have complete faith in you,' said Roscoe. 'If you've a hunch about a particular suspect, I'll trust your judgement. I've expressed doubts in the past about your personal initiatives. I wasn't enthusiastic about you going abroad on that case last year, but you proved me wrong. You always seem to resolve matters to everyone's satisfaction. So please take as much time as you need.'

'I don't want to appear foolish, sir, if the events of Valentine's Day didn't proceed in the way I believe they did. So I'd rather not say any more at the moment.'

'All right. Come straight in to see me as soon as you've got everything in order,' said Roscoe. 'Meanwhile, I can tell you we're one suspect down. Omar Khalid's just brought me some shocking news. You know Chester Crane, Makepeace's sidekick? His body was pulled out of the Grand Union Canal last night.'

'Oh my God,' said Sunita. 'I know he was a vile criminal, but that sounds horrific.'

'Yes. Taylor had him brought in for questioning a couple of days ago. As soon as he left the police station at Snow Hill, he was chased down the street and forced into a black Range Rover Evoque. His body was found four miles away, floating in the canal in Sparkbrook.'

'Someone clearly didn't like Crane speaking to Taylor and his team,' she said.

Chapter 47

A soft rain was falling on Monday morning, four days later, as Sunita Roy arrived at police headquarters a few minutes after nine o'clock. She managed to take the last remaining parking space before heading into the building and making her way into the CID office with a spring in her step.

The chief inspector was already in his room, briefing Hopkirk about an assignment. He quickly turned his attention to Sunita.

'Now we're going to hear the fruits of your labours, are we, Sergeant?' he asked as Hopkirk left.

'Yes, sir,' said Sunita, who was carrying a brown envelope.

'Before we start,' said Roscoe, 'I've had the results back from forensics on Dominic Jenks' gloves. The blood's his own, so that largely absolves him for the moment.'

'It was worth a try, wasn't it?' she replied.

'Definitely. Anyway, I'd better call Khalid and Dawson in, since they've both played key roles in this investigation.'

After the two detectives arrived, Roscoe sat down and Sunita placed her envelope on the desk.

'As you know, sir, I've spent a few days making numerous inquiries, which have taken me as far afield as Hertfordshire and Gloucestershire,' she said as she found a seat beside her two colleagues. 'But finally I believe I've got enough information to tell you who killed Lizzie Hope.'

'Let's hear what you've learnt, Sergeant,' said Roscoe, leaning back in his executive chair. 'Axel Makepeace was behind it, wasn't he?'

Sunita shook her head. 'I'm afraid, sir, we'd be making a mistake if we accused Axel Makepeace.'

The chief inspector frowned. 'Are you sure?'

She folded her arms. 'It wasn't him or any of his gang who murdered Lizzie. Let me explain. It all began when I was at the Crown and Sceptre pub on Wednesday evening last week,' she said. 'After Brett and I had spoken to Dominic Jenks, I stayed at the pub and had a chat with Roman Makepeace and then Tom Vickers showed up. Towards the end of the evening, I discovered a couple having a quiet conversation just outside the pub's back door. They were holding hands. I was astonished to find it was Roman Makepeace and his ex-girlfriend, Sophie Bishop.'

'Good God,' said Roscoe. '*She's* wasted no time.'

'I know,' said Sunita. 'I went back to watch the Urban Renegades and the more I thought about it, the more it occurred to me that Sophie might have had something to do with the death of Lizzie.'

'You mean she might have wanted Lizzie out of the way so she could resume her relationship with Roman?' said Roscoe.

'Exactly,' said Sunita. 'So, after thinking about it, I decided to confront them and find out what was going on. I found them sitting on stools at the bar at around 10.30 p.m. but they noticed me approaching from across the room and hurried off before I had a chance to speak to them.'

'So what happened next?' asked Roscoe. 'And what's in this envelope?'

'I'll explain in a second. I decided that, if Sophie Bishop was responsible for the murder, I'd have to break her alibi.'

'Didn't she say she was playing keyboards in a small theatre orchestra in Tewkesbury?' said Roscoe. 'It was a show involving dancers, singers and backing music so she would have had dozens of witnesses to support her story.'

'That's true. She claimed she was playing with the orchestra the whole night on Valentine's Day. But I've discovered that was an outright lie. Their performance that night was filmed. Some video clips were posted on Facebook and some on YouTube. I studied them all and two of them proved crucial. One, timed at 8.45 p.m., clearly showed, despite the lighting being poor around the orchestra, two keyboardists playing at the back of the stage. The second video I found was timed at around ten o'clock and showed only one person playing keyboards – a man.'

'Very interesting,' Roscoe observed.

'I went over to St Albans on Thursday morning and had a chat with the musical director who'd been in charge of the orchestra, Damon Seabrook,' Sunita continued. 'He confirmed my findings. He's revealed that, because it was Valentine's Day, they had a change to the usual programme. The show was due to start at 7.30 p.m. and finish at around 9.50 p.m. But that night, they brought on two acoustic guitarists to play some romantic ballads and the show finally ended at 10.30 p.m.'

Sunita brought out her notebook to refer to.

'Since Damon himself was there to play keyboards, they'd no need for Sophie to be there as well and she'd been aware of this for at least a week. He said he doesn't remember seeing her after a quarter past nine.'

Roscoe leaned back in his chair.

'But would she have had time to get from Tewkesbury to Worcester and kill her love rival?' asked Roscoe. 'She was in that photo we saw, taken that night at 11.15 p.m. How was that possible if she was in Worcester?'

Dawson, who had been listening intently, interrupted.

'Sir, aren't we forgetting one really important point?' he said. 'Sophie Bishop would have needed to have travelled up the M5 to get to Balmoral Gardens, but the road was blocked because of resurfacing work after a chemical spillage. The nearby A38 was the only alternative route and that was jammed solid with traffic. The whole area north of Tewkesbury was hit, as it had been the day before.'

Sunita nodded.

'I know that, Brett,' she snapped. 'But I'm convinced that not only did Sophie Bishop travel to Worcester that evening, she also made it back by a quarter past eleven so she could appear in a group photograph alongside Damon Seabrook and the five other members of the orchestra.'

She reached for the envelope on the desk and pulled out a colour photograph of seven musicians – some holding instruments – smiling towards the camera.

'That's Sophie in the middle,' she explained as she passed the picture round.

Roscoe leaned forward onto his desk and smiled.

'How on earth could she manage the journey then?' he asked. 'I don't know, Sergeant. I find this all very difficult to comprehend. Did she have a helicopter on standby, or a private jet? Did she hire a magician and get herself teleported to Worcester? Does she have a time machine?'

'Right now, I can't explain it,' Sunita replied. 'But I know for certain she was in Balmoral Gardens at around ten o'clock or ten thirty. Last Thursday, I presented Dr Ling with a specimen of Sophie Bishop's DNA and she's confirmed it's a match for the specks of saliva found on Lizzie Hope's kitchen table.'

'How on earth did you manage to obtain a sample of the woman's DNA so swiftly?' asked Roscoe.

'Tom Vickers and I obtained it on Wednesday night. As soon as the pair fled from the pub, I got Tom to collect the Corona bottle she'd been drinking from. Sophie had been drinking the beer out of the bottle and we put it straight into an evidence bag. Dr Ling found the woman's DNA on the lip of the bottle.'

'So we can prove that she was at Lizzie's house,' Roscoe continued. 'But we still haven't covered the vital question of how she travelled there. It's just occurred to me she could have made the journey by motorbike.'

'That's a possibility I have considered. But it's my firm belief she didn't want to run the risk of any sightings of her or any registration number – from a car or motorcycle – being picked up on camera,' said Sunita.

'I've seen videos of paramotor pilots flying through the skies under a canopy,' Roscoe continued.

'The light was too poor for that and train times didn't suit the operation either,' said Sunita. 'Laying the mode of travel aside, it's clear she came up with an audacious plan as soon as she realised there was going to be traffic carnage in the area over two days. She started carefully constructing an alibi that she believed was foolproof. I don't want to say more at the moment. I'm waiting for a phone call from a crucial witness. He's proved rather elusive but I expect to reach him later today and get my theory confirmed.'

'We're very close to solving this murder,' said Roscoe.

'Yes,' said Sunita. 'We know who did it and we also know why they did it. They only thing we don't know at the moment is how they did it.'

'Listen,' said Roscoe, 'we've got more than enough evidence to bring Sophie Bishop in for questioning and she's certainly got a lot of explaining to do. We could be dealing here with an extremely cunning woman.'

Chapter 48

Sunita Roy had driven for hundreds of miles and toiled into the small hours of the morning over recent days without a great deal of sleep. She was beginning to recognise that she had become so consumed by following her instincts on the case that she was partly neglecting her health.

As she and the chief inspector set off in his car for Sophie Bishop's home later that morning, she suddenly felt overcome by exhaustion. However, she knew she had to struggle on. She had to remain sharp and alert. The woman she suspected of Lizzie Hope's brutal murder had to be caught and brought to justice.

The chief inspector glanced at her several times while they travelled away from Solihull in heavy rain.

'You look shattered, Sergeant,' he told her.

'I *am*, sir,' she admitted. 'I hadn't appreciated it until now, but I feel drained.'

'Not to worry,' he said reassuringly. 'After we've got this lady under lock and key, you can have some well-deserved time off. So, this hectic round of interviews you've carried out all began after spotting Roman and Sophie had rekindled their relationship?'

'Yes. There was no mistaking it was them. They were holding hands beneath the moon.'

'They say the moon plays tricks with the emotions,' Roscoe remarked.

'It annoyed me to see them like that so soon after seeing Roman holding hands with poor Lizzie. I remembered how she'd doted on Roman and he on her. Sophie, when I met her, had made some critical remarks about Roman. She claimed their relationship had been in a rut. She insisted her new partner, Chris, was "much more husband material" and that he was a "sweetheart". All her words keep coming back to me and I realise she must have been acting. It was like being led by a dancing monkey.'

'It *does* sound like it,' he admitted.

'All the time her heart had been set on getting back with Roman. She must have felt intense resentment and jealousy while he was with Lizzie.'

'Which eventually boiled over,' said Roscoe.

'Exactly,' said Sunita. 'My father used to say that great anger is more destructive than the sword.'

'I'm impressed with your father's wise words,' said Roscoe. 'But why did she strike on Valentine's Day? It was known the motorway would be blocked that night. She could surely have selected any other night to carry out her gruesome deed, couldn't she?'

Sunita nodded.

'I believe she had been planning the murder for some time and the conditions that night were ideal from her point of view,' said Sunita. 'It was actually because the road was blocked that she chose that night. The highways authority announced on the Sunday that they'd be resurfacing the road and that it would take at least two days. She must have seen reports about this and realised this created the opportune moment for her. She thought it presented her with the perfect alibi – trapped in Tewkesbury by the traffic.

'She must have found out somehow that Roman had an early start the following morning. Don't forget that Sophie used to work for the coach firm, so probably knows several people who still work there. She probably knew that, after a Valentine's night rendezvous, Roman and Lizzie would part and Lizzie would be at the house alone.'

'So Sophie Bishop set up everything in advance?'

'That's right. I've just remembered something else. The landlady of the pub where Roman and Lizzie dined received a call from someone checking on the booking.'

'That's the Five Bells?'

'Yes. I'm wondering now if that could have been Sophie Bishop keeping tabs on the couple's plans.'

'Maybe,' said Roscoe as they neared the end of their ten-mile journey.

His car drew into the leafy street of small, detached houses.

'That's the one, sir,' said Sunita, recognising Sophie Bishop's grey composite front door. 'It looks like she's out.'

'How do you work that out?' he asked.

'There's no car. When I saw her three weeks ago, her white Fiesta was on the forecourt. She must be at work.'

After a further nine-mile journey to Dudley, the pair quickly found the sports shop that Sophie Bishop managed. It occupied the ground floor of a detached 1960s building on a busy dual carriageway. Roscoe stopped his car on the wide pavement directly outside and they entered the shop. An assistant in her early twenties with frizzy ginger hair immediately approached them.

'We're from Heart of England Police,' Roscoe explained. 'Is your manager around?'

'Is it Sophie you're after?' asked the woman.

He nodded.

'I think she's doing the accounts in her office. I'll go and see.'

A minute later, Sophie Bishop, looking smart and businesslike and with perfectly coiffed hair, walked towards them from the rear of the store. Unlike the previous occasion Sunita met her, she was wearing make-up.

'I hear you want to speak to me,' she said with a cautious smile.

'DCI Roscoe and DS Roy, Heart of England CID,' said the chief inspector. 'We need to ask you a few questions at police headquarters.'

'Why? What's this about?' asked Bishop.

'I think you probably know why we're here,' he continued. 'We're investigating the murder of Lydia Squires and believe you might have been involved.'

'Don't be ridiculous. I've never met the woman.'

'We believe you have,' he insisted.

'We also believe you had a notable meeting with her on Valentine's Day,' said Sunita, 'and that that meeting led to her untimely death.'

'That's complete nonsense. So am I being arrested then?'

'Not unless you make things difficult for us. But we need you to come and answer some crucial questions.'

'All right,' said Bishop. 'I'll just explain to Tracey that I'm going off to assist you and I'll get my coat.'

'We'll also need your house keys,' said Roscoe, 'because I'm afraid we're going to have to carry out a search.'

'This is crazy,' Bishop muttered as she fetched her long, grey coat and briefed her colleague.

* * *

Three hours later, at just after 2.30 p.m., the two detectives were making their way to Interview Room One at St James Street when Sunita revealed that she had received a crucial phone call and that she now had the final piece of evidence she needed.

The chief inspector nodded his head continually as she explained to him in detail her assumptions about how Sophie Bishop was able to travel to Balmoral Gardens.

'You're absolutely sure about this?' he asked after she had finished speaking.

'Yes, sir.'

'Well, it's very hard to believe. But, on reflection, what you're saying has a certain ring of truth about it, Sergeant. Now we've got a golden opportunity to put your theory to the test. Because, if my ears aren't deceiving me, that sounds like Miss Bishop's solicitor walking along the corridor towards us.'

Dipak Sharma, a stout, middle-aged lawyer who was wearing what Roscoe judged to be a slightly misshapen pair of glasses, stepped towards them with a broad smile.

'DCI Roscoe,' he said. 'Pleased to see you again. And DS Roy. I've been asked to represent Sophie Bishop.'

'Have you had a chance to speak to the lady?' asked Roscoe.

He nodded.

'Yes. We've had a little chat and we're ready to proceed. She thinks there's some kind of misunderstanding and that she'll be allowed home shortly.'

'That remains to be seen,' said Roscoe in a low voice. 'Anyway, I'll arrange for her to be brought up.'

Sophie Bishop's earlier glow of confidence appeared to have faded a few minutes later as she was led along the corridor to the interview room by two female officers. Her face seemed pale and it looked as though her mascara had been running – perhaps from crying – as she joined the detectives and Sharma.

After turning on the recording equipment, Roscoe outlined the suspect's rights.

'I understand what you're saying,' she said in response, 'but I seriously believe you'll be letting me go as soon as you've heard what I've got to say.'

Roscoe shrugged his shoulders.

'Now I need to ask you, Miss Bishop, about how you spent Valentine's Day,' he said. 'Did you go to work that day?'

She nodded. 'Yes, I finished at the shop early because I'd agreed to perform with Damon Seabrook's orchestra. We were providing the music for a show in Tewkesbury.'

'This is the Theatre Royal?'

'Yes. It's a show called *Dawn of Rock*, charting the history of rock 'n' roll down the ages.'

'So what time did you leave your shop?'

'Around four o'clock.'

'And at what time did you set off from your home in Northfield?'

'I left home just over an hour later and reached the theatre at about six,' she said.

'You travelled there in your Ford Fiesta?'

'Yes. There was a lot of traffic around Tewkesbury, which held me up a bit.'

'What happened when you reached the theatre?'

'Well, I found Mr Seabrook, who's the musical director, and we all began setting up our instruments. I don't really see why you're asking about all this.'

Sunita stared at Bishop across the table. 'You'll see why in a minute,' the sergeant explained.

'What time did the performance end?' asked Roscoe.

'Well, a normal performance of *Dawn of Rock* lasts two hours twenty minutes. But because it was Valentine's Day, Damon had some romantic ballads added and it went on until, I don't know, something like eleven o'clock.'

'The reason you're not sure is that you weren't there,' said Roscoe.

'What do you mean? Of course I was there,' she insisted. 'I was there, playing keyboards.'

'Not for the whole evening, you weren't,' said Sunita with a shake of the head. 'Mr Seabrook says your services weren't required after nine o'clock.'

Bishop winced at this but quickly regained her composure. 'If I could show you a photograph of me and my bandmates taken at a quarter past eleven, would that satisfy you?' she asked.

'We've seen that picture on Facebook,' said Roscoe. 'I'd be more impressed if you could show me a picture taken at ten thirty. But you can't do that, can you? Because you were in Worcester, stabbing Lydia Squires to death.'

'Please, phone Damon,' Bishop implored them, raising her voice. 'He could send you the picture with a time stamp on it. In any case, how could I get to Worcester in my little Fiesta when all the roads going north were blocked? I stayed and watched the show from the back of the theatre.'

'Don't try and lie your way out of this,' said Sunita, staring directly into their suspect's eyes. 'I managed to work out how you managed to get to Worcester and back. You travelled by speedboat along the River Severn.'

Chapter 49

Sophie Bishop, who was twiddling nervously with strands of her hair, glared across the table at the two detectives.

'You're suggesting I travelled from Tewkesbury to Worcester by speedboat?' she said. 'That's the most ludicrous suggestion I've ever heard. Everyone knows the speed limit on the river is six miles an hour. It would have taken the best part of three hours using any rivercraft.'

'That would be the case if you were obeying the regulations,' said Sunita. 'But you weren't. I've got a statement from a man who used to run boats along the river between the two riverside towns. He's confirmed that, although it would mean breaking all the rules of the river, it is possible to travel between Worcester and Tewkesbury in around thirty minutes.'

'This doesn't sound possible to me,' said Sharma. 'Anglers, birdwatchers and ramblers would quickly notify the river police.'

'When it's dark?' said Sunita.

Sharma interrupted. 'I know the theatre in Tewkesbury is close to the river,' he said, 'but surely, if your allegations were true, Miss Bishop would have had a problem once she arrived at the Worcester quayside. If she were to have visited the house of the murder victim and carried out this atrocious murder, how are you suggesting she made the final part of her journey after leaving the boat?'

'Balmoral Gardens is around a mile from the Worcester quayside in a suburb called Barbourne,' Sunita replied. 'So it would have been easy for her to walk that distance in a short time.'

'I was never there,' Bishop insisted. 'You've got the wrong person—'

Roscoe interrupted. 'I should point out we have DNA evidence that shows you were at the house. Tiny specks of your saliva were found on the top of the kitchen table, suggesting you spoke to Miss Squires across the table when she entered the room. You need to account for that.'

'Well, I can't explain that. There must be some mix-up in the lab. I'm innocent, I had nothing to do with any of this.'

Sharma waited for his client to finish before he glanced towards Sunita.

'Sergeant Roy,' he said, 'there's a serious matter that concerns me about these allegations. It's not everyone that can take command of a powerboat travelling at high speed along the Severn with all its strong currents, and especially in darkness.'

'I know,' said Sunita. 'That's why Miss Bishop's brother stepped in to help.'

'My brother?' said Bishop with a quizzical look.

'Yes. James Bishop. It didn't require a great deal of research to find out that he's one of Britain's powerboat champions and keeps his main vessel, *Aqua Raceboy*, at Upton upon Severn, eleven miles south of Worcester. He also knows the river like a seasoned waterman. So with him at the helm, you were able to make the journey to Worcester quayside, walk or run to the house in Balmoral Gardens, kill your love rival and make it back by river to the theatre in time for the group picture.'

Bishop glanced towards her lawyer. 'The woman's living in fantasy land,' she told Sharma.

Roscoe folded his arms and sat back in his chair. He stared across at Bishop. 'Can you confirm you've got a brother called James?' he said.

Bishop nodded.

'Yes,' she said.

'And is he a powerboat champion?'

'Yes, he is, but I haven't seen him for weeks. Anyway, no one would go to those lengths.'

'But it was a perfect scenario for you, wasn't it?' said Sunita. 'You were trapped in Tewkesbury by the traffic. You clearly thought you'd got away with murder.'

'Nonsense,' she sneered.

'Chief Inspector,' said Sharma, 'the traffic problems that have been mentioned – does this relate to the closure of the M5 motorway because of a spillage?'

'That's correct,' said Roscoe. 'The motorway was shut between Sunday night and Wednesday morning of that week. Other nearby roads suffered as a result. The police and highways authority gave advance warnings but many motorists remained unaware until they found themselves caught up in tailbacks.'

'I see,' said Sharma. 'My other question is this. Do we have any evidence that this James Bishop drove this *Aqua Raceboy* boat on the Severn that night? I mean, have you spoken to him?'

Sunita intervened. 'We're in the process of contacting him. However, I've obtained a written statement from a man named Terry Windsor, who lives in Riverview Cottage at Upton. His home is close to the Severn and he's told me he was disturbed by the sound of a craft hurtling up the river at around 9.40 p.m. on Valentine's Day. He looked out of his window and noticed the distinctive blue and white colours of James Bishop's boat.'

She continued, 'I should also tell you that, on that Tuesday night, Sophie Bishop was seen leaving the theatre shortly after a quarter past nine with a man who's been identified as James Bishop. We've a witness who was standing outside the Riverside Tavern in Tewkesbury. This is beside the river, three minutes' walk from the theatre. He saw them heading towards the *Aqua Raceboy*.'

'Where they set course for murder,' Roscoe muttered under his breath before turning towards his colleague. 'Sergeant, do you have any other points to make?' he asked.

Sunita paused to collect her thoughts.

'Only that we believe this crime came about because of your obsession with Roman Makepeace, didn't it, Miss Bishop?' said Sunita.

'Is that true?' Sharma asked her.

'No,' she replied. 'Of course not. I was in a relationship with Roman until last year but I've moved on.'

'That's completely untrue,' said Sunita. 'On Wednesday last week, I caught sight of you holding hands with Mr Makepeace at a pub in Queensbridge, so you've clearly revived your relationship with him.'

Roscoe glared across the table at their suspect. 'Miss Bishop, we've accumulated a great deal of evidence which points to you creating a daring scheme to eliminate your love rival and win back the affection of your former boyfriend. I believe you travelled to Worcester in your brother's boat with the intention of murdering Miss Squires. You must have been breaking all the rules of the river, travelling at speeds of more than thirty miles an hour. You had no thought for other river users as you hurtled past like a rocket. Then you broke into Miss Squires' home and used a knife from the kitchen drawer to brutally stab her to death.'

He waited to see whether his scathing words had elicited any reaction. There was none. Bishop simply sat gazing across the table with a cold expression.

'Sophie Bishop,' he said, 'I'm formally charging you with the murder of Lydia Squires in Balmoral Gardens, Worcester on the night of 14 February. You don't have to say anything but it may harm your defence if you don't mention, when questioned, something you later rely on in court. Anything you do say may be given in evidence.'

'I'm not going to comment. This is so utterly ridiculous,' she insisted.

* * *

After Sophie Bishop had been sent back to her basement cell, the chief inspector and his sergeant returned to his first-floor room in CID.

'Excellent work, Sergeant,' Roscoe said. 'I was especially impressed by your evidence from the guy living by the river. How did you know about Bishop's brother?'

'You know that I called our family history expert last week?' she replied. 'I got him to do some research. He's produced a family tree, which is here.'

She produced a computer printout from her pocket and placed it on Roscoe's desk.

'This shows Sophie Bishop was born on 12 December 1989 in Birmingham to Thomas and Jennifer Bishop,' she explained. 'Her brother, James, was born on 10 July 1987.'

'That's very valuable information,' he said. 'Tell me something. Why do you think Sophie Bishop didn't come to the house with a weapon? She'd gone to a great deal of trouble planning the murder. Why rely on the chance that she might find a weapon there?'

'All I can think is she didn't want to be caught holding a weapon in the street by witnesses,' she replied.

Roscoe nodded.

'Sergeant, there's something else I've been wondering about all afternoon,' he said. 'Do you think Roman Makepeace might have been complicit in the murder?'

'There's no evidence of that,' she said. 'I think the anguish he felt over the loss of Lydia was genuine and that, once he'd recovered from that loss, he gained solace by reconnecting with his former girlfriend – which no doubt delighted Sophie.'

'I tend to agree with you,' said Roscoe. 'There seems no suggestion that Roman Makepeace had anything to do with the death. However, we need to bring James Bishop in. If he was aware of his sister's intentions, he could be in the frame for conspiracy to murder.'

Chapter 50

The tall, ginger-haired man, clutching an open umbrella, hurried along the rain-lashed street towards the magistrates' court.

Roman Makepeace, a normally placid man, arrived at the entrance of the modern building in Worcester red-faced and irate.

The chief inspector and his sergeant were sheltering inside the crowded reception hall, waiting for Wednesday morning's court session to begin. Sunita recognised Makepeace immediately and held the door open for him.

'Is it true you've arrested Sophie?' he demanded while folding his umbrella.

After glancing at Roscoe, Sunita led Roman to a quiet corner of the foyer.

'I realise this may have come as a shock to you, Roman,' she said gently when they were on their own.

'Bloody right,' he said. 'You must be mad. Wasn't she in Gloucestershire that evening?'

'She tricked everyone,' Sunita explained. 'She managed to get to Worcester during a long break from the stage.'

'Have you really charged her with Lydia's murder?' he asked.

She nodded.

'Roman, we've got a strong body of evidence against her,' she said.

Roman shook his head and stared down at the floor.

'When I saw online yesterday that Sophie was appearing in court, I couldn't believe it,' he said. 'It doesn't make...' He paused in mid-sentence and gazed at Sunita.

'I'm so sorry,' she said, patting his arm.

'I've just been thinking about some of the nasty things she's been telling me about Lydia,' he continued.

He turned away and gazed through the window at the rainswept pavement outside. When he turned back seconds later, Sunita thought she could detect tears forming in his eyes. She also wondered if she could detect a whiff of alcohol on his breath.

'Lydia meant everything to me,' he said. 'I've never met a woman that I cared about so deeply. If you're right and Sophie's been lying to me all this time...'

He stopped speaking again and raised his hands to his face.

'God, what a nightmare,' he said. 'She definitely came to Worcester that night?'

'Yes,' said Sunita softly.

Roscoe stepped towards them. He patted Sunita on the shoulder.

'Sergeant, we ought to go in now,' he said. 'The usher's opened the doors.'

She nodded and followed the chief inspector through the reception area towards Court Three, leaving Roman alone in the foyer with his troubled thoughts.

* * *

The usher's voice roared out, 'All rise.'

The chief inspector glanced towards his sergeant.

Like everyone else present, they rose to their feet at a quarter past ten and watched as a door opened at the back of the courtroom. Three magistrates, two men and a woman, trooped in solemnly and took their seats beneath the royal coat of arms.

'What have we got this morning?' asked James Arnold, the chairman of the bench, a corpulent man with grey hair and glasses.

The legal advisor, a blonde woman in her thirties sitting at the desk in front, turned to him and they held a quiet discussion.

The day before, Roscoe had sent a file on the Lizzie Hope case to the Crown Prosecution Service, who had approved laying a murder charge against Bishop.

'That's Clare Robbins, the neighbour, over there,' Roscoe said in a low voice, pointing to the public gallery at the side of the court. 'And I'm pretty certain that's Dominic Jenks from Urban Renegades a few seats away.'

Sunita nodded.

'No sign of Roman Makepeace yet,' she whispered.

'Bring up Sophie Bishop,' Joanne Bennett, the legal advisor, demanded.

All eyes became fixed on the open, wooden dock as footsteps could be heard on the stairs beneath. Sophie Bishop, still in the business suit she had been wearing at the time of her arrest, emerged, accompanied by three dock officers.

Gone was the smart appearance of the confident sports shop manager. The lady standing uneasily in the dock had straggly hair, a pale complexion, hollow eyes and a haggard look.

'Are you Sophie Jane Bishop?' Bennett asked.

The defendant nodded. 'Yes,' she said quietly.

'Is your date of birth 12 December 1989?'

'Yes.'

As she spoke, Sunita noticed Roman Makepeace rising to his feet, wild-eyed and agitated. He must have previously been sitting out of view in the back row. Now he moved to the front.

Sunita noticed Roman's eyes were staring at his ex-partner in the dock.

All at once, he stood up and screamed at her, 'I can't believe you killed Lydia, you bitch. You're a monster.'

Bishop began trembling and grabbed hold of the metal rail in front of her for support. She called back, 'I love you so much, Roman. I did it for us, my love. We were meant to be together. I couldn't let that harpy take you away from me.'

'Silence in court!' Bennett hissed.

The chairman peered across the courtroom at the heckler.

'I won't have interruptions in my court,' Arnold declared. 'If that gentleman shouts out like that again, he'll be removed. Miss Bishop, you must also control yourself in a court of law.'

Sunita noticed three uniformed constables had arrived. They were standing close to the public gallery.

Bennett again attempted to read out the murder charge but Roman had not yet finished.

'Sophie, you've ruined my life,' he yelled. 'I hope you rot in hell.'

Arnold gestured towards the three uniformed officers.

'Sergeant, remove that man,' he bellowed.

The detectives watched as the constables grappled with the highly emotional spectator and bustled him out of the chamber.

Roman's anguished words had had a profound effect upon the defendant. Bishop slumped down in her chair, with her head in her hands, as more tears streamed down her cheeks.

Chapter 51

Tom Vickers was smiling in anticipation. He watched from his car as his partner hurried from her house in Shawley Green, slamming the front door behind her, and hauled back the passenger door.

'It's all right. We're not late,' he told Sunita as she took her seat beside him and they set off on Saturday afternoon.

'Cocktails with the guvnor,' he remarked. 'Guess I'll have to be on my best behaviour.'

'Yes, please don't drink too much, Tom, and let yourself down,' Sunita said with a frown. 'Anyway, I'm not sure if it's cocktails. The invitation was simply for drinks with the Roscoes.'

'He obviously wants to show his appreciation for your work on the Worcester murder case.'

It began to rain ten minutes later as their car passed ploughed fields on the northern edge of the town. They turned into narrow Woodside Way, which was flanked on one side by a row of ash and beech trees with buds bursting on the boughs, and parked in the Roscoes' drive.

After the pair had stepped round the front lawn, Sunita pressed the doorbell.

'Good to see you both. Come in,' said Roscoe as he drew back the door.

'Very kind of you to invite us over,' said Sunita, who was smartly dressed in a yellow tunic and loose-fitting dark trousers beneath her coat.

'Yes, good of you, guv,' said Vickers.

'Pleasure,' said Roscoe, taking their coats. 'If you'd both like to go into the living room, I'll get some drinks.'

After Roscoe had poured Sunita a glass of white wine and a lager for Vickers, Helen appeared in the doorway.

'Hello, you two. Has Gavin told you our news?'

The guests shook their heads.

'We're grandparents at last.'

'That's wonderful, Helen,' said Sunita with a broad smile. 'Congratulations.'

'Yes. A little boy,' said Helen. 'It's been a little touch and go. He's arrived about four weeks early.'

'When was he born?'

'Early this morning at Warwick Hospital,' she continued. 'Five pounds fifteen ounces.'

Vickers shook Roscoe's hand.

'Is it true you've reserved a place in the police cadets for him, guv?' he asked with a grin.

'Not yet,' said Roscoe, smiling back. 'But he's making his presence known in the maternity ward. I don't think George and Amanda are set for a quiet life.'

'Amanda OK, guv?'

'Yes. She's fine.'

'I've got some snacks in the kitchen. I'll just fetch them,' said Helen.

She returned with plates of sandwiches, sausage rolls, chicken goujons and a courgette quiche.

'I hope you're both peckish,' she said while arranging the plates on the dining table by the patio doors.

The visitors glanced at each other and nodded.

'Any name yet for the baby?' asked Vickers.

'They haven't finally decided,' Helen replied. 'But they're talking about calling him Grant with the middle name of Dennis after my father and Amanda's grandad.'

'Please pass on our best wishes to George and Amanda,' said Sunita.

When they had all sat down, Vickers spoke about the court appearance of Sophie Bishop.

'I saw something about it on Midlands TV,' said Vickers. 'Press photographers were trying to snap her picture through windows in the prison van.'

'Yes, I saw that,' said Roscoe. 'There was quite a stir. Look, the reason I invited you over here was that Norris and I thought you did a terrific job over the case, Sergeant.'

Sunita, who was sitting on the settee beside Vickers, smiled and nodded.

'Thank you, sir,' she said.

'Norris is recommending you for a commendation for your dedication and professionalism at this year's chief constable's awards,' he said.

'Brilliant.'

'She's also asked me to thank you for your work on the Councillor Portman case and for gently persuading Jackie Perrins to give evidence against Axel Makepeace. She makes an ideal witness because of her knowledge of the West Side Gang and Todd Styler's past dealings with them.'

'I thought she only knew about day-to-day street dealing.'

'According to Taylor, she was once taken to Axel Makepeace's home by Styler and on one occasion she was an accidental witness to a shooting. He says they're on the point of arresting him – thanks to Jackie's evidence.'

'And Roman?' she asked.

'He's likely to be charged with extortion.'

Sunita shook her head.

'I hope she stands by her decision to provide evidence, sir,' she said.

'Taylor says he's had his suspicions for some time about a certain member of his team – a guy he feared might be cosying up to the West Side Gang. He'll tell me more about this after the arrest. Makepeace must be livid.

Not only did he lose his drugs shipment. He now realises Taylor's got an insider working as a gang member but can't work out who it is. Taylor's convinced that poor Lizzie was a good operator and her covert assignments remained covert.'

After more drinks were poured and consumed, finally, just after four o'clock, the two guests said their farewells and emerged into the cold, damp country air.

'Well, Inspector Vickers,' said Sunita, slipping her arm through his, 'the day is still young. I sense a scene of bright lights, relaxing music and the buzz of the crowd is beckoning us.'

'Are we going out dancing or to see a show?' he asked as they stepped round the lawn towards his car.

'No. I've got something in mind that's far more exciting than that,' she replied. 'Shopping.'

THE END

If you enjoyed this book, please let others know by leaving a quick review on Amazon. Also, if you spot anything untoward in the paperback, get in touch. We strive for the best quality and appreciate reader feedback.

editor@thebookfolks.com

www.thebookfolks.com

More fiction in this series

MURDER ON OXFORD LANE (Book 1)

A budding chorister doesn't return home from practice but his wife doesn't appear concerned. DS Sunita Roy becomes convinced he has been murdered but she has her own problems in the form of an ex-boyfriend who won't take no for an answer. Will she keep her eye on the ball when all expect her to fail?

THE CROSSBOW STALKER (Book 2)

When a serial killer armed with a crossbow terrorises the West Midlands, Chief Inspector Gavin Roscoe suspects a motive of jealousy and revenge. But as the number of victims increases, the connection initially established between them wears thin. DS Sunita Roy has a different theory and resolves to pursue her own instincts, come what may.

MURDER OF A DOCTOR (Book 3)

Police search for the identities of people seen near the scene of a doctor's murder. And it seems like an open and shut case when a father with a grievance against him can be placed nearby. But DS Sunita Roy wants to dig deeper, and with an internal affairs investigation ongoing, she'll have to tread carefully.

OUT FOR REVENGE (Book 4)

There's a noticeable change of atmosphere in the city when a dangerous prisoner is released. He has plans to up his drugs business. But someone will quickly put an end to that, by putting an end to his life. Detective Sunita Roy has the unenviable task of hunting down the gangsters who were likely responsible. But when the cops close in, they'll have an even bigger problem than they first imagined.

HEIR TO MURDER (Book 5)

Miles Kenworth makes the lives of others in his apartment block a misery with his loud music. One day the woman next door hears a commotion and enters Miles' flat to find him lying dead in a pool of blood. The man from upstairs is standing over him. It looks like a straightforward case until DS Sunita Roy opens a can of worms…

IT NEVER RAINS (Book 6)

Midlands detectives race against the clock to find a boy taken from the home of a Premier League football player. Having shot dead his bodyguard, the kidnappers clearly mean business, but the police are soon at loggerheads with a specialist officer sent to assist. As relentless rain swamps the area, can DS Sunita Roy keep her head above water and crack the case?

All FREE with Kindle Unlimited and available in paperback.

More fiction by Tony Bassett

SEAT 97

Journalist Nick Colton lands the scoop of his career when a concertgoer sitting next to him is shot dead in front of his eyes. But the gunman escapes amidst the chaos, and Colton's investigation into the murder will see him treading a dangerous line through London's unforgiving streets.

FREE with Kindle Unlimited and available in paperback.

Other titles of interest

MURDER IN THE NEW FOREST by Carol Cole

When a woman's body is found on the ground next to her horse, it seems an unfortunate accident had occurred. However, DI Callum MacLean, newly arrived in the picturesque New Forest from Glasgow, suspects differently. But hunting a killer in this close-knit community, suspicious of outsiders, will be tough. Especially when not everyone in his team is on side.

THE GIANT'S CAUSEWAY MURDERS
by Robert McCracken

A lull in cases sees father and daughter private investigators
Sidney and Ursula Valentine surveying potholes for the
council. When a woman asks them to look for her missing
sister, their spirits are lifted. But after finding a dead body,
and being told tall stories about lottery wins and missing
treasure, their hopes of easy money are dashed.

All FREE with Kindle Unlimited and available in paperback.

www.thebookfolks.com

Printed in Great Britain
by Amazon

60214234R00143